THE STRANGER
AT THE DOOR

The Urban Chronicles

The Mercy Seat
The Stranger at the Door

THE STRANGER AT THE DOOR

By

Henry O. Arnold

Dedication

For Derri Smith
Founder of End Slavery TN
Now
Ancora TN

Acknowledgments

Gratitude begins with my parents, Henry and Bernie, and ends with my wife, Kay, daughters, Kristin Pearson and Lauren Zilen, sons in-law, Derek Pearson and Erik Zilen, and grandchildren, John Erik, Clara Laurie, and Patton Blair.

Jenaye Merida and Karen Longino of Working Title Agency/Media for their wisdom, guidance, and support.

Miralee Ferrell, Publisher of Mountain Brook Ink, and editor for *The Stranger at the Door*, who worked her legendary magic and brought this novel to a higher level of literary craft.

Tim Pietz, publicity manager for MBI who continued making the public aware of this novel long past the normal course. And Kristen Johnson, the MBI office manager whose tight ship approach to the production of this novel kept us always on schedule.

To Lynnette Bonner for the book cover design for *The Stranger at the Door* and *The Mercy Seat*.

Derri Smith for her bravery to start a ministry to help young women escape the slavery of human trafficking.

Landon Arnold for his SWAT tactical expertise.

Ben Pearson for his expertise in all thing's photography.

Jillian LaFave at Robotic Fox for her fabulous web design work.

Jim Reyland and Chase Benzin at Audio Productions, Inc/Nashville for making my audio book sound terrific.

And finally, to God…I have been carried on His shoulders all my life.

Chapter One

Leandra paced the cluttered room like a lioness, growling under her breath. She paused in front of the window of a squalid interior room that looked out upon the expansive factory floor of a recycling facility. Through the broken glass she could see her people gathering around the mounds of trash awaiting the recycling bins. These mounds had been scooped up and piled off to the side clearing a wide-open space for her test. Her people had gathered to put her on trial.

But were they really her people? Not yet. This was her second attempt. She had failed her first effort to survive the gauntlet, fallen halfway through the line, slipped on the splashes of her own blood and sweat. She could not fail this time. She would stay on her feet. The lioness would take the pain and endure to the end of the line. She would prove her mettle to the unbelievers.

Leandra turned from the window. Her eyes caught the images Esteban had spray-painted on the large wall. The grimy, besmirched wall had become Este's canvas, covering it with fierce Aztec warriors, male and female, in extravagant costumes and posing each one in supple dance motion, or in the warlike stance of a warrior ready for combat. She was getting ready for combat.

The tools of her lover's trade were stacked neatly on metal shelving in one corner of the room, twelve-ounce cans of spray paint, every color imaginable in service to Este's imagination. In the middle of these vibrant designs floated a large, fierce-looking skull with a red wing painted on each side. Inscribed between the two wings in gothic-heavy script were the words "Death Demon."

Next to the skull stood a female warrior wearing a lion-skin covering with a jeweled leather belt tied around her waist. Leandra had been Este's model for this portrayal. She pressed her palm upon the wall and scraped her fingers along her image. If she was ever to have the privilege of the Death Demon being tattooed onto her arm, she must prove herself tonight. She must not break. She must not fall. She must prove herself to be the lioness warrior Esteban had envisioned her.

Leandra spun around when the door opened. The sound from the crowd gathering on the warehouse floor exploded in her ears, a hellish racket designed to strike fear. Esteban braced his hands against the doorframe, a human buffer to the rupture of beastly sounds. His furrowed brow and the flexing muscles in his jaw revealed his anxiety. It had been less than a month since her first attempt to walk the line. Some of the bruises on her legs and arms still showed discoloration on her brown skin. Some of her cuts had not fully healed.

Este's distress was palpable, and she loved him for it, but now was not the time for love. She would not allow herself to feel any affection for this man—all affection must be cast aside. She was a lioness readying herself to survive the line. No love would be expressed for her on the line, so she could not be careless and indulge any tenderness for Esteban. She would not allow her heart to fall victim to an unguarded moment. Her heart must be steeled if she were to take the punishment. She would delay any gratification of tenderness. If she survived the beat down, Este would smother her with tenderness.

"You ready?" Este cast an anxious look onto the warehouse floor.

Leandra nodded and shook her bare arms as if casting off feasting mosquitoes. She began to hop back and forth on the balls of her feet.

A head emerged behind Este, and he stepped aside to allow for an unencumbered entrance of his older brother. Beltran stole into the room, skulking around as if he might spy something he'd want to pilfer. Leandra lived in fear that Beltran would demand her affections. He always was on the lookout to snatch what did not belong to him. In his mind everything belonged to him. It was the privileges of leadership, so no object or human was safe around him. He took what he wanted when he wanted and discarded it when the object or human no longer held interest. Leandra's only protection from Beltran's advances was Esteban. The younger brother stood as protector, but tonight even Este could not protect her.

"You like it here, don't you?" Beltran asked waving his arm around the interior.

Leandra said nothing. She stood still out of respect and fear of what Beltran might do. Before being brought into the fold of the Death Demon gang, she had been in constant survival mode. From sheltering with criminal parents until a juvenile judge slammed the gavel against her blood relation's delinquency, to running through a slew of foster homes, to homelessness, and finally, to this grungy room in a recycling factory, her life had been one long escape from one combat zone to another. Despite this, here she stood, the fight still in her heart, and she would continue to fight until she died.

"So this is the deal," Beltran said. "Don't break. You don't break the line, you don't go into the stable, and little brother here gets to keep you." He snapped the side of her head with his middle finger like smashing a fly. When she flinched, Beltran snickered.

"That was just a love tap, baby. You about to have the hard smackdown."

Leandra started bouncing on her feet again, a bold recovery against the thump to her head, a defiance against a top dog's ruling of the consequences were she to break.

When Beltran marched out the door, Este stepped aside for his big brother to pass. He kept his head bowed and did not look at him. As soon as Beltran blew by, Este extended his arm ushering Leandra out of their room and into the arena.

There was an eerie silence when she entered the vast piles of recyclables and the monster machinery required to make trash usable once again. In the middle of the factory floor was the cleared space. The Death Demons quietly formed two ranks into a human gauntlet. She could not call them brothers or sisters. Not yet. If she survived the line, they could become her "cousins." Then after that, there was but one more initiation before she could be called a Death Demon and wear the red-winged skull on her flesh.

When Este found Leandra on the streets, she immediately accepted his offer to go with him to the recycling center. Anywhere was better than the fighting to survive the dangerous existence lurking at every unfriendly corner, in every dark alley. As a favor to the little brother of the leader of the Death Demons, she had been allowed to remain. Now was the time to earn her place. But she was no fool. If she lost this second opportunity to prove herself, Leandra would be back out on the streets or be thrown into the horrors of the stable for later use on the circuit. She had to get to the end of the line. She did not want to be homeless again, or worse, be forced into working the slavery of the pipeline. That life was worse than the beat down she was about to experience. The door of opportunity was open, and she intended to blast through it.

Beltran waited for her at the head of the double line waving for her to approach.

Este leaned in and whispered, "I will be waiting for you at the end. Keep your eyes on me." Then he hustled over to his place at the end of the gauntlet.

Leandra kept bouncing on the balls of her feet using the momentum to make her way over to Beltran.

"It is three minutes to midnight," he said tapping his high-priced watch, stolen by a gang member seeking his favor. "Last time you fell in two minutes. Never made it to the halfway point. If you make it this time, I figure it will take you past midnight. The other side of midnight is your fate or redemption."

Beltran stepped away from her. The moment he raised his hand the squadron of Death Demons erupted into curses of her name, forecasts of her defeat, the rattling of chains, and the banging of batons and pipes upon the concrete floor in rhythmic drumming. All hostile broadcasts meant to strike fear and herald her failure.

Leandra looked at Este at the other end of the human passageway. Focus on Este, eyes on him, endure the blows, stay on her feet, do not lose sight of Este. The only rule to this ritual was to stay on your feet and get to the end of the line.

Beltran dropped his arm. Propelled by her quick start, Leandra avoided the first attempts to crush her. She leapt over the chains whipping around her legs. Her agility got her to the halfway point before sustaining any blows. But beyond that point, the remaining Demons along the line got wise to her quick moves. Each side of the gauntlet anchored their stances, and when Leandra bolted into the second half of the double column, the Demons unleashed their blows upon her head, back, shoulders, and arms. Leandra kept her eyes on Esteban. She could not hear what he was shouting for the ringing in her ears and the brutal treatment upon her body, but when he waved his arms for her to come to him, his urgent gestures boosted her courage.

Then from out of the corner of her eye, Leandra saw the long chain veering toward her, chest high, not down low at her legs so as to trip her. This long, heavy chain had one purpose, to stop her dead in her tracks and knock her onto the factory floor. For one split second Leandra took her eyes off Esteban and grabbed the hawser flying toward her. The Demon who flailed the chain cursed when Leandra yanked the linked weapon from his grasp and used her momentum to swing the chain in a full circle scattering the last Demons on the line as they ducked to avoid being struck. Then the warrior lioness flung the weighty shackles across the open space scattering her attackers. Her victorious running of the gauntlet brought a stunned humiliation upon the vanquished Demons, the chain crashing onto the hard surface of the floor echoed her victory. She indulged a brief smile when she heard the metal bouncing off the solid flooring. She had been triumphant. The Demons were scattered. The last thing she saw before she collapsed was Esteban rushing toward her with open arms.

Chapter Two

Kenda Crane was no stranger to chaos. Being the pastor's wife of an inner-city church, a mother of three teenage kids, and a high school drama teacher with numerous musicals and dramas under her belt, there was little that phased her. But staging a Christmas pageant at The Mercy Seat church for the first time bumped her into a different category. It was a daunting sight to witness the pews in the church filled with people from her community, each player dressed in what Kenda could only loosely call, biblical attire.

Most of the wardrobe was pulled from personal closets. Bathrobes or mau-maus, sandals or bare feet, strips of cloth wrapped around the head and tied with string to hold it in place, some bits and pieces of colored fabric strategically attached to liven up an otherwise drab costume. Kenda's only stipulation for wardrobe adornment was "no gang colors or insignias." Other than that, whatever was taken from the closet, or could be found on the racks at thrift stores, or what her youngest daughter, Carrie, could scavenge was acceptable unto her sight. Carrie's dumpster diving skills went into overdrive the moment Kenda appointed her wardrobe mistress.

On a Sunday morning in early November, Kenda announced that she was considering staging a Christmas pageant for the community and wondered if congregants would be interested in supporting such an endeavor. The response was immediate, akin to a movement of the Spirit with a breeze of hallelujahs and applause blowing through the sanctuary. The congregational adrenaline rush could not be denied.

Now she was in the thick of it. She had more cast members

than needed, but she didn't have the heart to deny anyone wanting a role to have their moment on stage. An abundance of shepherds, wise men—who said it had to be just three wise men, break the tradition—angels, oh my, the angels. Her ensemble of earthly angels must have rivaled the ranks of the original heavenly host. A bustling population of citizens in Bethlehem were gathered in the city for a Roman census, after all.

A Mr. and Mrs. Inn Keeper with a horde of staff—but there could only be one Joseph and one Mary. Maxwell reluctantly agreed to play Joseph. Their middle daughter, Corley, would have made an excellent Mary, but Kenda wanted to keep her nepotism to a minimum. A Mary had yet to be chosen, and Kenda was on the lookout for the perfect young female to play the role. With only a week before opening night she was not in a panic, but on the verge.

When her son, Carlo, volunteered his services at the dinner table one night before the start of rehearsals, Kenda and Maxwell could not believe what they were hearing. Nor did his sisters. Corley was the first to recover from the shock and seize an opportunity. Corley suggested that she and her big brother be co-stage managers to keep the chaos of rehearsals and three performances from spilling out into the city of Richland.

Carlo was warm to Corley's idea, and as a bonus, not only did he suggest that his girlfriend, Lin, might want to be involved, but he offered his photography services to document rehearsals and performances posting them on The Mercy Seat's social media sites to advertise the pageant to the community. This was a new Carlo and Maxwell and Kenda were hard pressed not to overreact with joy.

It was a new day in the Crane household. Everyone was different since the incident. Everything in the Gardens was different, in all of Hells Canyon, but the most visible difference was at The Mercy Seat church. There were those in the community who were critical of the way Lady Justice had favored the white man once again. Over time those voices were silenced by a different mindset.

After the incident The Mercy Seat became the church to attend, and her husband the pastor to follow. It was near celebrity status, a status her husband detested. Kenda did not have to convince Maxwell to deny the media interviews, or the book offers, or the speakers' circuit, or, of all the absurdities, movie deals from several different companies. The power of Maxwell's "no" only riveted everyone's attention.

All things had been created new after the incident. It was not long before the service on Sunday was full, standing room only, and then flowing out into the parking lot. People living in the Gardens projects and Hells Canyon neighborhood who had never darkened the door of the church now attended without fail.

The years Maxwell had spent befriending all these new churchgoers hoping to convince them to come to The Mercy Seat out of a desire for God, had coalesced after her husband had been released from jail. The hordes came out of a desire to see him, to be able to boast that they were members of Pastor Maxwell Crane's church. It was no longer The Mercy Seat church. It was her husband's church, and it was crushing him. Kenda had to watch her beloved husband hold it together on the outside, but she bore witness to a steady nosedive of his heart and soul with each passing day.

Once the parishioners gave Kenda their resounding affirmation for a Christmas pageant, she went to work writing a script. She wanted to include a scene between Mary and Elizabeth when Mary comes to visit her cousin with the astounding news of the angel Gabriel's visit and the events that would follow. Kenda may not have her Mary, but she did have her Elizabeth. After she had written the scene, she went to the church office while Maxwell was on one of his Hells Canyon walkabouts and handed Rosemary the two-page scene.

Rosemary scratched the back of Ezekiel's head where he sat purring contentedly in his mistress's lap while she quietly read the dialogue.

"Kenda, this is so good," Rosemary said once she had finished.

"Do you mind reading it through with me, Rosemary? It will help me hear how it sounds, and I can see if something doesn't ring true."

"If you want to, but I don't know. I'm no actress. How do you want me to do it?"

"Do it like Rosemary."

After they finished reading the scene tears were flowing from Kenda's eyes.

"Was I that bad?" Rosemary laughed. "I told you I was no actress."

"On the contrary, my dear, you are a natural."

The shared experience stirred the hearts of both women. Kenda immediately offered the role of Elizabeth to Rosemary, and Rosemary immediately began to express her doubts.

"Oh, Kenda, I don't know. I don't know. I've never done anything like this."

"The Mercy Seat has never done a Christmas pageant. First time for everything."

"But still, I mean, I mean, I don't know what I mean." Rosemary gave out a nervous chuckle and looked down at Ezekiel. The cat had meowed his annoyance at the lack of scratching while Rosemary had been distracted reading the scene with Kenda. "What do you think, Ezekiel?" she asked her feline soulmate. "Think I should do this part?"

Kenda was shocked when Ezekiel turned his head and focused his cat eyes right on her, and out of an inspirational thought, Kenda made a brilliant offer to Rosemary.

"What if you had Ezekiel sitting on your lap during the scene?" Kenda said.

"Can we do that? It's not in the Bible, is it?" Rosemary asked.

"Well, just because cats aren't mentioned doesn't mean they weren't around. I say we take a little theological license. What do you think?"

Kenda sat back in her seat when Ezekiel's head swivel back around and looked into the eyes of his mistress. It had to be a sign of approval, and both women chose to accept it as such.

"Well, if Ezekiel thinks we can, then I guess, I guess we can."

That day the deal was sealed.

Daunting as the number of the multitudes were, Kenda smiled as she looked out over the church auditorium. Her cast was almost complete. The excitement among the company was palpable as they waited for their director to call for rehearsal to begin. Kenda spent the first few rehearsals giving out scripts, assigning parts, reading through the story, and giving minimum stage directions. She did not want to overwhelm all these marvelous people with too much instruction. Let her bear the numerous headaches. Above all, this was to be a joyful time for everyone involved. If she succeeded in that, then the audiences would be caught up in the joy coming from the stage. What else was Christmas about if not joy?

Kenda's biggest hurdle would be to move clusters of angels, shepherds, wisemen, and Bethlehemites on and off the stage. The Mercy Seat stage platform could barely accommodate the pastor and worship band. Kenda had spent much of her early rehearsal period creating a traffic pattern in the hope of avoiding a bottleneck or personal injury.

Kenda took the mic from off the stand to address the players.

"Okay, this is our third rehearsal. We've got six more before our first show."

There were groans, titters of excitement, and happy applause among the flock.

"I can feel your excitement and your nerves," Kenda said. "But we can do it."

Kenda waved her prompt list in the air.

"We are going to get through the main crowd scenes tonight so you can learn your entrances and exits and on-stage blocking. I will work on the smaller scenes another night that will not involve most of you. So, let's put the first big crowd scene on its feet, which is when Joseph and Mary enter Bethlehem. Everyone in that scene, come on down."

Kenda lowered the microphone and waved for Corley to come over as the cast rose from their seats in the sanctuary and began moving to the stage.

"Have you seen your dad? Is he in his office?" Kenda asked.

"I don't think so. Maybe he's outside."

"Go check please. I'll get Carlo to help me wrangle the cast."

Corley scooted for the center aisle leading to the front of the church, careful to avoid bumping into the citizens of Bethlehem who were fanning out toward the stage like human streams.

Kenda split the group into two sections and sent half to each side of the platform where they would walk up the three steps to get onto the stage. This was the first test to see how everyone could navigate this bustling crowd scene.

When she turned back around Corley was there, her head lowered and arms crossed in front of her. Her daughter was trying not to cry. Kenda shut off the microphone, put it back on the stand, and drew Corley to her side.

"What is it, baby?" she whispered.

"When I opened the door I saw Daddy leaning against one of the front columns. I could hear him crying. I couldn't tell him it was time to start. I just couldn't."

This was not a surprise to Kenda or the kids, though she had kept the frequency of Maxwell's spontaneous breakdowns from them. She had witnessed more than her share. Since the incident these episodes came upon him without warning and varied in severity. She knew her husband and was sure that in private, these episodes could be full-on crying jags, and that Maxwell desperately tried to spare her and the kids the bewildering, deep grief he was going through.

No one in the family talked openly about what had happened to cause her husband to go to jail even though it had been a short stay. The Crane household was unable to resolve the varied and confused feelings they all were going through. After months of living in this low-simmering pot of not knowing how to refer to what happened or what anyone was feeling, Kenda chose to reference what occurred as "the incident," and took it upon herself to handout the lifejackets when she saw anyone in the family start to go under.

Kenda and the children knew all the details. They had seen all the outward support from the community and even the brief condemnation. Her family shared the pain of the incident, the collective level of guilt. Kenda had tried her best to keep the family from descending into some circle of emotional hell. She hoped the Christmas pageant might provide an escape route out of their shared despondency.

Maxwell had refused medication. He refused professional counseling. Her husband had argued that there was theological cause for this grief and that God was dealing with his soul. But did God have to take a jackhammer to her husband? He had many one-on-one sessions with their dear friend and Rector of the cathedral, Rendell Hardy. Without ever revealing what her husband had expressed to Reny, he would text Kenda after each session simply to encourage her.

No one could fully know what Maxwell was going through. No one except Pete, her brother. Maxwell and Pete had served together in Afghanistan in the Marine Corp, where Pete was on a special forces team and her husband was a chaplain for the unit. Kenda believed that these two men both understood trauma on a visceral level. Her brother had stepped up and was lending his shoulder for his Marine brother. Kenda was so grateful for Pete's aid and comfort.

After Kenda kissed Corley on the top of her head, she noticed Carlo and Lin going over the script with some of the cast members. She waved for Lin to come over and then whispered into Corley's ear.

"It's gonna be okay, baby. Daddy just needs time."

Corley nodded and then allowed Lin to lead her away.

Kenda looked down the aisle at the front doors of the church. Her daughter had just told her that her husband was outside weeping. It took everything within her to keep from telling the cast to take five and let her rush out the doors and wrap Maxwell in her arms, but that would draw more scrutiny than she wanted. This would have to wait. She would deal with this later. The citizens of Bethlehem were awaiting her instructions.

Chapter Three

Maxwell cracked open the right-side door of the front entrance of the church and peeked inside the sanctuary. He knew he needed to be in there helping Kenda, being a supportive husband, and seen by those present as their pastor, but he did not have the grit. In the weeks following the incident, he had been able to prepare and deliver his sermons, but for the last few months, he couldn't find it within himself to study his Bible and work up even a short homily for the Sunday crowds. Rosemary had to stop scheduling his meetings and Rendell had lined up guest pastors to fill-in while he took personal time. He was still a presence on the grounds, but when he entered the sanctuary, it took everything within him to keep from fleeing.

He could see the swarm of people buzzing around Kenda as she directed them into their positions. Maxwell placed his foot inside the vestibule but then stopped. He was distracted by a metal screeching sound. He swung the door open and closed, and above his head he could see the source of the sound. Cold temperatures and age could be blamed. A shot of 3-In-One in the dried out, hydraulic dampers inside the manual door closer and a spray of WD-40 on the door hinges would be a temporary fix. Everything about The Mercy Seat church was a temporary fix. The back-check facility on the ancient brass arm had given out long ago. It should be replaced. So much about this structure should be replaced. The squeaking metal was all the excuse he needed to keep from continuing into the building.

Maxwell could hear Kenda talking on the mic directing the townspeople moving through Bethlehem. He should be ready to make his entrance as Joseph with whatever stand-in Kenda assigned for Mary. There wasn't that much to the role of Joseph. When Kenda began writing the script she told him she would write a scene between Joseph and the angel, but Maxwell did not want to say anything. He would make his entrance and exit, be a fatherly presence for the Holy Family tableaux, but let others do the talking. The heartwarming disarray of rehearsal in progress from the front of the sanctuary almost brought Maxwell to tears. The house of the Lord was full of people enjoying themselves, preparing to celebrate the birth of Christ, and still he could not enter. Maxwell allowed the door to close.

He flipped on the sconce lights on the front portico and slipped behind one of the columns. Maxwell took a pack of smokes from his coat pocket and a lighter. It had been his street currency. Since the incident, it became his own bad habit, something to occupy his troubled mind, to calm his troubled nerves, to soothe his troubled heart. He thumbed the spark wheel on the lighter a couple of times before the flame held, and he cupped his hand around the flame to shield it from the damp cold to light his cigarette. He held his hand before the flame, first for the warmth and then for the burn. He waited for the burn to register, and then waited another couple of seconds before releasing the valve and extinguishing the flame.

He wrapped his hand around the column, wiggling his fingers and letting the wind cool the sting of his skin. It was a strange and exhilarating sensation, this hot and cold tingle on his flesh. Maxwell took a deep drag off his cigarette and looked up and down the four-lane street in front of the church. There was very little traffic. The air was just cold enough to confuse the atmosphere. At any given second, there were flakes of snow, then drizzle, then icy rain. Few citizens of Richland would be out on such a night.

Maxwell noticed a painter's van approaching the church with metal ladders stacked on top. It stopped in the middle of the road and sat idling. Maybe the driver needed assistance. He pushed himself off the column to offer his help, but then another vehicle came from behind forcing the van to accelerate. The tires spun until it gained traction and drove off. Instead of following the van, the black SUV pulled into the church lot and parked in the handicapped spot. When the driver opened the door to get out, the interior light illuminated the face of his brother-in-law. Maxwell smiled and took another drag, then waved the glowing cigarette to let Pete know he was there.

During the months following the incident, Pete had gone through a strenuous regime of physical therapy to get back to a level of normalcy. Normalcy for Pete was beyond the scope for most mortal men. Maxwell made regular visits to the VA where Pete spent his time recovering and regaining his strength after the brutality inflicted upon him by Richland's corrupt police officers who had given themselves over to the dark side. It was the one thing Maxwell could do even in his current muddled state—encourage and support his best friend.

Maxwell could make the case that in some way Pete nearly gave his life for him. All the circumstances were somehow related in Maxwell's jumbled mind. He had been unable to sort it out with any clarity. Maxwell would witness Pete's weekly progress, growing stronger, yet felt himself a world apart, slowly fading in the dark.

Pete two-stepped his way up the sidewalk holding out his cane like a chorus line dancer.

"Show off," Maxwell said.

"Next stop, Broadway," Pete replied.

"Not sure I'd buy a ticket to that show." Maxwell moved away from the column.

"When are you going to build a wheelchair ramp for me?" Pete asked.

"When you start coming to church."

Maxwell took another drag off his cigarette and lobbed the burning stub at Pete. He batted it away with his cane generating an explosion of glowing embers in the air that survived only a milli-second in the moist air.

"This the way you greet all your parishioners?" Pete asked.

"Just the ones who park in handicapped spots without their tags."

"I never got one of those blue tags," Pete said. "Couldn't mentally adjust to the thought of being disabled."

When Pete took the three steps up onto the front porch he winced in pain.

"The leg still tender?" Maxwell asked.

"Yeah, still pinches. Another week and I will mount this stick on the wall." Pete gave his cane one last twirling flourish then propped it against a granite column.

When they heard the sounds of the worship band playing, they both turned toward the church doors.

"Bethlehem is rocking it tonight," Pete said.

"I think that is the instrumentation for the townspeople to move about the stage with purpose," Maxwell said.

"Shouldn't you be in there?" Pete asked.

"Yeah. Maybe. I don't know. I'm on break from rehearsal." Maxwell braced his shoulder against the column of the portico.

Just then the stained glass front windows began to rattle from the vibration of the band in a full crescendo.

"In-coming. Sounds like the whole building might explode," Pete commented.

"Kenda is a pro. She has everything under control," Maxwell said. "What are you doing out on a night like this?"

"No law says I can't drive at night. Let me bum a cigarette."

Maxwell pushed his shoulder off the column and pulled the lighter and pack out of his coat pocket. He tapped out two ciga-rettes and handed one to Pete, then flashed the lighter and fired up the smokes. He looked out over the sidewalk and could tell the surface was getting slicker.

"I need to salt down the porch and steps before rehearsal gets out," he said stepping over to a corner of the porch and grabbing a box of salt ice.

"When did you start?" Pete pointed to Maxwell's cigarette.

"Ever since…you know…ever since," Maxwell said and raised his pack of cigarettes like a spokesman for the brand and said, "I've used these things as street currency for so long, I thought it was time to spend some of the church budget on myself; a simple, low-cost pleasure to calm the demons."

Maxwell stuck the cigarette into his mouth and reached into the box of ice salt and began to scatter the crystals over the steps and down the sidewalk.

"Isn't that bad for your recovery?" Maxwell pointed to Pete's cigarette.

"Just bonding with my brother," Pete said. "And I don't inhale."

Maxwell salted the walkway to the parking lot and back. The street and neighborhood were unusually quiet. Except for the hissing sound of freezing drizzle hitting the pavement and the few cars that moved cautiously along the slick road, the rumble of Christmas music from inside the church was all that was audible.

"I didn't know church plays could be so loud," Pete said.

"Catch a performance," Maxwell said. "And wear your combat ear plugs."

When Maxwell finished scattering the salt, he stepped back onto the porch and placed the box on the windowsill. He turned to see Pete glaring at him.

"You haven't seen her yet, have you?" Pete asked.

"Straight to the point, brother," Maxwell responded.

"Straight is all I know, brother," Pete countered.

Maxwell knew he could not duck out of this question. He knew Pete would wait him out. His brother would stand in the wet and cold all night if it came to that. Pete's face was stern like a prophet ready to go deep, knead his soul, and strike his dark heart with a blaze of truth.

Maxwell could not speak the word. He just dropped his head and shook it.

Pete responded with a firm squeeze of Maxwell's shoulder.

"You know when we were in-country and we raided the wrong house or arrested the wrong suspect or worse, we went back to the family to express our condolences, try to make amends. It helps."

"Yeah, I know," Maxwell tried to pull away from Pete, but the grip on his shoulder only tightened. Yes, Pete's strength was nearly back. "The timing isn't right."

"I'm calling you out on that. The timing is never right, that's why it's time."

When Pete released Maxwell's shoulder it was as if he was sending him forth to face what he had been avoiding since the incident.

"You sent us out on many missions, brother. Now I'm sending you out."

"So you're a chaplain now," Maxwell scoffed. "That's rich."

"She could have lied. I mean, it was her son that died, but she told the truth and saved you," Pete said. "That was a righteous act, and you walked out of jail a free man."

"None of this brings her son back," Maxwell said. "I walk, and as a bonus, I get to keep my son. Where is the righteous justice in that?"

"We walked the hard road together in Afghanistan," Pete said, not softening the hardness in his voice. "We came back to the world and we're still walking it but on home turf."

He was back in the world, but it did not feel like home. He was on a road, but one he had never traveled. He was alone, without a guidance system, without a guide.

Carrie burst out the door startling Maxwell with her unexpected entrance.

"Daddy, I came as quick as I could."

His attention was so diverted he forgot the standard reaction.

Maxwell looked down into a pair of bright eyes and a smiling face. It took a moment for his brain to send the signal of recognition that this was his youngest daughter. He was supposed to say something. What was it?

Like an acting partner who had forgotten their lines, Carrie lowered her voice and prompted her partner's memory, "And not a moment too soon."

In an instant the familiar words.

"Right, right, and not a moment too soon."

Carrie took Maxwell's hand, but he winced when she pinched his singed flesh.

"What happened to your hand, Daddy?"

"Nothing, honey. Scratched it just now scattering the salt ice."

Carrie did not question, just accepted the explanation at face value, but her expression scrunched up when Maxwell put the cigarette back to his lips for one last drag.

"If Mama Rose knew you were out here smoking, there'd be…" and she paused until her father removed the cigarette from his lips.

"Hell to pay." Maxwell finished her sentence, and then released the smoke from his lungs. "I know. Our secret, okay, kid?"

"Okay." Carrie's uneasy smile reflected an ambivalence at the burden of keeping this covert information. "Mom needs you inside to help set up the manger."

"Be right in."

"Good night, Uncle Pete."

"Good night, Carrie."

Carrie disappeared inside the church building, and Maxwell and Pete returned to an awkward silence. They each took a final drag and discarded the cigarettes in the wet front yard of the church.

"You want to come see your sister work her Christmas

magic?" Maxwell offered.

"Not tonight. Another time, maybe."

"Come on inside," Maxwell cajoled. "You won't get struck by lightning."

"I'm not so sure standing next to you."

"Ha. Ha. Funny. I get it." Maxwell reached for the door handle.

Pete stopped him from opening the door. This time Pete's fingers clasped Maxwell's forearm with a firm gentleness.

"How about you? You back in the pulpit?"

Maxwell chuckled and shook his head. For the last several weeks of his sabbatical from preaching, while the church was empty, he had walked around the pulpit making his way from the side door entrance to the opposite corner of the sanctuary to get to his office. He had often paused in front of the pulpit, gazed upon the two pieces of driftwood found while beachcombing years ago, formed into the shape of a cross, and suspended on the back wall of the church. He had walked all around the sanctuary, between the pews, up and down the middle and side aisles. He meandered from one side of the sanctuary to the other, knelt at the altar railing mumbling rote prayers and passages of scripture—the words off his tongue bringing no lasting comfort to his heart.

Or he might pause to muse on the stained glass in the windows, then no longer pausing, then no longer musing, then no longer praying or whispering righteous words. The sacred words turned to ash. The images of stained glass dissolved into blood and tears. Yes, he had approached the pulpit. He had moved toward its short stairway leading up to the stage, but he could no longer raise his foot to take that first step. He could not imagine being on that stage, behind that pulpit with his Bible and sermon notes spread out in front of him. He could no longer raise his eyes upon the people, open his mouth to the congregation, and utter any words that would not be false, empty, void of any resemblance to God.

His heart was empty and so his words would be.

"I took a son from his mother. That does not preach." Maxwell waited for Pete to let go of his arm before he opened the door. "I better get inside."

After one final squeeze, Pete released his grip and headed back to his vehicle.

Before Maxwell went inside, he noticed Pete's walking stick up against a column.

"Hey, Pete, you forgot your stick." He waved it toward Pete.

"Keep it. A souvenir of my past life."

When Maxwell opened the door the light from inside the sanctuary made him hesitate. His eyes burned and he lowered his head. The light had exposed his nakedness and shame. The sanctuary was not the place of welcome and refuge he had once enjoyed. He looked back at Pete and saw him open his car door.

"Thanks for stopping by," Maxwell called out.

Pete gave Maxwell a stiff salute before he stepped inside the church.

Chapter Four

From the vestibule, Maxwell took in the vision of rehearsal in progress. The whole stage was a buzzing hive with the citizens of Bethlehem, the floor in front of the stage was crawling with an army of shepherds, and angels hovered in the wing space, but there was no wing space. The space between the front row pews and the side entrance from the parking lot and the entry to his office were completely blocked. Where had these people come from? The Mercy Seat had never enjoyed such enthusiastic increase, and this Christmas pageant and all the volunteers from the neighborhood were an outgrowth of that happy energy.

When Carlo posted a beautiful graphic advertising the performance dates on the church's webpage, Rosemary told Maxwell the phone had not stopped ringing. She couldn't get her regular work done. The pageant was expected to draw crowds from the Gardens and the Hells Canyon community. Even Rendell said he would bring a contingent from the Cathedral for one of the shows. Never in his life did he expect to see such an influx of people flowing into The Mercy Seat. Should the Fire Marshal decide to drop in for a show, he would close the place down.

Maxwell focused in on Kenda giving her directions to the attentive eyes and ears of the cast. *How does she do it,* he wondered? *How does my wife take disorder and create order?* It had to be like God hovering over the formless void of creation pondering what wonderful things might emerge from the imagination of the Creator before stirring the pot. Kenda could stir any pot and something beautiful appeared.

Maxwell saw Carlo signaling for him to come down to the

stage where he stood next to his mother. What a turn in their father and son relationship. He never thought he would see this, a smiling Carlo waving for his father to join him. Was this a deceptive vision? Were his eyes playing tricks? His son wanted him close, but it had come at a cruel cost. Maxwell forced a smile. He did not want to rebuff his son in any way and walked down the aisle.

Kenda turned around just as Maxwell was navigating through a cluster of sheep and shepherds sitting on the floor in front of the stage.

"Right on time," Kenda said, and gave him a peck on the cheek.

There was a rolling moan among those who witnessed the affection between the pastor and his wife. That was one thing Maxwell held onto, the tangible affection of his wife even if he struggled to return it.

"I saved you a spot downstage just left of center," Kenda said pointing in the direction of the stand-in Mary and Mr. and Mrs. Innkeeper. "Once you arrive in Bethlehem, the Holy Family will be escorted by the Innkeepers to the stable."

"The stable is…" Maxwell asked, unable to figure out where in this morass of people his wife would place a stable.

"Still a mystery, but I'm thinking the scene might be played where we're standing now, in front of the stage."

"I see. And what about the shepherds and sheep?" Maxwell inquired. He had no ability to see into the mind of the visionary.

"Along the side aisle until time to move. That way they can slip over to the manger once the angels make their appearance in heaven. Simple."

"Simple, yeah." Maxwell shook his head in wonder but could not help giving her a smile. She was stirring the pot.

"Do you mind taking your place between Mary and the Innkeepers so I can see if the picture in my head matches with reality?" Kenda asked.

Maxwell hopped onto the stage from the floor and took his

place where Kenda had requested. He felt ill at ease to be in the pulpit. He had not publicly addressed the people for weeks now. He had not looked out over the congregation from this elevation, preached for them, read Scripture, or prayed for them. He did not have to say much in this scene, other than request lodging for his pregnant wife and himself. He could do that, at least. Nothing sacred about those words. It was not a sermon. He could say his couple of lines and head to the stable. He was an integral part of the Holy Family, but no demands other than window dressing. He could do this.

Once Kenda was happy with the stage picture, Maxwell could exit. She needed to block the scene with the shepherds and the heavenly host. Maxwell made his way off stage right, maneuvered around the worship band, and slipped into the church office.

He shut the door and leaned his back against it, but he was not alone. The words of Elizabeth, the cousin of Mary, were being hurled into the air in a frantic rhythm with strange emphasis on odd syllables that were unintelligible utterances. *Had Rosemary decided to speak her lines in tongues,* Maxwell thought?

"Rosemary, are you practicing?" he asked.

"Lord have mercy, Maxwell!" Rosemary exclaimed spinning around in surprise. She almost lost her grip on Ezekiel tucked in his usual position against her side.

"Sorry to interrupt your creative process." Maxwell held up his hands.

"I am so over my head." Rosemary started fanning her flushed face with the pages of her script. "I don't know. I don't know."

"Kenda has an eye for talent. You will be perfect."

"I don't know. I don't know." Rosemary paced the floor while continuing to fan herself. "The idea of saying these words in front of people. I've only memorized Bible verses. Now Kenda has me doing this." Rosemary paused from aerating her face and raised the script to the ceiling.

Maxwell pushed off the door and scooted over to his desk.

"Rosemary, you know your Bible. When you stand and pray for the church and community, more Scripture comes out of your mouth than anything else. I suggest you think of saying your lines like a prayer. See if that helps."

Rosemary's expression turned thoughtful. She lowered her arm with the script.

"I hadn't considered that." She compressed the lines on her face in deep thought. "I usually close my eyes when I pray. You think that might help?"

"It might be nice if you looked at Mary when you talk to her, once we get one, that is. But we have more time. You just keep practicing."

"This being an actor is hard work, isn't it Ezekiel?" Rosemary adjusted Ezekiel to the other side of her body. "You know Kenda said I could have Ezekiel on stage with me during the scene."

"She did tell me that. I think it's brilliant."

Maxwell glanced at Ezekiel who appeared indifferent to his mistress's agitation. He had grown used to her exhilaration. New cause this time, but same excitement.

"Ezekiel would calm my nerves to be sure." Rosemary snuggled Ezekiel up to her face. "Oh, and if you need to use the church office phone, I unplugged it. I can't get any work done with it ringing all the time."

"Don't intend to use the phone, so it's all good." Maxwell pulled the chair out behind his desk.

"It won't bother you if I keep going over my lines?" Rosemary waved her script at him.

"You keep right on rehearsing. I'm used to it. This is standard procedure in the Crane household." Maxwell plopped down in the chair.

The front page of the *Richland Examiner* lying on his desk stared him in the face. The one-word headline read "CON-VICTED." Beneath the headline were the pictures of Barton

Young, former Mayor of Richland, and Bill Grant, former president of United Bank and Trust. "Two out of three," Maxwell mumbled. "One more to go." There was still the trial of former police commissioner, Joe Cassia. He was putting up more of a fight than Barton and Grant.

The mayor and the bank president pled guilty and sweetened their deal by turning on Cassia. Kingpins of the city brought low by personal greed and lust for power. The newly appointed police commissioner, Cynthia Peale, pictured at a press conference vowed to root out all corruption in the department. Maxwell knew this was easier said than done, but he hoped Blind Lady Justice would do her righteous best.

Once named "Person of the Year" by the *Richland Examiner*, the newspaper had given Maxwell plenty of attention. Countless other news outlets over these past many months had done the same. He was grateful not to see his image or name associated with these three, but the incident tied them together.

The forged iron chain of linked events weighed upon his shoulders. There was no escaping that. He had tried to get back to normal life once the charges of involuntary manslaughter had been reversed and he had been released, but there was no normal to be found. He was walking on turbulent waters in gale force winds. There was no shoreline he could see, no personal Savior extending a hand. Perhaps this was the tradeoff for getting out of jail. He could walk the streets, but would have no peace, no personal happiness. The injury to his soul was a moral injury with no visible entry wound.

The parallel universe in which others might be of help was, at present, useless. How many times had he said he was sorry to God, to Kenda, to the kids, to Rendell, to Pete, to Rosemary, to himself. Was there a magic number of "I'm sorry's" to be reached? If there were, it had yet to be attained, and he had lost count. The repetitive nature of the mantra brought no serenity. No matter how often he said it, the memories around the incident were never expelled, the screams of his kids never quieted, the curses of his dying victim never silent, the cries of horror from the mother watching the life go out of her son always ringing in his ears.

If it had been some arbitrary accident, something that could be looked upon by reasonable people and agreed that, though cruel, the randomness of life had created this incident, he might be able to claim that he had been as much a victim as the other party. But that thought was illusive and meaningless. Maxwell had to accept the fact that he had gone to the victim's home, called him out, shouted at him to keep away from his son. He made a conscious choice borne out of the impulse to protect a child and willing to do harm to the one who would do harm to his child. If only there were some ritual he could go through as a form of justice that might bring about some consolation, some closure. He was living in a first-person state of sorrow.

He ran his hand over the front page of the newspaper smudging the ink over the burned spot. He licked his finger and smeared the printer ink into the singed flesh blending the shades together. Maxwell closed his eyes, leaned back in his chair, and just listened to Rosemary speaking her lines as Elizabeth, calmer now, with no excited pounding of syllables, greeting the virgin Mary when she came to visit. "You are blessed among women, and the child you bear is also blessed." What beautiful words, Maxwell thought. Just to be told you are blessed.

Maxwell awoke with a start. He looked around the office and saw Carlo waving from the office door. Rosemary was putting on her coat and tucking Ezekiel inside the lining.

"Is rehearsal over?" Maxwell asked.

"Yeah. Everyone has gone," Carlo said. "Lin is going to spend the night so she doesn't have to drive home. They're all waiting at the front."

"I need to hold your arm when you walk me to my car," Rosemary said to Carlo.

"I salted the porch and sidewalk before I came in," Maxwell said, his voice hoarse and his mind befuddled.

Maxwell rose from his seat and placed his hands on the desktop until he got his bearings. "How long was I asleep?" He glanced around, but Rosemary and Carlo were already out the door.

It was a surprise to Maxwell that he could have slept through the remainder of rehearsal. After adjusting his eyes, he stepped around the desk and made his way to the exit. He flipped off the lights and closed the office door. The sanctuary lights were already turned out, but the light was on in the vestibule where everyone was waiting for him.

Once he locked the front door of the church, the family, Lin, and Rosemary with Ezekiel in tow, all huddled together against the cold, and in one amoebic shape, gingerly made their way down the sidewalk to a chorus of crunching sounds of the salt ice beneath their feet. The company stopped in their tracks the moment they heard the sounds of skidding brakes of a vehicle on ice and human shrieks.

The vehicle skidded to a stop on the highway in front of the church and the backdoors of the van flew open. A female screaming at the top of her lungs jumped out. She did not get very far before she slipped and fell on the slick pavement. A man leapt out of the van and grabbed her by her neck. He began dragging her back to the opened doors, but the woman screamed and fought back causing the man to slip. He cursed and yanked her hair but continued toward the van's opened doors.

The little company froze in place on the sidewalk in front of the church.

"Let her go!" cried Maxwell. He was in the middle of this group, and he grappled with his family, forcing them to release their hold on him so he could run to the scene. Once free of their grip, he still could not move swiftly over the grass and parking lot due to the slick coating of ice and drizzle. He kept shouting. If nothing else his shouted demands to let the woman go might be enough until he got there. Once he got to her what would he do? He didn't know. He was all impulse, no rational thought. He heard the screams from his family, but he could make no distinction between their screams, his own, or the woman who violently fought against her assailant.

Just before he reached the road the man let go of the woman and leapt into the back of the van. The vehicle instantly pulled away. The spinning tires sprayed chutes of ice and water before the treads could grip the road. When Maxwell got to the woman he could see inside the van. It was crowded with people yelling and screaming, but the interior was blacked out and he could not see how many passengers it held. The man leaned halfway out of the back of the van and was able to slam the doors closed as the vehicle surged forward, gaining enough traction to race down the street and out of sight.

There were no other vehicles on the road that might have seen the incident, to flag down or to glimpse the license plate number on the vehicle. Was there even a license on the back doors? Maxwell could not remember and gave it no more thought.

When he knelt beside the woman, she gripped his arms and began to sob. She wore torn jeans, a thin black tee-shirt, and a cheap rhinestone jacket. She had lost one shoe, the one she had on was slip-on canvass.

When Carlo raced up beside him, Maxwell saw the look of horror on his son's face as he stared at the trembling young woman he held in his arms.

"Son, help me get her inside The Mercy Seat."

Chapter Five

Maxwell and Carlo lifted the young woman to her feet. She needed to be brought to safety, out of the elements and out of sight in case the people in the van decided to turn around and come back for her. Maxwell did not want to put his own family in jeopardy should that happen. They must hurry.

"Corley, get the keys from Rosemary and unlock the doors," Maxwell shouted, and Rosemary dug the keys out of her purse and handed them to Corley.

Maxwell felt the woman's body quaking. She was unsteady on her feet, and with only one shoe, it made for slow going to get her off the road. The tremors were so violent that it was difficult to hold onto her arm, and he clasped his free hand upon her back. At his touch, he was surprised to feel a jolt instantly rise above the existing flow of constant trembling. It was like an electric shudder produced by fear not cold.

"Hold her arm tight, Son," Maxwell said, and then he addressed the woman. "Don't be afraid. We'll take care of you."

Maxwell could not remember the last time he had said those words. He could not remember the last time he felt those words. He could not remember the last time he had helped calm someone's fears or was compelled to make an offer of aid and reassurance. He could not find within himself the effort required to muster compassionate energy. It seemed an impossible task. Until now.

Maxwell and Carlo lifted the woman over the curb and onto the frozen grass in the front church yard. Maxwell gave one last look in the direction of the fleeing van. The road was still empty. The van hadn't turned around. At least not yet.

They moved across the slick grass and onto the front steps. Corley held the door open, and Maxwell could see the rest of the women standing inside the vestibule with Kenda pressing Carrie and Lin into her side and Rosemary beside them.

"Kill the front porch lights," Maxwell said as soon as they crossed the threshold into the church, and Kenda immediately reached over to the panel and flipped off the lights. "Shut the door and lock it."

Maxwell gave one last look outside as Corley pulled the door closed. The street was empty. They had made it inside The Mercy Seat without being seen—he hoped.

"You want me to turn on the lights in the sanctuary?" asked Kenda.

"No, keep it dark. Make the church look vacant," Maxwell answered.

He didn't let go of his grip on the young woman's arm, but he could tell that she was weakening and her legs were beginning to go limp. She couldn't stand or walk for much longer. All her energy had been spent busting out of the back of the van and fighting her assailant to keep from being pulled back into the vehicle.

"Let's get away from the front door," Maxwell said.

He and Carlo held onto her as they limped down the center aisle. This unexpected father and son rescue team of a bent and trembling castoff pulled from the currents of a dark and sinister stream. The rest followed behind. When they reached the front row, Maxwell directed Carlo to place the young woman on the pew. Corley knelt down and helped the woman lie back on the cushioned bench. Kenda bent over and took hold of the woman's ankles and stretched out her legs. She removed the single shoe and began to massage her feet. At Kenda's tender kneading, she began to moan. To Maxwell's ears it sounded like a whimper of sorrow from a wounded animal.

"I've got a blanket in the office," Rosemary said. "And I can zap some apple cider in the micro, get something warm inside her. Carrie, help me get the blanket."

"There is a flashlight in my top desk drawer, Rosemary," Maxwell said as she and Carrie hurried to the door of the church office. "Bring it back with you."

Maxwell placed his arm over Carlo's shoulder and nudged the two of them to step away. Lin knelt beside the young woman stretched out on the pew and took her trembling hands, enveloping them in her own. Corley remained at her head and massaged her neck and shoulders.

Maxwell looked around the dark sanctuary. A muted glow from the streetlights seeped through the stained glass windows giving the sanctuary a spectral ambience. He could hear the soft whispers of prayers and affection uttered from the three angels lending their warmth to comfort the young woman. All sounds that came from this stranger were sighs and moans, with an occasional sob. She had a voice. She must have a voice, but Maxwell heard no words from her lips. What would she say? What would her first words be to them? Where had she been? What horrors had she witnessed?

"Dad, what are we going to do?" Carlo asked, keeping his voice low.

Maxwell could tell his son was trying to disguise his anxiety. But what struck him in his son's question was the "we." What are we going to do? This was an inclusive question, one that invited all to participate in the search for answers and solutions. His son wanted his father to be present once again within the family.

"Not sure yet. We must hear from her. She arrived with a story. We must learn it."

Rosemary and Carrie rushed out of the office and moved in beside them. Carrie handed Lin the blanket and she gave one end to Corley. Kenda continued to rub the girl's feet as Lin tucked the blanket around her ankles. Corley draped the blanket over the woman's shoulders and then lifted her up so she could drink the cider. Rosemary handed Corley a mug of cider, and she carefully placed it beneath her trembling lips.

"Careful," Rosemary said. "It's a hot brew."

All listened to hear the first slurps. Would she be able to drink? Could she stop shivering enough to take a sip? Could she accept this kindness from strangers and not fight back like they had seen her do in the street outside the church?

When Rosemary handed Maxwell the flashlight, he chose not to turn it on. There was enough light coming through the stained glass to see the shadowy forms gathered around the woman. A beam from the flashlight could cause a reaction from her that might do more harm than good. All attention was focused on her, but no one needed to see what they were doing. The gentle whispers and prayers and comforting hands in the darkness did not need illumination.

When the young woman took her first slurp of cider, everyone was able to exhale a sign of relief. There was life, the push to survive, and Maxwell wondered what else she had endured and lived through before ending up in front of The Mercy Seat.

After a few more swallows, Corley lowered the cup for the woman to catch her breath, but she instantly said, "No, please. More."

Her first words were spoken in a harsh rasp, but Maxwell could detect in her voice, that while strained, she spoke with determination.

"Good girl," Kenda whispered. "Drink slow. All will be well."

His wife might be talking softly to this young woman, but Maxwell hoped Kenda's words could soothe her soul along with the hot cider.

He handed Carlo the flashlight and knelt beside Kenda. He allowed the woman to sip a little more, and when she pulled her head back and began to take deep breaths, he decided it was safe to speak. He used the same tone as his wife.

"My name is Maxwell Crane. My family is here along with

very close friends." Maxwell spoke as though he were calming a frightened animal in hopes of persuading it into believing it was safe to come out of hiding. "Would you tell us your name?"

The woman was struggling, only able to take quick breaths. Maxwell could tell that Corley was bracing the woman's back with one arm while she held the mug of cider.

"Carrie, take the cider from your sister," Maxwell said.

When Carrie reached to take the mug from her sister, the woman pulled her hands from beneath the blanket and grabbed the mug taking several swallows before surrendering as if she would not have another opportunity to taste this restoring brew.

After she had finished drinking, she let go of the mug and Corley handed it off to Carrie before slipping onto the pew so she could use her shoulder and arms to help the woman lean against her and continue to sit upright.

The sanctuary was filled with her raspy breathing, and when she gradually began to calm, Maxwell quietly spoke to her once again.

"You were very brave tonight, and we are thankful that you escaped when you did…that we were all here to help."

"Thank you." She spoke with a breathy weariness. "Thank you."

"We would like to help you more." Kenda rested her hand on the girl's ankle. "We'd love to know your name."

Except for the young woman, Maxwell and the others held their breath. All were waiting. Maxwell did not want to further upset this foundling who had arrived at the doorstep of their church in such dramatic fashion. It was important to learn her name and speak it with love and sympathy. Maxwell suspected that when she heard her name spoken before, it sparked danger within her and a fear of punitive consequences. If the name was uttered now, it would signify trust.

"Honey, you are in a safe haven." Rosemary spoke gently in her soft husky voice. "You're in the house of the Lord, in the hands of His people, and in the heart of His heart. He knew your name while you were still in your mama's womb. Speak it now. All will be well."

Only Rosemary could declare such true words of comfort and for those words to be believed. If a miracle could be worked, Rosemary could speak it into existence. Maxwell need not do anything more. Patience was required now, and only Rosemary's kind voice could add to this coaxing offer with a hymn.

"Are we weak and heavy laden,
Cumbered with a load of care?
Precious Savior, still our refuge—
Take it to the Lord in prayer;
Do thy friends despise, forsake thee?
Take it to the Lord in prayer;
In his arms he'll take and shield thee;
Thou wilt find a solace there."

As Rosemary's voice trailed off, Maxwell saw the young woman raising her head in the shadowy light as if she might be expecting a heavenly appearance brought on by Rosemary's singing. She took a deep breath and exhaled toward the ceiling before lowering her head to address those alongside her.

"Leandra," she whispered. "My name is Leandra."

Chapter Six

The speaking of her name cleared the air like the utterance of a strange tongue during a time of worship. Maxwell waited to hear if Leandra would put forward anything in addition to her name, but this was all she had to offer. More patience was needed. There was more to learn from Leandra before deciding what should be done.

Between serving in Afghanistan to being the pastor at The Mercy Seat and tending to the Hells Canyon community, Maxwell had enough life experience that he should never be surprised by the unexpected, but the dramatic arrival of Leandra at the front door of the church had shaken him. Once he saw Leandra escape from the back of the van, his instincts kicked in and he ran toward danger, not from it. The last time he reacted in such a fashion someone had died, and he trembled at the vivid memory of that tragic moment. He was thankful the group around Leandra was shrouded by the sanctuary's vague darkness so they could not see his own shaky demeanor.

When Maxwell felt Kenda lean closer to him and place her hands on his back, he knew the shadows had not obscured him from his wife. What a blessing she was, is, and always would be. Even in the darkness she had sensed his distress, and her strong hands began to massage his arms and shoulders.

"You have a beautiful name, Leandra," Maxwell said, and then he waited, not so much to see how she might respond, but he waited on himself. He needed more time for Kenda's strong touch to calm the quaking inside him. He needed the jumbled memories in his mind to stop and dissipate. Leandra's arrival was a new state with a new reality that would require something from him that he had lost within himself since the incident. Leandra was like a spirit moving over the waters calling to his soul to rise from the deep.

Rosemary began humming "What a Friend We Have in Jesus." The lyric was not necessary. The confident droning was enough of an underscore for this moment. Leandra had breached a violent world and escaped into a new one. Rosemary's gentle voice had to be a palliative glaze over Leandra's heart. It certainly had that effect on his own soul.

"You are safe now, Leandra," Maxwell said, and he believed it. Inside this sanctuary she was safe, they were all safe, but Maxwell knew they could not stay here forever. Eventually they must emerge, and it was better to do so under the cover of nighttime. But what to do for Leandra? What to do with her?

Carlo took his iPhone from his back pocket and the screen lit up. Maxwell could see Leandra flinch in the soft pixel glow. He reached over to block the light from the phone with his hand.

"Dad, don't you want to call the police?" Carlo asked.

"Not yet, Son." Maxwell kept his voice calm as glass.

The idea of contacting the police seemed to unnerve Leandra. She pulled away from Corley's grasp, sat upright and began to moan while rapidly shaking her head.

"No, no, no," she repeated over and over. "No. They will come for me. They will find me. Too risky. Too dangerous. They will come after me."

This panicked response even caused Rosemary to cease her purring melody. She was being drowned out by Leandra's sobs that were on the verge of a full-blown wail.

"Leandra, who are 'they'?" Maxwell asked. "We want to help you. If we know who those people were in the van, then—"

"No. Please no. Don't want to go back there…don't want to go back."

Leandra collapsed back into Corley's lap and put her hands over her face.

Maxwell did not want to consider what might happen if she

did go back to that world. It might be worse for her than what she had previously experienced. Whatever that world might be, he did not want to increase the risk of a harsher life for Leandra.

"Daddy," Corley whispered as she stroked the top of Leandra's hands that still covered her face and muffled her whimpering.

"What, honey?" Maxwell said.

"Maybe we could…maybe we could take her home with us. You know, until it is safe for her, until we know what to do."

This thought sobered Maxwell. The idea did not come from him or Kenda or Rosemary. It came from his daughter. She saw the stranger at the door, the stranger who had already found a resting place in his daughter's lap, and Corley was ready to take her in. How will it be safe, he wondered? When will we know what to do?

"Maybe give her time to heal, time to feel protected," Corley said.

His daughter's words went deeper than Maxwell imagined, bypassing his head and began pulsating inside the chambers of his heart.

"She could have my bed. I could sleep on the foldout in Carrie's room."

Corley was way ahead of him. She was thinking through options beyond what Maxwell even contemplated. Carlo as well. In spite of Leandra's understandable reaction to his son's suggestion to call the police, it was something he had not yet given serious thought. Getting her off the street and learning her name was as far as he had gotten. Carlo had helped him carry her inside the church. Rosemary had sung an uplifting hymn. Kenda had massaged her feet. Carrie had brought her a hot drink. He, at least, had gotten her name.

A stranger had arrived in the sanctuary and lay before the altar of the Lord, and Maxwell, his family, along with Lin and Rosemary and even Ezekiel had been privileged to share this incomparable experience. Now they shared in finding a solution to this quandary even if only a temporary one. She had just escaped a worse predicament, and now lay in the sanctuary of The Mercy Seat.

Maxwell did not want to make a unilateral decision regarding Leandra's future. He had made so few decisions since the incident that he felt out of practice. This core group had helped him to this point. Without them his heart and mind was as wobbly as a new-born colt.

Maxwell leaned his head toward Kenda. "What do you think?" he whispered.

"This is like Mary and Joseph looking for a safe place in Bethlehem," she answered. "But we can do better than a manger in a stable."

This was what Maxwell needed to hear. He took Kenda's hand into his own. The offer would come from them both.

"Leandra, you are welcome to come home with us, if you would like," Maxwell said. "We would love to have you."

Leandra continued to breathe through her fingers, wet with tears and saliva until she finally lowered her hands and wiped them on the blanket.

"I got nothing but what I'm wearing." She raised her head off Corley's lap.

"We have everything you need," Kenda replied.

In the shadows there was just enough light for Maxwell to see the apprehension on Leandra's face. How could she not be fearful even with this offer of refuge? Given the life she knew, how could she not be hesitant to accept a new reality, a new extreme, albeit one that was just the opposite of what she had escaped?

"It would be an honor to have you with us for as long as you need," Maxwell said.

Leandra grabbed the back of the pew with one hand and pulled herself up. Lin stepped back so Leandra could swing her feet onto the floor.

"You have a nice family," Leandra said. "I don't want to wreck it."

If she only knew what he had done to wreck the family unit, Maxwell thought. Her presence would completely change the dynamic in the Crane household, Maxwell believed. Everyone's focus would shift from him to Leandra, and that would be a relief.

"We all know what it is like to pick up the pieces of a broken life," Kenda said. "Allow us to help you start picking up the pieces."

Leandra sighed as if such a decision was like lifting an immense weight but then she said, "I'll come home with you."

Rosemary raised her head and arms to the heavens," Thank you, Jesus. Thank you, Lord. This child has been lost and has now been found."

Maxwell rose to his feet and pulled Kenda beside him.

"We walked to the church tonight, Daddy," Carrie said. "Can she make it?"

Maxwell and everyone watched as Corley hurriedly unlaced her gently used and thoroughly sanitized, pink, combat boots Carrie had found on one of her dumpster dives that fit her perfectly. Then she knelt in front of Leandra.

"I bet these should fit." Corley pulled off her boots and began to help Leandra slip her feet into each one.

"I'd drive you home, but my car is chock full of gift baskets for the shut-ins," Rosemary said. "Ezekiel has to sit on my lap and not in his buckled in cage."

This was not a hardship for Ezekiel. Maxwell knew the cat preferred being tucked into the warm side of his mistress over the cage.

"All good, Rosemary," Maxwell said. "We'll cut through the Gardens like always. Be home before you know it. Carlo, would you and Lin help Rosemary to her car?"

Carlo and Lin escorted Rosemary out the side entrance. Maxwell stood at the door to be sure there was no one in the parking lot or on the highway. Once Rosemary and Ezekiel got into her car and drove onto the empty highway, Carlo and Lin returned to the side entrance.

"Did you see the van or anything else in front of the building?" he asked.

"Nothing. The street is empty," Carlo answered.

Maxwell looked inside the dark sanctuary. "Rock and roll, ladies. Let's go."

Kenda helped wrap the blanket around Leandra's shoulders as they made their way to the side entrance where Maxwell held the door open.

"Carlo, turn around." Corley approached the door in her sock feet.

When Carlo turned around Corley jumped onto his back.

"What are you doing?" He staggered forward as if his legs were unable to bear the weight. "You're killing me."

"Stop whining, big brother. It's like when we were kids." Corley slapped him on his rear end. "Now tally-ho."

Carlo whinnied like a horse then gingerly bounced in a circle around the slick parking lot as Carrie and Lin walked on either side of Leandra toward the Gardens projects.

After Maxwell locked the side door he put his arm over Kenda's shoulder. They stood side by side watching their kids and Lin walking the stranger toward their home.

"What have we done?" Maxwell whispered.

"I don't know, but I'm glad we did it."

Chapter Seven

Kenda quietly opened the door of Corley's bedroom, carrying a tray of breakfast food. Eggs, bacon, toast with butter and honey, a glass of orange juice, a small pot of hot water, and a selection of teabags and a packet of instant coffee. Kenda could not tell if Leandra was a tea drinker or preferred coffee. She hadn't asked Leandra her preference the night before when she left the young woman in Corley's bedroom.

When they had gotten home last night Corley insisted that Leandra take her room to give her some privacy. Kenda had the family stay downstairs while she helped Leandra settle into Corley's bedroom. She didn't want everyone looking at Leandra like she was a frightened exotic creature, which, to the Crane family, she was. She assumed Leandra had been looked at in all sorts of ways, none of them good or kind, and she did not want her family looking at this young woman with even benevolent curiosity. Kenda had Maxwell get her a glass of water, and then she led Leandra upstairs.

While Leandra stood in the doorframe of Corley's bedroom with the blanket she had been given at church wrapped tightly around her, Kenda switched on the desk lamp and lowered the blinds on the window. She waved for Leandra to come in, then Kenda set the glass of water on top of the dresser and pulled open the top drawer. She took out black flannel pajamas with a picture of William Shakespeare on the front and a "Will Power" caption above Will's wrinkled face. The top and bottom had been stuffed in the drawer, so Kenda shook them out and tucked the pajama top under her chin.

"This is futile," Kenda said after a few attempts to smooth out the wrinkles. "I tell Corley not to cram her clothes in the drawer, but does she listen? Least they're clean."

Leandra was not even looking at her and Kenda chuckled nervously. She followed Leandra's eyes as they roved over the walls of the room taking in all the posters and pictures and books and scripts, trinkets and knickknacks on bookshelves, and furniture with an open closet overflowing with a teenage girl's wardrobe. When Kenda observed the awed expression on Leandra's face, it dawned on her that something like a home and a private bedroom with such largess had not been a part of Leandra's short history. Back at the church when she had told them she had nothing but what she was wearing, Kenda could only imagine her life didn't include something like what consumed her field of vision with such wide-eyed wonder.

"Most of this stuff we got from thrift stores in the neighborhood or Carrie's dumpster dives." Kenda did not want Leandra to get the wrong impression, that they had a lot of money or that they indulged the wishes of their kids. She found herself comparing the lives of her children with her perception of the life they had rescued. She wanted to make Leandra feel equal and normal as if shopping at thrift stores and scavenging through dumpsters were the equalizers with the world of this young woman. There was nothing equal or normal about this situation, and Kenda could not avoid the discomfort creeping over her heart.

Kenda laid the "Will Power" pajamas on the bed and neatly folded them. She was glad that Corley had at least made her bed that morning, and she pulled back the sheet with an electric blanket between it and the coverlet. She placed the pajamas on the pillow and picked up the controls for the electric blanket.

"You might like this." Kenda held up the controls. "Corley turns the dial up to broil thirty minutes before getting into bed. Just turn the dial like so."

She demonstrated the mechanics, and while Leandra gave

Kenda her attention, there appeared to be no comprehension on her face of how the electric blanket operated.

"I'll set the temperature at Corley's preferred heat and warm up your bed, and you can adjust it when…once…you know, to your own liking."

Kenda set the controls on the edge of the desk next to the bed. She was not sure she was getting through. On some level Leandra was shell-shocked. She had escaped from a horrible situation and in an instant found herself in the home of perfect strangers standing in the middle of a strange teenage girl's bedroom, one she might have had were the circumstances different. The stranger had been taken in by strangers. *What if this child was my child,* Kenda wondered? Then she quickly dismissed the thought that was too awful to ponder.

"May I get you anything else before I say goodnight?" Kenda asked. When Leandra just shook her head and kept her eyes fixed on the controls of the electric blanket, Kenda took that as her cue to exit. "Well then, sleep as long as you like. We are on Christmas break, so we have no schedules to keep."

When Kenda slipped by Leandra, she had to resist the desire to embrace her, at least give her a motherly touch on her shoulder, but she chose not to. Better to give it time, and she quietly closed the door behind her.

When she came down the stairs, she found the family seated around the dining room table. As soon as they saw her the quiet conversation stopped and everyone waited. They expected a full report of the last few minutes, but what could she tell them? Kenda had done all the talking. She had pulled down the bed, laid out the pajamas, given instructions on how to use the electric blanket. She had tried her best to make the stranger feel welcome. But she felt like a failure, and when she tried to speak, the tears began to flow, which only made it worse. By her tears, the family would only assume that Leandra had told her more than she could bear, which was not the case. She would only be confessing her own thoughts and feelings that were convoluted at best.

"She never said a word to me. I turned down the bed and left her standing in the middle of the room," Kenda said struggling to gain control of herself. Then she looked at Corley. "I couldn't help but think of all the times I put you to bed, read you stories, listened to you when you needed to talk, kissed you goodnight, and now this…this…"

"Miracle," Corley interjected, and then she jumped up and moved to hug her mother.

Kenda wrapped her arms around her daughter. Maybe Corley was right. The appearance of this stranger was a miracle, but for what purpose and to what end?

"If we are going to wait to call the police, should we at least tell Reny?" Maxwell said. "It might be good to let him know, get his counsel."

"Yes, we should," Kenda said wiping her eyes. "But let's get a little more of her story. If we learn more then we will know how best to help her."

"Mom, I want to pray for her," Corley said.

Kenda pressed Corley to her side. There was a guest in their house like no other, and their collective response had been to bring her in, give her shelter, clothe her body, quench her thirst, and now pray for her well-being. Out of the mouth of her daughter came the tender words of thankfulness for this miraculous arrival, for the miracle taking place within their hearts, and for the hope of a future miraculous conclusion for the destiny of their guest, whatever that should be.

The first thing she noticed after she had gently opened the door of Corley's bedroom the next morning was the glass of water she had left on the dresser the night before. It had not been touched. Exhaustion must have taken over. Kenda tried to keep the dishes from rattling on the tray as she eased into the bedroom. The lamp on the desk was still on and the morning light bled through the cracks of the closed blinds. She could see the form on Corley's bed and hear the throaty breathing of deep sleep. Kenda did not want to awaken Leandra. Sleep was more important than food or drink, and she knew the fierce struggle of last night's trauma had taken a physical toll.

She tiptoed over to the dresser and set the tray of food on top. On the floor beside the bed she noticed two piles, one was the church blanket Leandra had been given to cover herself, and next to it lay the rhinestone jacket, her jeans and tee-shirt, and one shoe, the only items she had to her name. Kenda knelt down to pick them up but stopped. Was this a mother's natural response to gather dirty clothes and toss them in the washer or was it to gather up the molted skin of a former life and toss it away?

As Kenda's eyes adjusted she forgot her questioned impulse to grab Leandra's belongings the moment she caught sight of her bare back as she slept facing the wall. The "Will Power" pajama top had ridden up to her shoulders during the night. What she saw nearly took her breath away, bruises, scaring, and a crudely etched tattoo on the bicep of her right arm that read, "Daddy's Girl." She knew she could never unsee what she had seen, and she could never hear that term again and not think of it as a cruel endearment. Last night the blanket had kept these sights hidden, and she put her hand to her mouth to block the sob rising into her throat.

Kenda returned downstairs. She would not reveal what she had seen, and she was not sure what if anything she would tell Maxwell. This information might need to be held in her own heart for a time until she figured out what should be shared and not shared.

When she returned to the kitchen Kenda informed the family that their guest was sound asleep, and the order was given that until their guest awoke, no one was to go upstairs, and everyone was to speak in whispers. They must move through the house as quietly as possible, and if the kids required the bathroom they had permission to use the one in the master bedroom. Up until then it had been off limits to all but the parents. The Crane children almost keeled over to hear their mother break her cardinal rule proclaimed the moment they took possession of the house–they were denied access to her bathroom. Yes, the arrival of this stranger was becoming more of a miracle by the hour.

Supper was served early on rehearsal nights, and it was always takeout. Neither Kenda nor anyone else in the family had the energy or time to cook. Tonight the menu was Mexican from the second-generation family local El Azteca, a Crane favorite located in the heart of Hells Canyon. While life for the Crane household had taken on a new dimension with their unexpected guest, it had not, however, come to a complete stop or changed course. Kenda had a Christmas pageant to mount, and the show must go on. There was a cast of thousands with a lot of moving parts, and she had to use every minute of rehearsal to see that these untrained yet eager volunteers from the church and the neighborhood were in synch. Kenda and the family must get to the church and be ready when the cast began to flow into the building.

The aromas of authentic Mexican cuisine filled the downstairs when Maxwell entered the house and set the sacks on the dining room table. The table was set with drinks poured as the family passed the steaming dishes amongst themselves. At first, no one noticed Leandra. She appeared like a ghost until Kenda looked up from her plate. She cleared her throat with that motherly, attention-grabbing sound, and all eyes turned to the disheveled young woman, barefoot, hair mashed and matted, wearing Corley's black "Will Power" pajamas standing in the entrance to the dining room off the hallway.

How to greet her, Kenda wondered? She had already drawn

everyone's attention, but by the crimson flush of her face, Kenda knew Leandra needed to be absorbed into the family dinner as quickly as possible and with no fanfare.

"I'm sorry," Leandra mumbled. "I just woke up and didn't know what to do."

Kenda immediately rose from her chair as did Maxwell.

"No, no. It's fine," Kenda said. "Are you hungry?"

Leandra looked like she needed to ponder the question before she answered.

"Did you see the breakfast tray I left for you?" Kenda asked. "I'm sure the food's cold by now."

Maxwell pulled out the empty chair next to Corley and invited Leandra to sit.

"Where's the other girl?" Leandra asked remaining in place.

No one responded to her question. Kenda realized her family was apprehensive, not knowing how they should relate to her. She was unsure herself.

"Oh, you mean Lin, my brother's girlfriend," Corley said. "She drove home around noon once the roads were clear. Come on, sit down by me. You like Mexican?"

"I love Mexican," Leandra replied, but she remained frozen in place.

"Great. There's plenty." Corley rose and offered Leandra a plate. "What do you like?"

"Everything," Leandra said, but when the family found her answer amusing, Leandra flinched.

"We have loads of everything." Corley began dishing black beans and rice onto her plate, then grilled vegetables and chicken strips and held it up to Leandra. This seemed to be what she was waiting for, and she moved to take her seat at the table.

Leandra dove into her plate. She shoveled in fork after fork, barely inhaling, with loud swallows in between. When she lifted her glass of water to wash down the food, she noticed everyone staring at her and she paused.

"I am so glad you're hungry." Kenda tapped her fork against her water glass drawing everyone's attention away from Leandra.

When the family went back to eating Leandra took a couple of swallows of water and set her glass back down.

Kenda noticed her staring at the remaining food on her plate. It was that same far-away stare she had seen last night in Corley's bedroom.

"Looks like you got a good night's sleep," she said. "I hope the bed was comfortable."

"What were you all doing at the church last night?" Leandra asked, and then took another drink of water.

The question seemed to come out of nowhere, but it did have a perfect logic. Kenda was the last person she had spoken to once they got home, and other than offering Leandra the names of everyone in the family, there had been no explanation as to why they happened to be in the right place at the right time.

"We're putting on a Christmas pageant at The Mercy Seat," Kenda said. "We had just finished rehearsal and we were the last to leave the church."

"Christmas pageant. Is that like the baby Jesus story?" Leandra asked.

"Yes it is," Kenda said. "We have rehearsal in about an hour."

"You should come with us." Corley seemed hit by sudden inspiration. "We could put you to work."

"What would I do?"

"Oh trust me, there will be plenty to do," Kenda said.

"Is that cat lady going to be there, the one who sang last night in the church?"

"You mean Rosemary," Maxwell answered. "Yes, she will be there along with her cat, Ezekiel. They are inseparable, and I know she would be glad to see you."

Leandra went back to staring at her plate as if contemplating what all this meant.

"This is a lot to take in right now," Kenda offered, but she believed she should at least acknowledge the unusual circumstances in which they all found themselves. "I know you've come into a new world that might seem overwhelming, but we want you to know that you're safe here and welcome. We'd love you to come with us."

Leandra blinked her eyes, raised her head, and took in the family seated around the table, finally coming to rest on Corley next to her.

"You got something I could wear?" Leandra said, her fingers pinching at the "Will Power" top.

"Closet full of possibilities," Corley said with excitement. "Let's go."

Both girls jumped up and headed toward the hallway.

"Can I come with you?" Carrie asked with that look of not wanting to be left out.

"Of course," Corley said. "You can help us pick the outfit."

Kenda noticed her son and husband watching the girls race down the hallway and disappear up the stairs. Then they both turned and looked at her.

"I think it's best she come with us," Kenda said. "Certainly safer."

"I can't imagine what she's been through," Maxwell said.

"We can't erase her past," Kenda said. "But maybe we can give her a fresh start. It's worth a try, wouldn't you say?"

She gave her husband an expectant glance, expectant and hopeful that there may be two opportunities here for a new beginning. Maybe a secret contained in this miracle arrival was a new start for her husband, as well. Kenda saw the old Maxwell in action last night running to rescue Leandra, bringing her back inside the church, and gently coaxing her to say her name. Maybe a new life for Leandra would bring a new life for her husband. She could only hope.

"Yes, my dear," Maxwell whispered. "It's worth a try."

Chapter Eight

As soon as the side door of the church opened, Rosemary was standing at the entrance with Ezekiel in his customary perch. She was all smiles as the Crane family and Leandra stepped in out of the cold. Rosemary had arrived early to open the building and let in the first arrivals for rehearsal. If it was up to Rosemary, the church would be open twenty-four-seven. She wanted God's house available for anyone day or night. She often described The Mercy Seat as the messy emergency room of the kingdom of heaven, a welcoming shelter for the estranged and disaffected. One did not have to be "put together and buttoned down to walk through these doors." It was like Jesus welcoming the blind and lame into the Temple once he had cleaned house and driven out the money-changers.

"Come into God's house, baby," Rosemary said reaching out her hand to Leandra and guiding her toward the office.

Rosemary had gotten a call from Maxwell ahead of time that they would bring Leandra with them to rehearsal but thought it best if she could stay in the office until she felt safe to come and watch. Maxwell said that they did not want to bring undue attention to Leandra if everyone saw her as a guest of the Cranes.

"We'll be right out here if you want to come and watch," Corley said, stopping at the door of the office as Rosemary and Leandra stepped inside.

"Thank you, Corley," Rosemary said. "We may do that when it comes time for my scene. Ezekiel and I have a lot of rehearsing to do before I have to get on the stage."

"Carrie or I will come get you when Mom's ready to do your scene."

"I've been lifting my prayers to heaven for the Lord to get me through this."

"You'll do great, Mama Rose," Corley said, turning back into the sanctuary.

Rosemary closed the door to the office and looked back at Leandra standing in the middle of the room wearing a bewildered expression.

"A church office in a church. Not what you're used to, I suppose," Rosemary said.

Leandra shook her head and tried to smile but her face could not maintain it.

"You'll do fine here, honey. It will be fine." Rosemary instinctively knew to take small steps even with her encouragement. Leandra came from a life unimaginable to her. It was not necessary for Rosemary to know where this young woman came from. All she knew was that she had come out of the darkness and into the light.

Rosemary's task was to make Leandra feel safe until she could take a deep breath, until the surface of her heart would be calm, and until she would not always be looking over her shoulder for potential danger. Rosemary had to believe there was a different future for Leandra, and as a member of the hospitality committee, to welcome her into a new life.

"Those must be Corley's clothes," Rosemary said pointing to the ensemble of black jeans, sweater vest with a white turtleneck underneath, along with the pink, Doc Martin boots. "You two are about the same size. They fit you real nice."

"Could I have more of that apple drink you gave me last night?" Leandra asked.

"Coming right up." Rosemary was most happy when she had a task to serve.

She had learned to do everything in the office with one hand, Ezekiel tying up the other hand most of the waking hours. She filled a mug with water from the dispenser, ripped open the packet of apple cider powder, poured it into the mug, set it in the micro and put the timer on for two minutes.

"Let me get you a chair." Rosemary went around behind Maxwell's desk and dragged his chair to where Leandra stood.

Rosemary had not seen Leandra in full light. Her long dark hair cascaded around her shoulders. Her skin had isolated blemishes, and there was a scar that cut her right eyebrow down the middle. Rosemary did not want to imagine how that might have happened. Leandra had a pleasant face though clouded by hardship. If she could smile, Rosemary thought, her face might have an air of beauty. Leandra looked like a regular young girl, maybe early twenties, but there was nothing regular about her.

"Please take a seat, honey," Rosemary said just as the dinger went off on the microwave. She set the mug on top of the microwave and stirred the cider with a spoon. "This is my favorite winter drink," she said before handing Leandra the mug.

Rosemary did not want to stare at Leandra while she cooled the hot cider with her breath, so she grabbed the pages to the scene between Elizabeth and Mary off her desk.

"I liked that song you sang last night," Leandra said.

Here was a second memory mentioned from the night before, but for the life of her, Rosemary could not remember singing any song. She was having enough trouble remembering her lines in the play. It had to be a hymn. That was all the music she knew.

"Well, I'm glad you liked it." Rosemary turned around to look at Leandra, and she could feel her face flushing with embarrassment. "But I'm sorry. I don't remember singing last night. Do you recall anything about the song?"

"There were some strange words I'd never heard, but something about taking it to the Lord in prayer."

"In prayer." Rosemary immediately remembered the song she sang as she repeated those last two words with Leandra. "I was singing 'What a Friend We Have in Jesus.' It was the first thing that popped into my mind."

"I guess," Leandra said shrugging her shoulders. "Would you sing it again?"

Rosemary could hardly believe her ears, and maybe for the first time in a long time, she had no word of response. Something was happening that she couldn't explain in any other way than divine. Last night this terrified young woman was a lost wave that crashed onto the shore of The Mercy Seat. It took a moment for Rosemary to emerge from her amazement and offer a response.

"I will sing that hymn for you, if it is the last thing I do, but I have a request of you before I do that."

Rosemary could detect the surprise and apprehension on Leandra's face, and she almost regretted her forwardness, but she chose not to retract her words. Maybe it was time to entice this young woman to take another step into the light.

"Sure, I guess," Leandra responded. "If I can."

"I believe you can." Rosemary held out her script to Leandra. "Kenda calls it 'running lines.' These lines have been flying all through my head like blind birds and never come out right. If you could follow along, make sure I'm saying the right words, and then read what Mary says so I can hear it. That would be a big help."

Rosemary saw Leandra's hesitancy to take the pages, and she felt a twinge of regret that she might have overstepped. When Leandra took the pages and began looking them over, her eyes marveling at the lines, her lips trying to mouth the words, Rosemary became anxious at the possibility that Leandra might not be able to read very well, or not at all. Rosemary was preparing to give Leandra a pass, but then she began to speak.

"Auntie Elizabeth, are you home?" Leandra said reading directly from the script.

Rosemary was taken aback and forgot what came next. She had not heard anyone say Mary's lines because Kenda had yet to find someone to play the role. It was not until Leandra looked up from the page that Rosemary realized she was to speak her line.

"Oh, shoot, yes, what is it? What do I say?" Rosemary asked

snapping her fingers in irritation at herself.

"Mary is that you? Have you come all the way from Naz…Naz…something? I don't know how to say it." Leandra looked up from the script.

"Yes, of course. Nazareth," Rosemary responded before answering with Elizabeth's line. "Mary is that you? Have you come all the way from Nazareth?"

Rosemary rushed through her line and Leandra immediately picked up her cue.

"Yes, Auntie," Leandra read. "I had to come find you. No one would believe what has happened to me. No one but you. I can't tell my parents. I dare not tell Joseph. I don't know what to do. I'm afraid of what people will do and say when they find out what has happened to me. You are the only one who would understand."

The surprises just kept coming. Rosemary marveled at what she heard. Not only could Leandra read, but she read as if she understood what she was saying and why she was saying it. There was an urgency in Leandra's voice, with an added twinge of fear at the prospect of what might happen to Mary. It was an uncanny ability to inhabit a role.

Rosemary dropped into her seat without taking her eyes off Leandra. "Child, what have you done to me," she whispered, awed as if she had discovered a lost, ancient treasure. Then an even bigger miracle happened. As soon as Rosemary settled into her seat, Ezekiel leapt out of the crook of Rosemary's arm, and in one bound, jumped into Leandra's lap forcing her to set the mug of hot cider on a table behind her.

"My Lord, the Son of God must be standing at the door, ready to come get His own," Rosemary said, her voice quivering and her eyes becoming misty. Ezekiel had never willfully sought out the lap of another human being, and Rosemary had to tamp down a stab of jealousy. Her very own companion had left her for another.

"What's the matter?" Leandra asked looking first at Rosemary and then into the face of Ezekiel nestling in her lap. Leandra held up her hands, as surprised by Ezekiel's sudden move as was Rosemary. "What did I do?"

"Nothing, child. You were just being you," Rosemary offered. "I've had nothing but the jitters for days over this part." She weakly waved her hand in the air. "I was holding onto Ezekiel like he was a lifeline. I guess he got tired of absorbing my nerves and needed to find a calmer leg to light on to get some peace."

When the door opened into the office, the hubbub of cast members brought Rosemary out of her daze.

"Mama Rose, we're on a ten," Corley said. "Mom says we'll pick up with your scene after the break."

Rosemary barely swiveled in her chair to look at Corley.

"Honey, would you ask your mother to step in here for a minute?" she asked.

"Sure thing," Corley said, and she disappeared leaving the door open a crack.

Rosemary turned back and noticed that Leandra still held her hands in the air. She looked confused, not knowing what she should do with Ezekiel's intrusion.

"It's all right, child," Rosemary signed. "He just needs his ear's scratched."

Leandra's empty hand slowly descended, and she began to rub the back of Ezekiel's head.

It was Ezekiel's contented purring that got to Rosemary. This was what it must feel like to be jilted, Rosemary mused. She felt the weight of her empty hands and the sudden absence of the one she had devoted her love and attention to for so long. Out of the blue the object of her devotion sought the affection of another. Rosemary assumed this was a sign from the Lord, maybe a double sign, hold loosely all things in this life, even her precious Ezekiel. This young woman had arrived at the door of The Mercy Seat for a purpose no one could have imagined.

"You wanted to see me?" Kenda stuck her head through the door.

"I would like you to listen to this." Rosemary pointed to Leandra and her beloved Ezekiel resting on a stranger's lap. "Honey, would you please read Mary's lines again. I'll come in with my cue this time."

Kenda stepped into the room and closed the door behind her. Then Leandra began to read, and Rosemary leaned toward her and gave her line right on cue. After she spoke, Rosemary leaned back and let Leandra read the words of Mary the way she had done before, but this time she added the extra business of scratching behind Ezekiel's ears while she said her lines. When she was finished, Leandra looked at the two women.

Rosemary swiveled in her chair and faced Kenda. She did not have to say anything. She had given Ezekiel his freedom and set Leandra up in the best possible way to show she was perfect for the role of Mary.

"That was wonderful, Leandra." Kenda moved a little farther into the room. She looked at Rosemary, and the "mother" of The Mercy Seat nodded her approval.

"Leandra, you read those words beautifully. Who knew, right?" Kenda glanced at Rosemary who responded with a whispered 'Amen.' "I know this may sound unusual, but would you consider being the Mary in our Christmas pageant? There are only a few more rehearsals left before our first show, and I think you are perfect."

"I don't know," Leandra said. "What do I have to do?"

"You will need to memorize your lines, but my girls would love to help you. And you have a few scenes, like with Rosemary who plays your Aunt Elizabeth."

"The one we just read?" Leandra asked.

"Yes," Rosemary said beginning to recover from Ezekiel leaving her in the lurch and warming to the idea of the three of them being in the scene together. "We will have Ezekiel on stage with us. Now that I see he has warmed to you, I think it will work."

As much as Rosemary wanted to restore Ezekiel to his proper

place at her side, she did not want to disrupt this delicate moment of Leandra coming to her own decision and making a choice that might enhance her life, maybe even change it. Rosemary imagined Leandra probably had few choices in her life, and they were all centered on survival.

"Once you and Joseph are in Bethlehem and have the baby Jesus, you would need to hold the baby and place him in the manger," Kenda said.

"You mean I have to hold a live baby," Leandra said daunted by the prospect.

"There are a few mothers in the church with newborns, and they have volunteered their babies for a performance," Kenda answered.

"Look, I never held a baby and I'm no virgin," Leandra blurted.

While this news took no one by surprise, Rosemary was at a loss for words. She had come to the end of her capacity to effect the desired outcome. She had made the discovery of raw talent and introduced her to the director. Now she really did want to snatch Ezekiel into her arms if for no other reason than to hide her own discomfort.

"Leandra, I don't know all the reasons why God brought you to our front door," Kenda said. "But here you are. You needed shelter and we needed a Mary. I think you have a natural talent, and you're right for this part. We'd love to have you in the pageant, but I don't want to add stress to your life. Please, feel no pressure."

Ezekiel caught Rosemary's eyes. He shook his head and looked around, and as if he had awakened from a dream and realized he had somehow wandered into unfamiliar territory, he jumped onto the floor and into the waiting hands of his mistress. Rosemary lifted him to her chest and began to stroke Ezekiel from his head all the way down through the end of his tail. He had come home, and Rosemary was whole again.

"We have people from all over the neighborhood flowing in

and out of our church," Kenda added. "You would be welcomed by everyone. You think you'd like to play the role of Mary?"

It thrilled Rosemary to hold Ezekiel close and observe Leandra's face as it began to show signs of accepting the offer. Leandra's outward gaze went from bafflement to becoming her own person with the power to make her own choice.

"Yeah, I'll do it. Why not?"

"Hallelujah." Rosemary looked at Kenda. "We have us a Mary."

Chapter Nine

It was unsettling for Maxwell to have a fourth female in the house, especially given the life he assumed she must have had leading up to the dramatic circumstances of her arrival. While the whole family had embraced the idea of taking her in, Leandra was the center of attention, which changed the natural routine of the household. Then the added factor of mounting the pageant increased the family dynamic to a sense of urgency. So many things to get done in so little time, and this raised his level of discomfort. Maxwell was used to the normal chaos of production at home when Kenda did her high school plays, but this production was at The Mercy Seat and involved the whole family right down to his role as Joseph.

Maxwell could not remember agreeing to doing the role. He must have said "yes" at some point, but he had no memory of any conversation with his wife where such an agreement was made. In spite of his uneasiness, he had to admit that not only was his family enjoying this shared experience, but the pageant was also bringing the church community and the neighborhood together in a special way. At each rehearsal, Maxwell could see the delight and pride on the faces of the cast and worship band as they interacted in creating this experience. Was this not the whole point? Was not this his desire as a pastor to have The Mercy Seat be an oasis in the midst of a community that had more than its share of hardships? To provide opportunities for people to gather in joyful fellowship?

Still, Maxwell felt like an observer, not a participant, of everything going on around him. He watched himself move about in the familiar places of church, home, and neighborhood as a stranger not only to himself but to others. For the day-to-day life, he would be in the here and now with everyone, speak when spoken to, join in on a required activity like collecting the take-out dinners, doing laundry, attending play rehearsal, but he was never fully present. He was a wax figure on exhibition, an exterior recognizable to others, yet only able to relate on a surface level. He was unable to break through the invisible barriers restricting deep personal connection.

His awkwardness was most obvious with Leandra. When Kenda had shared with him the scarring and tattoos she had seen on Leandra's arms and back that first day after they had taken her in, he could not get that out of his mind. Given the close quarters of their house or at church, Maxwell did not know how he should act around Leandra. A father? A pastor? Some kind of a therapist?

He had little conversation with her since that first night, allowing Kenda and the girls to take the lead on that front, while he remained in the background. From what little he knew about the male-dominated world from which she escaped, Maxwell did not want to give her any reason for her to believe he was like them. He said the same to Carlo, but his son was so smitten with Lin that it was not an issue.

Maxwell agreed that all the familial effort made on Leandra's behalf would give her the possibility of a new start in life. That process began now in their home but would continue with people better qualified to facilitate positive opportunities for Leandra. He and Kenda concurred that until they could decide the best course of action to help Leandra that they would confine themselves to church and home. The short walk through the Gardens projects to and from both locations would be the only brief forays into the outside world.

The days since her arrival flew by. Maxwell took pleasure in how Kenda and the girls had embraced Leandra as their own personal mission to help her feel comfortable in this unusual world she had fallen into.

To his surprise, when it came to portraying Mary, Leandra was a natural. After a few rehearsals she overcame any timidity she had about accepting the role. She took direction well from Kenda, and Corley and Carrie were constantly helping her with her lines and character motivation. In the few scenes he and Leandra had together as Joseph and Mary he had to remind himself not to stare in wonder at how well she was doing. She was an example to him. Here was someone coming out of a traumatic life and engaging with a new one. Why could he not do the same? Why was he having such difficulty emerging out of the recent trauma in his life and finding his way?

Maxwell witnessed Rosemary take Leandra under her wing the moment she agreed to play Mary. When the cast members observed how kind and caring she treated Leandra during the rehearsal time, they all embraced her as well, no questions asked. Such was the way of The Mercy Seat church community—few questions were asked and none of them pried. Rosemary led by example.

Even though the story of the pageant centered around the biblical miracles of appearances by heavenly angels, the implausible births of an elderly Elizabeth and a virgin Mary, and the eastern star guiding wisemen to the manger, Maxwell had to admit that the biggest present-day miracle of all was seeing Ezekiel in the arms of Leandra. Every time they rehearsed their scene, Ezekiel would jump from Elizabeth's lap into Mary's arms. Only Maxwell could appreciate such a phenomenon. All the years he and Rosemary had worked together it was rare to see any physical separation between feline and mistress. It was a "till death do they part" symbiosis. To his astonishment, the arrival of Leandra produced this miracle. However, when it came time for Leandra to deliver Mary's song of praise at the end of their scene, Kenda had insisted that Leandra give Ezekiel back to Rosemary. The virgin Mary holding a cat while reciting the Magnificat was too much poetic license.

The start-time for the first two public performances had to be delayed because of crowd control. People arrived an hour early just to get a seat. Maxwell had not even considered offering tickets to the shows. They were not charging an admission fee, so why issue tickets? The performances were free and when the church doors opened a flood of humanity poured into the sanctuary. There were no extra chairs to set up along the side aisles or in the foyer, but that did not discourage anyone. Maxwell instructed the ushers to tell the people if they wanted to stand for the performance they were welcomed to do so. Both side aisles were jammed all the way down to the front row pews which made it difficult for the shepherds and wisemen and citizens of Bethlehem sitting on the floor to make their entrance and exit. Once the foyer reached capacity the church doors were closed and they could begin the performance. If the Fire Marshall arrived, he would not even be able to enter to give the order to shut down.

The standing room only problem continued into the third and final night of the pageant. Maxwell had saved an entire pew for Rendell and the people he was bringing from the cathedral to see the final show. He would not have done that for anyone else. He owed this man so much. He could not have survived this long without Reny's aid and comfort and spiritual guidance. Reserving a pew was a small payback for the abundance of kindness he had received from this man.

Even though turning people away was something Maxwell never wanted to do, he decided to take the long view and consider it a blessing. If Rendell and those members from the cathedral saw firsthand the excitement and appreciation the people who lived in Hells Canyon and the Gardens had for the church, then perhaps the cathedral's movers and shakers might be more persuaded to lend their influence in altering the proposed gentrification of the neighborhood. Maxwell would welcome such a miracle, and maybe packed houses would help nudge that along in a positive way.

After securing the pew for Reny and the cathedral crowd, Maxwell slipped out the side entrance before the front doors were open and the hordes rushed to their seats. He needed a smoke before the show began. The cast and band were crammed into his office getting into costume. They were basking in the success of the first two performances and excited about this final one. He would slip back in once everyone had vacated his office to get into costume and see if Kenda needed any last-minute help. He caught her eye before going out the door and gestured that he would be in the parking lot. She knew exactly what he was about to do and she pressed her fists into her sides and shook her head. Maxwell returned her look of disapproval with a helpless shrug. His wife was indulging his new habit but he did not want to abuse her tolerance. He'd promised her it was a short-term fix to help him through this bumpy time, but he was not sure he could keep his promise.

Most of the audience was from the neighborhood and would walk to the church even on a cold night in December. But the parking lot was still full. Cars were even pulling onto the basketball court adjacent to the parking lot. This was another miracle Maxwell had never seen, an overflowing parking lot. He pulled a pack of smokes from his jacket pocket and lit one as he ambled toward the alley behind the church.

"How long is my sister going to let you keep sneaking out for a smoke?"

The voice he knew. It was not his conscience. It was Pete.

"She hates it, but I'm getting away with it for now."

Maxwell held up the pack of smokes but Pete declined the offer.

"The kids were wondering if their Uncle Pete would show up," Maxwell said.

"Wouldn't miss it." Pete tucked his hands under his arms for warmth.

"It's another standing room only house." Maxwell pointed to the people streaming from the parking lot toward the front entrance of the church.

"If the church thing doesn't work out, maybe you could go into show business." Pete splayed his fingers and waved his jazz hands.

"I think both worlds have more in common than people realize."

"You excited about all this?" Pete waved a hand over the gathering crowd.

Maxwell took a drag from his cigarette and looked away.

"Your silence indicates not so much," Pete said.

"No, I'm into it," Maxwell said. "Kenda and the kids are loving it. The community loves it. The church is jammed. What's not to be excited about?"

Maxwell shivered from the cold and wrapped his arms around himself to hold in some warmth. He could not explain why he did not want to make eye contact with Pete. He had not seen him since they visited on the church steps the night of rehearsal, the night Leandra came into their lives. How many days ago was that? Maxwell could not remember. He had been to war with this man, married his sister, considered him as close to a brother as he could possibly have, yet tonight, he was not capable of small talk or big talk even with someone he loved.

"How is your house guest?" Pete asked.

Soon after they brought Leandra home with them, Maxwell and Kenda decided they needed to solicit some advice. They wanted to honor Leandra's panicked request not to call the police and felt they could not yet bring Reny into the conversation. Rosemary and Lin could be trusted not to reveal any details of the situation or Leandra's personal life, but outside of the small group who had witnessed the dramatic episode in front of the church that night, they could only think of Pete. He had agreed that this sudden incursion into their lives was beyond their skill set and they needed to actively seek professional help, the sooner the better. But he accepted the fact that the timing was tricky and needed to keep everything on the down-low until arrangements could be made for her transition.

"Kenda and the girls have really embraced her," Maxwell answered. "And Rosemary has taken her under her wing in a way I have never seen before."

"I'm not surprised. All of them have big hearts. And what about you?"

"Like you suggested, staying on the sidelines." Maxwell shrugged his shoulders. "I will support, but I'm letting the ladies take the lead."

"Sounds like you're staying clearheaded about this." Pete tapped his forehead with his finger.

"As soon as this pageant is over, we're getting her into some kind of program."

"The sooner the better. This is not normal, you have to admit. A young girl, age what? Early twenties, you say?"

"If that," Maxwell replied. "It's hard to tell given the world she's come from. But older than Carlo for sure."

"I don't want to spook you, Maxwell, but given her world and how she came to you, none of it makes sense. Jumping out of a van full of people, I mean…"

"I haven't told anyone but you about what I saw inside that van. I don't want to scare my family." Maxwell heard Kenda call his name and he hid the cigarette behind his back.

"Come on. It's time to get into costume." Kenda had the side door propped open with her foot to keep the cold air from blowing into the sanctuary.

"Do you have an extra costume for your brother?" Maxwell shouted. "You could make him a wiseman."

"More like a wise guy," Kenda motioned to Pete. "Come on,

big brother. I love to see you quaking inside the church."

"Let the torture begin," Pete started toward the door opening his arms to his sister.

Maxwell used Pete as cover to flick his cigarette away without Kenda noticing, then he caught up with them as they stepped inside the church.

Kenda pointed to the "Reserved" sign at the end of the front row.

"I can see you squirm on the pew," she said and kissed her brother on the cheek.

"So this is your way of winning my soul to God." Pete smiled at his sister.

"Face it, Brother. I'm never giving up on you, and neither is God."

"She's got your back, Pete, whether you like it or not," Maxwell said patting him on his shoulder.

Pete threw up his hands in a gesture of surrender and then worked his way through the shepherds and townsfolk on the floor to his spot on the pew.

"The wisemen can't find their props," Kenda said.

"What a terrible thing to show up at the manger empty handed," Maxwell said, which got him a playful slap on his arm. "I think I saw them behind my desk last night before we went home. I'll check."

"We'll have to hold the show again tonight," Kenda said as they watched the people filing into the sanctuary. "But if you could get the props for me, I'd appreciate it."

"Done," Maxwell said and began to work his way toward the church office.

When he got around to the other side of the stage, he saw that the door to the office was halfway open, and the lights turned off. This was unusual. The door was always open and the lights were not turned off until right before the show started. When Maxwell opened the door and flipped on the lights, he saw someone in costume with their back to him talking on the office phone. The person was as startled as he was when the lights came on, but Maxwell was more startled to see Leandra turn around with the receiver of the church phone pressed inside the headdress of her costume.

Maxwell could hear a muffled voice coming through the phone line but could not tell if it was male or female, and Leandra cupped the mouthpiece with her hand.

"Please keep looking. I want to find her," Leandra said, then quickly hung up.

Leandra was nervous, that was clear, but Maxwell did not want to interrogate her, not with the play about to begin. He did not want to appear threatening in any way.

"I've been trying to find my mother for a while now," Leandra offered breaking the silence. "I hadn't seen her in forever. Don't know if she's in town, or gone, or dead."

"I hope she's not dead," Maxwell managed to say.

"Me too. Just trying to find out." Leandra took a small step away from Maxwell's desk. "Wanted her to know I'm getting out of the life."

"Daddy, I came as quick as I could," Carrie said as she stepped into the office.

Maxwell did not give the expected response. Carrie was dressed in the generic garb of a citizen of Bethlehem. Both she and Corley chose to be in costume so they would not be conspicuous as they guided the different people groups to their various places during the performance.

"Yes. Yes." Maxwell finally picked up his cue. "And not a moment too soon."

"Come on," Carrie said with a twinge of frustration. "You need to get into costume. We'll be starting soon."

Leandra bolted from the desk. Carrie and Maxwell moved aside as she rushed by.

"Carrie, would you get the props for the wisemen and take

them to your mother," Maxwell said. "They're behind my desk."

"Sure," Carrie said. She dashed over to the desk, gathered up a tray of props, and scooted to the door. "Hurry up," she said leaving Maxwell still standing at the door.

Maxwell had never heard mention of a mother, either from Leandra or Kenda or the girls. Leandra had offered little personal history in the time she had lived with them, and she had never made a request to try and contact her mother or anyone outside the world she had escaped. The pageant had consumed most of their waking hours and Leandra had been absorbed in the furious activity of mounting a show. Now Pete's words hit him. Was there reason to mistrust? Reason to sense danger?

Maxwell moved over to his desk. How long had she been here alone? Who could she be talking with about her mother? Was anything missing on his desk or in the office? He scanned the top and then went to the other side and opened a drawer. He kept nothing of value inside the desk, but still he checked. He knew Rosemary had a petty cash box squirreled away somewhere, but he didn't know where she kept it.

Then the feeling of self-reproach struck him, expelling his initial reaction of mistrust and suspicion. This was the natural response to a stranger, and he knew what it felt like. Such judgmental attitudes toward Leandra were not good. What was good was that she wanted to find her mother. It was good that she felt comfortable enough to begin the process with a simple phone call. If her mother were out there, that might be a new beginning for Leandra that would provide a happy ending to her sad story. But for now, the show must go on, and he was still in his street clothes.

"Get it together, Maxwell," he muttered. "Time to suit up."

Chapter Ten

Maxwell stood with Mary and the baby Jesus as the wisemen lay their gifts before the holy child. Instead of watching in awe as the oriental royals presented their offerings, Maxwell kept his eye on Leandra. She was indeed a natural, speaking her lines, interacting with the others, especially with Rosemary who had shined as Elizabeth, thanks in part to Ezekiel. At first, Kenda had just been relieved she had discovered a Mary, but when Leandra took to the role, Kenda couldn't help sharing a feeling of pride at how she might have facilitated a fresh start for this young woman. Maxwell wasn't sure, but maybe the acting was too good. He knew he needed to tamp down his suspicion, so he shifted his gaze and looked out over the sanctuary. The aisles were full, including the center aisle. Young children sat on the windowsills. The foyer was crammed. To accommodate anyone else, they would have to hang off the rafters.

Maxwell appreciated the unique beauty of the one-hundred-year-old building, from the stained-glass windows to the fine maple pews to the hardwood floors, the exposed oak beams, the plaster walls and ceiling. But when it came to improvements, the budget constraints did not allow for many modern upgrades. There was no state-of-the-art technology.

When it came to theatrical lighting, there was none. There were two choices for the sanctuary lights—on or off. There were no light adjustments to signify scene transitions or special lighting to highlight special moments in the play. All the action was done in full view and left up to the collective imagination of the audience to accept all changes of locale. From Maxwell's observation, no one in the sanctuary seemed to mind including Jeff Anderson. He and his wife Lindy were seated next to Rendell. Maxwell had not known who Reny was bringing with him from the cathedral, but the Anderson's had made the cut.

Why had Anderson come to the show? The last time Maxwell and Anderson had shared a moment it had not gone well. Maxwell stormed out of the top floor of Anderson's tower offices when the mayor announced the razing of Hells Canyon and the Gardens. According to Anderson's new architectural design, there would be a new world order of the neighborhood that included a brand-new Mercy Seat building in a different location than its present one. Anderson had just taken the position of chair of the Mercy Seat Ministries, at the behest of Reny, and Maxwell had accused Anderson of doing so only to assure that his empire could control this great reimagining of Richland's poorest quarter of the city.

Even though Kenda had shared with Maxwell her brief but important conversation she had with Anderson concerning the future of Hells Canyon and the church, Maxwell had been too self-absorbed after the incident to consider a potential change of heart in Anderson. Given the political upheaval in Richland, the city council had stalled final approval of plans for a revitalized community, but as far as Maxwell was concerned, the wrecking ball would start to swing once things got back to normal.

He could not imagine Anderson had come to the show tonight out of any Christmas spirit or benevolent motivation. The lowly condition of the building would only reinforce Anderson's original plan to tear down the church and construct a new one. Good money after bad, Maxwell was sure of it, and he did not want to hang around after the show and have Reny compel an uncomfortable reunion.

As soon as the bows were taken and the cast began to mingle with its adoring public, Maxwell slipped off the stage and took cover in his office. He peeked out of the office and saw Kenda and Rosemary receiving their much-deserved praise from Rendell and his cathedral guests. Leandra was tucked in between them smiling like the star she had become. There were so many people Maxwell guessed it would take a while for them to exit the building, so he grabbed his smokes and moved to the rear door of the office that opened onto the small plot of ground behind the church. The back-yard was little more than open-air storage for the aged church van, a weathered picnic table, and a charcoal grill chained to the table leg.

When Maxwell lifted the lid on the grill the hinges were so rusted it fell onto the ground. He could not remember the last time this grill had been used and he did not bother to pick it up. It was not worth carting off for scrap metal. The timeworn H-VAC unit connected to the back of the building rattled and gasped. The alley cut between the church and the Gardens projects. This little plot of property illuminated in the bright moonlight was nothing more than a mini slum environ.

Maxwell sat on the tabletop and pulled out a cigarette. Just before lighting up, he remembered he was still in costume. Kenda would kill him if he burned a hole in the robe with a hot cigarette ash, but the need for a smoke overrode his concern for his wife's wrath, so he fired up his lighter, took a drag and held the cigarette at arm's length. He listened to the wheezing H-VAC pumping the warm air into the church. If it would only last until spring, he hoped to convince Reny to invest in a new one.

He noticed a car driving down the alley then coming to a stop at the back of the building. The security light hanging from the back of the church was too weak for Maxwell to tell the make of the vehicle or the passengers' identity. But when the backdoor opened and the interior lights revealed the occupants, his heart sank. Jeff Anderson hopped out of his Bentley and instructed the chauffeur to pull off onto the grass but keep the engine running. Before Anderson closed the door, he heard Lindy instruct her hus-band to tell Maxwell how much she enjoyed the show.

He slipped off the table, but the back of his robe caught on the edge, and he heard a ripping sound. Maxwell tried to detach the snagged robe, but Anderson's approach forced him to stop his efforts and turn to face him. He could not feel more humiliated. Here was a multi-billionaire architect and commercial development tycoon, dressed to the nines, while he in his first century robe was fixed to a weather-beaten picnic table. Like the outdoor grill—modern man meets rusted-out relic. Why could not Anderson dress like a normal person? If he was going to come down from Mt. Olympus, and take in a show with the common folk, he could at least dress more like the citizens of Hells Canyon.

"Bravo, my friend. Bravo." Anderson ambled toward Maxwell applauding with his gloved hands. "Lindy and I loved your little show."

"Little show," Maxwell muttered under his breath, and then he quickly dropped his cigarette behind him, snuffing it out on the ground with his sandaled foot.

"Man, the crowds," Anderson marveled. "I couldn't believe it. The Richland Performing Arts Center could learn a few lessons from you. You pack them in like that on the other two nights?"

"Yeah. We did, actually."

"And you didn't charge admission?" Anderson asked.

"It was a gift to the community," Maxwell answered.

"You could have raised a lot of money for the community."

Maxwell could not help himself. He laughed. "The Mercy Seat community doesn't have a lot of money…in case you haven't noticed."

Maxwell did not bother to fill the awkward silence that followed. He looked at the Bentley and cocked his ear but could not hear the sound of the engine. A lot of money spent on a quiet engine.

"Reny tells me that more people have been coming to The Mercy Seat church lately, in the last few months since…since, well…," Anderson let his words drift away.

Maxwell's spine began to heat up. "In my house, we call it 'the incident.'"

"I can't imagine," Anderson replied. "It must have been really bad. I'm sorry."

"It was a bad time for a lot of people," Maxwell said.

"You think you know who your friends are and then they turn out to be drug dealers with cartel connections." Anderson raised his hands.

"Yeah, Richland elite, Armani suits, and fancy cars and all the time they were saturating my neighborhood with drugs. Who knew? You should pick better friends."

Maxwell recognized he was the one without the Christmas spirit, not Anderson, but he couldn't help himself. The man in front of him could only be charged with poor choices of business partners, nothing more.

"You're right. I should be more careful next time," Anderson responded. "Guilty by association. At least they'll go to prison— out with the bad, in with the good, let's hope."

"Then you should feel really guilty standing next to me," Maxwell said.

"When I came to The Mercy Seat with Reny on the day everything went down, I spoke briefly with your wife about rethinking the whole Hells Canyon redesign, possible changes in direction, find a way we might capitalize on the situation," Anderson offered.

"Capitalize on the situation?" Maxwell could not believe his ears. "You mean we might capitalize on someone's death?"

"Poor choice of words. It's not what I meant, Maxwell. I didn't mean that."

"Well Jeff, that is the way it sounded to me. I'm not used to killing people. I admit, I never once thought of him as good. I never even thought of him as ever being human, you know, a child of God. Diego Sanchez was a snake coiled around my son's neck. I wish my son had never hooked up with him. I had murder in my heart. I wanted him gone, but I just didn't want to be the one responsible for it happening. But he's dead now. His mother is alone, and I go to sleep at night with her screams ringing in my ears."

There it was. The true confession that entangled him since the incident had exploded out of the deep pit of his gut. Maxwell spoke truth to Jeff Anderson, the deepest truth he had kept to himself all this time. He had never fully confessed the abysmal turmoil of his soul, not to Rendell, or Pete, or Kenda.

The scene in front of Diego's apartment with his mother on the porch screaming, his own kids screaming and watching from the side of their building was a constant loop in his mind. He had acted on impulse and death was the result. Now he had spoken from his heart. Out of the abundance of the heart the mouth speaks, and his outraged breath had carried the fury of his personal guilt. Why he chose to speak now and to Jeff Anderson of all people he could not explain. He was shattered. The ghost of the buried dead had been in pursuit and finally caught up to him. His body began to tremble under an intense sensation of freezing cold as if he had smashed into a drifting piece of ice floe.

"Daddy. Daddy, we're headed home."

Maxwell heard the familiar voice and snapped his head in its direction. He saw Corley, Carrie, and Leandra dressed in their biblical costumes standing in the parking lot.

"I thought you were going to help your mother strike everything," Maxwell said, his voice raw from divulging the truth of his heart. He wished he could go home, or back inside the church, or just evaporate into the cold air, but he was held in the prison of the moon's silver spotlight.

"Leandra is really tired," Corley said. "Mom said we can come back in the morning and pack everything up."

"What about Carlo and Lin? Where are they?" Maxwell asked.

"Inside with a bunch of their friends from school." Carrie waved toward the church.

"They'll be right behind us, Daddy," Corley said. "Just a hop, skip home, and we're gonna crash as soon as we get there."

Maxwell was unable to process what was happening. His

body felt ridged with cold, that if he stood there much longer, he would become enveloped in his own private ice age. Yet in his fragmented mind he sensed a danger at the thought of his girls going home with Leandra. He was not sure why he sensed this was not a good idea, but he was held in the bewildering grip of his confession to Jeff Anderson. He was the anonymous priest in the confessional booth, and Maxwell marveled at his exposed vulnerability to a man be barely knew. That and the cold. He was too frozen and needed more time to thaw before his mind would become fully clear.

"Straight home, then," he said trying to keep his chattering teeth from flying out of his mouth.

Maxwell watched the girls walk down the alley that cut through the Gardens in the direction of home. When he turned back, he was surprised to see Anderson standing perfectly still before him. He had said nothing for the last few minutes. He had waited. Perhaps Anderson had more to say, but Maxwell didn't want to hear it.

"I am so sorry," Anderson said. "I didn't know…it was that deep. I should have…should have come by sooner. Reny said you were in a tough spot, and I just didn't want to intrude. No excuse. I should have reached out. I'm sorry."

Anderson began to step away but then he stopped. He extended his arm and laid his hand upon Maxwell's shoulder, giving it a firm squeeze.

"Anything you need," Anderson whispered. "Anything."

Anderson returned to the Bentley and got into the back seat. The quietness of the departing vehicle made Maxwell feel as if he were watching a silent movie. When he looked up into the moonlight he finally broke. His eyes began to sting the instant his tears hit the frigid air.

Chapter Eleven

Corley had convinced herself that the arrival of Leandra was no accident. She could not fully explain why she felt so drawn to Leandra but was persuaded the two of them were developing a special bond in the short time she had come into the life of the family. Corley had gladly given Leandra anything she wanted to wear from her closet. She had given up her bedroom convinced that Leandra had rarely if ever had a moment of privacy or nice clothes to wear.

Leandra turned up with the clothes she wore, clothes bought by those who used her for one purpose, clothes from a life Corley knew would be difficult to forget, but this limited offering of her bedroom and her wardrobe was a small yet positive step toward a new life. She and Leandra were so close in size that everything she had fit Leandra. In spite of Corley's garments consisting mainly of secondhand purchases, the fact that Leandra took such pleasure in getting these new outfits gave Corley immense delight.

Given the timing of Leandra's arrival and the chaos of putting on the pageant, Corley had not had much one-on-one time with Leandra except in assisting her with the role of Mary. Corley recognized Leandra's natural abilities, and she was devoted to helping her succeed in the role. She was the family thespian after all, and Corley spent time coaching Leandra, hoping to make her feel as comfortable as possible on stage. Even her mother couldn't devote the time to one individual because of the million details of doing the play, and with the success of the show and Leandra's achievement as Mary, Corley felt like she was walking on air as the three of them made their way home.

Now that the pageant was over, Corley was looking forward to spending the remainder of the Christmas break getting to know this unusual person who had been dropped on the doorstep of The Mercy Seat. Leandra had shared little of her life during this brief period, perhaps out of shame or an inability to articulate the details of her story. There were no long conversations. Corley could only wonder and speculate about the life Leandra led and how she got to this point. But who knew the future, Corley reasoned? Wherever Leandra might end up, Corley imagined they could continue the friendship.

"We normally have a cast party at school when we close a show," Corley said as they walked out of the Gardens projects and onto the street toward their house. "But given the size of the cast and the logistics, it was impossible."

"We were lucky to get out alive," Carrie said, and then she scooted over to the first dumpster on the street and took a peek inside.

"Carrie, do you have to stop at every dumpster you pass?" Corley asked.

"Every time it's like a treasure hunt." Carrie pushed aside some trash bags and leaned over the edge for a better look. "Can't get a better bargain than free."

"You should do a commercial for the dumpster diving business." Corley and Leandra breezed past the dumpster leaving Carrie balancing on her stomach half inside the dumpster door.

"Wait. Look. Look what I found!" Carrie shouted, the echoes of her excitement bouncing inside the metal receptacle.

Corley and Leandra stopped and turned as Carrie skipped around the dumpster proudly holding two linen HarperIman dolls. "Look at these. Two HarperIman dolls in mint condition. You know how expensive they are? I can't believe I found them in—"

Bright headlights from the vehicle behind Carrie turned her petite stature into an instant silhouette. Corley raised her hand to her brow to deflect the intense high beams. She noticed that Leandra had dropped her head, and she thought she heard her whisper something, but then lights from a second vehicle came on from behind her. When Corley turned to face the second vehicle, she noticed that the front porch lights on her house were on. They were always on. The only time they went out was when her daddy or brother had to replace the bulb. What a strange thing to think of as the dark forms leapt out of the side doorway of a van and began their menacing approach. Corley spun around and saw more dark forms burst out of the other van and rush toward Carrie.

"Run, Carrie," she screamed, but her little sister had already been surrounded by the forms and were lifting her off her feet.

What Corley could see, what she was amazed to see in these bright headlights were floating skulls. She squinted in disbelief, and then turned back and saw the same floating skulls behind her coming from the second vehicle. These were Day of the Dead skulls attached to human forms dressed in black.

Carrie was hoisted in the air, kicking and screaming, the HarperIman dolls flying out of her hands, as the Day of the Dead skulls lifted her above their heads and moved back to the open side door of the van.

"Put her down," Corley shouted, but then she heard Leandra scream. When she spun back around, she saw an arm tightly wrapped beneath Leandra's neck as she fought to get away.

"Don't hurt her," Corley screamed as she rushed toward Leandra. She was able to grab the arm of the skull clasped around Leandra's neck and tried to pry it away. If she could free her friend, then maybe together they could rescue Carrie.

Then Corley felt the sudden blow against the side of her face. There was a flash of light across her eyes brighter than the lights of the vehicles and she dropped to her knees and clung to Leandra's legs. She lost all coherent thought. She was all muscle and visceral impulse trying to rescue her friend. She did hear Leandra cry out not to hit her again, and then Corley was lifted off her feet. She lost all physical strength and did not try to resist as she was tossed inside the van. She had suffered a vicious blow, but she was determined to remain conscious. What remaining strength she had, she used to stay conscious.

"Carrie," she managed to utter. "Where's my sister?"

Carrie suddenly fell on top of her crying and screaming as the van door slammed shut and the gunned engine propelled the van down the street.

Corley reached her arm around Carrie and tucked her sister into her side.

"Where is Leandra?" Corley managed to ask.

"The other van," Carrie said between her hyper sobbing.

Then her arms were pulled behind her back as were Carrie's and plastic restraints were wrapped around both their wrists. A strip of tape was then slapped over their mouths and a black hood was forced over her head. Carrie vanished from her blurry sight. The black forms disappeared. The Day of the Dead skulls vanished. All was black now and all she could hear was Carrie's muffled voice crying and calling her name. She felt a moment of relief to know that her sister was with her. They were together and they would get through it together. Whatever this was, they would be together. And then even the sound of Carrie's subdued voice faded with the blackness.

Chapter Twelve

Maxwell was wiping his eyes with the sleeve of his costume when he heard Rosemary call his name. He didn't want to go back inside the church office until he had composed himself. He had wanted to avoid Reny and the others, but even the backyard of the church was not a sufficient hiding place. He'd been found by the one person he least wanted to see, yet the encounter had unexpectedly begun to revive his heart.

Maxwell remained still trying to understand what had just happened, an initial easing of the grip of guilt he'd suffered for such a long time. His furious confession was like the primitive practice of bleeding a patient to improve their health. And with the unforeseen gesture of a hand upon Maxwell's shoulder, it was a touch of mercy he never expected from Jeff Anderson.

"I'm coming, Rosemary," Maxwell said. "Just needed some fresh air."

"It's too cold to be standing out there," she scolded. "Now come inside."

Maxwell chuckled as he started to move toward the back door, but he was instantly stopped when he heard the ripping of cloth and felt the snag of his garment. Now he had to laugh out loud. Maxwell carefully worked the hem of his costume free from the gnarly edge of the tabletop. He poked his finger through the tear as he examined the damage in the moonlight. If Kenda was going to be upset with him for his carelessness, at least he had the benefit of a little relief for his troubled soul thanks to Jeff Anderson's kind touch.

He closed the back door and stepped inside the rear entrance into an empty office. He figured Rosemary must have gone back into the sanctuary. Piles of costumes were strewn all over the floor, deflated wardrobes of angels, shepherds, and wisemen, abandoned as if the players had been raptured leaving behind their clothes. Maxwell seized the moment to slip out of his costume. He wore a pair of hiking shorts and a sweatshirt beneath the robe. He slipped on cargo pants, socks, and his hiking boots before Rosemary stepped back into the office with Ezekiel under her arm.

"Rosemary, I just have to say when you meet the real Elizabeth in heaven, she will tell you that you did her proud."

"Whew, I hope so. Hardest thing I've done in my life."

"Now that the show is over, I know you'll be glad for Ezekiel's undivided attention." Maxwell reached for his phone on top of his desk.

"Did you notice what happened during my scene tonight with Mary?" Rosemary asked.

"Can't say that I did." Maxwell glanced at his screen for messages.

"During rehearsal and in the first two shows, Ezekiel always jumped into Leandra's arms when she came on, but tonight he sat in my lap not moving a muscle."

"Who can know the mind of a cat?" Maxwell said in tantalizing wonder. He stuffed his phone into his back pocket and draped his robe over his lap. The sooner he confessed to Kenda his costume mishap the better.

"Go on with you," Rosemary said. "Don't be teasing me or Ezekiel."

"Far be it from me," Maxwell said placing a hand over his heart.

Kenda was beaming as she walked into the office with an armload of costumes. She dropped the costumes beside where he sat and raised her arms. "Our first successful Christmas pageant in the books. Thank you, Jesus."

This solo exaltation of thankfulness got an "amen" from Rosemary. When Kenda gave Maxwell a big kiss, he saw Rosemary smile as she shielded Ezekiel's eyes.

"First Christmas pageant?" he responded as if taken aback. "I was hoping this might be our one-and-done Christmas pageant." Maxwell pulled Kenda into his lap.

"Are you kidding me?" she said. "Everybody loved it, cast and audience. This was a big deal for The Mercy Seat. Don't be a bah-humbug."

"Well, I don't want to stick a pin into your exuberance, but I have a confession to make." He lifted the hem of his costume with its jagged thread wound. "I'd like to blame this on Ezekiel, but I cannot tell a lie."

"How did you do this?" Kenda exclaimed, unable to hide her disappointment.

Maxwell was about to come clean when Carlo appeared in the door of the office.

"Mom and Dad, I was wondering if Lin and I could grab a bite with our friends from school," Carlo said gesturing into the sanctuary. "Promise we won't be out late."

The sinking feeling in Maxwell's gut came not by drips but in a painful rush.

"The girls said you and Lin were going home with them," Maxwell said.

"I never told them that," Carlo responded. "We haven't seen them."

The sinking went deeper into his stomach.

"Did you tell them they could go home?" Maxwell asked, looking up at Kenda.

"I said we could come back tomorrow and put the sanctuary back together before church this Sunday, but I didn't say anything about them going ahead of us."

The sinking feeling began to unnerve him, but he did not want to cause a panic. He eased Kenda off his lap as he rose to his feet.

"You can go out with your friends once we've checked on the girls," he said.

"Maxwell, what's wrong?" Kenda asked.

He knew Kenda had picked up on his alarm though he tried his best to conceal it.

"Probably nothing." Maxwell did his best to keep his voice calm. "Just a miscommunication I had with the girls."

"You saw them after the show?" Kenda asked.

"I was outside in the back talking to Jeff Anderson when they walked by. I remember them saying they were tired and were heading home."

"They said nothing to me about going home." Kenda brought her hand to her mouth as if trying to stifle the sound of her distress.

But Maxwell heard the quivering in her voice, and it set him off.

"Carlo, come with me." He knocked over the chair scrambling to the back door. He dashed outside looking to see his son rush past his mother who followed at his heels. He knew not to tell her to stay calm. She would never be calm. He knew not to tell her to wait at the church. That would be a useless directive. And he knew he could not wait for her. He must race ahead. He must find them. Since he was the last one to see them, he had to be the first to know they were safe.

"You call the minute you find those darlings," Rosemary shouted, and that was the last thing he heard before his simple prayer took control of his lips, "Please, God. Please, God. Please, God."

Yet he could not pray and run and call out the names of his girls and breathe and keep this hurried pace. He had never been one for exercise. His walkabouts through Hells Canyon were enough for him, but in the amount of time Maxwell had been smoking, it was enough to create this restriction in his lungs. He was surprised by his inability to get a deep breath. It was harder than normal. Sure, there was adrenaline pumping through his veins, but he could feel his body running out of gas. He had gotten through the Gardens projects but began to slow down when he hit his street, his house within sight at the end of the dead-end road beside the electrical sub-station. His running legs weakened, and he was now staggering. From the church to within a hundred yards of his home, he had not seen the girls, nor had they answered his panicked calls for them to respond.

When he could not go any farther, he bent over gasping and hoping not to pass out. When Carlo slowed down to check on him, Maxwell waved him forward. "The house. The house," he said through his winded breathing. If they were just in the house, then all this rush of fear and energy would be for naught.

He watched Carlo bolt across the front yard and leap onto the porch. He tried the door and found it was locked. That was a good sign, and Maxwell began to feel a little relief. The girls were inside the house, doors locked, probably listening to songs from their current favorite female artist with the sound at eleven because they were the only ones in the house and no one to complain about the volume. Please God, let it be so.

Maxwell was able to stand up straight, but his legs were too shaky to move forward. He saw Carlo unlock the door with his key and rush inside calling out his sisters' names. Maxwell knew their big brother would be furious with them for scaring everyone to death. When Carlo disappeared inside the house, Kenda stumbled up beside him and clasped her hands around his arm.

"I couldn't go any further. I was about to pass out," Maxwell wheezed.

"Where is Carlo?" Kenda panted.

"In the house," Maxwell answered. His mouth had gone completely dry, and he ran his tongue over his chapped lips for a little moisture. "They said they were going straight home. This is so unlike them."

"Why did you let them go home by themselves?" Kenda said. "We never do that."

"I thought Carlo was right behind them, I thought he was…" Maxwell stopped. How could he explain his emotional state from his conversation with Anderson behind the church office? He had hoped to be able to share that moment with Kenda and have her help him process it. In that moment with Anderson, he was too confused to really pay attention to the girls' wish to go home. But now he was even more confused. His lack of attention to his daughters and the idea of their possible disappearance converged into Kenda's words, "Why did you let them go home by themselves? We never do that."

"No," he said weakly. "We never do that."

The primal roar from Carlo's voice shook him to his core. He looked at the front porch and saw the dark form of his son backlit by the porch light standing with his hands cupped around his mouth funneling the names of his sisters into the night sky as loud as he could shout them. If the girls were anywhere close by it would be impossible for them not to hear their brother calling their names, even over the constant electrical hum of the sub-station. His son didn't have to tell him that his daughters were not inside the house. Carlo's shouts told all.

Maxwell began to feel Kenda loosen her grip on his arm as she slid down his side onto her knees. The resonance of Carlo's screams shot into the atmosphere had pierced her and she began to wail. Maxwell tucked one arm around Kenda's waist and prevented her from a complete collapse onto the street. He knelt beside Kenda listening to her weep, listening to Carlo scream, and hearing his own breathing turn from a steady panting to one of a desperate cry.

From the glow of the streetlight near his house, Maxwell could see a piece of fabric lying on the pavement. He released his hold on Kenda's shoulders and crawled over to the cloth. He recognized it immediately. It was a head covering with a strip of faux leather pinned to it. Leandra wore it as Mary. Could it have fallen off on their walk home? Could she have removed it and then accidentally dropped it?

He tried to stand but could not. It took everything in him just to turn on his knees and face his wife. Carlo and Kenda were beginning to run out of steam, their deep cries and wails draining all their strength. Maxwell too was growing weary—the adrenaline rush he'd experienced moments ago was leaving his body depleted. He crawled back to Kenda.

He struggled to his feet, then lifted Kenda to his side and steadied her on her feet. There was not enough room in his soul to contain the current of pain that descended upon him. It was double agony as he felt his wife's pain cascading on top of his own. He raised the headdress Leandra had worn for Kenda to see, creating a sudden revival of tears and cries pouring out of Kenda's mouth. His heart became like crushed glass, the sharp splinters piercing the weakened muscle with a thousand jabs.

"Let up on me," Maxwell shouted to the heavens. "Lord, release Your grip. Have mercy."

He felt Carlo crash into his back and wrap his arms around him and his mother. Maxwell was the center of this family trio coughing and gasping and bawling. He was packed between his wife and his son, the tremors of their grief hurtling shock waves through his body. Where were his girls? Where was Maxwell when they needed their father's protection? Where was God?

Chapter Thirteen

Carrie lay still and could tell that the driver was going at normal speed, not as abductors fleeing the scene of a crime. No light seeped through the hood over her head. All she could hear was the rumbling tires of the vehicle as it moved along the street. She stretched her head toward the front of the van, listening for any voices. Carrie did not know how many abductors there were—it had all happened so quickly—but certainly enough to subdue the three of them and throw them into a van against their will, enough to hold them down, tie their hands behind their backs, tape their mouths shut, and cover their heads with hoods. All she could re-member was being surprised by the Day of the Dead masks, and that when she yelled for help, her sister had tried to rescue her only to be felled by a vicious blow. If Carrie hadn't screamed her sister might not have been struck in the side of her face.

The skulls had not spoken during the abduction. They were voiceless. They were swift, and they attacked with overpowering force. Carrie made a valiant effort to fight back, but the strength of the skulls was superior. Once she was thrown into the van, her mouth taped and the hood tied over her head, the strength drained out of her. The skulls were silent now with no verbal communica-tion coming from the front of the vehicle.

When she laid her head back down, she realized that the floor-ing of the van was not bare metal but covered in some type of car-pet. She lifted one leg and moved it from side to side to feel what might be nearby. In one direction her leg banged into the side of the van. She had not encountered another human, nor had she been scolded for moving about, so perhaps no one was watching. Then

Carrie extended her leg upwards. She was unable to touch the ceiling and concluded the van must have a large interior. Once again, she had not drawn unwanted attention to moving her leg, so she stretched it in the opposite direction. The second she felt a body—it had to be Corley's body, who's else could it be—she tapped her foot along the figure to determine its position. When the body remained still, Carrie began to tug at the body with her heel and attempt to call her sister's name through the tape over her mouth, but there was no response.

How could her sister respond? It took a moment for Carrie to realize that while she might be calling her sister's name, with the tape over her mouth, it must sound like distressed grunts. Carrie felt she was losing her nerve, but she refused to descend into panic. It was hard enough to breathe with the tape covering her mouth and a hood over her head. The front of the hood was already wet with her tears and rheum which made it that much more difficult to breathe. But she had to know, to be sure Corley was not dead.

Even with her hands tied behind her back, Carrie inched her way toward her sister until she felt she was more or less shoulder to shoulder with Corley. It became more difficult for her to take a deep breath, so she paused to steady her breathing. Once she relaxed, she rolled up onto her side and threw her leg over Carrie's body pushing herself on top of her sister. It was a shock and a great relief to Carrie when her sister instantly began to thrash about. She was alive. Carrie had not caused her death by screaming for help, and she still had some fight left.

Carrie slipped off Corley. She must be struggling to breathe like her and being on top of her sister would only made it worse, so she rolled back onto the floor of the van but laid her head upon Corley's chest. She wanted to hear her sister's heartbeat. She wanted Corley to know it was her head resting on Corley's chest and that they were together and would stay connected no matter what this was and no matter how it all turned out. Behind the strip of tape covering her mouth, Carrie began to utter the words, "I love you, Sister. I love you, Sister."

When she felt the adhesive tape over her lips slightly loosening, she thought it best to say no more for fear that when the abductors did remove the hood from her head and saw the tape had come off there would be trouble. When Corley began to settle down and breathe normally, Carrie realized her sister understood it was her. The attempt to bond with her had succeeded.

Carrie felt her anxiety begin to subside, but she did not allow herself to relax. With her head resting on Corley's side, Carrie wondered if her sister could feel the flow of her guilt and grief at having caused one of the kidnappers to strike her? Once their hoods were removed and the tape peeled from their mouths, the first thing Carrie would express would be her sorrow at having caused this pain, this unfair and unwarranted pain.

Why was this happening? None of it made sense. She concentrated on the moments leading up to their abduction. They had been taken by surprise, but this could not be an accident. This was not a group of delinquents who just happened upon three girls and made a snap decision to kidnap them. The culprits were lying in wait. They must have known where they lived. They must have known when they were coming home.

The three of them had followed the same route through the Gardens they had always taken from their house to the church. Nothing unusual in that except Carrie could not remember ever walking home from church without a parent or her big brother. But she was with her sister and Leandra, and her father knew what they were doing and said he was okay with it. He did say it was okay, didn't he?

Carrie had always enjoyed a certain freedom in the Gardens. The residents knew her as the dumpster diver girl. She'd never felt any fear or ever been threatened since her family had moved into the neighborhood years ago. But now the world she thought she knew had turned against her.

She felt the van slowing down, making frequent stops, and

taking several different turns. Carrie was so disoriented it was impossible to have any sense of direction and she had no concept of time as to how long she and Corley might have been riding in the van. It did not feel as if they had been driving long enough to be far from the city of Richland, or they might be headed to some remote spot. But where were they taking them? Was it some suburban neighborhood on the outskirts of town? It was impossible to know.

Carrie lifted her head again for any verbal clue, but the kidnappers remained silent. And where was the other van with Leandra? Were they driving the two vans together or did her abductors drive off in another direction? She was thankful to at least be with her sister.

Her anxiety level began to rise when the van came to a complete stop and did not move forward. She lowered her head back onto Corley's chest and listened to her heartbeat. It too had quickened. The van wasn't moving, but the engine still emitted a low rumble. No voices inside the van. No outside noise of traffic. When the engine was turned off, Carrie raised her head. She held her breath so she might detect a clue of place and persons, but all she heard was both doors on the vehicle opening followed by the side door of the van sliding back and the cold air rushing inside. A pair of hands forcefully grabbed her shoulders and dragged her out of the vehicle. She groaned at the pain.

The abductors set Carrie on her feet, and she shivered at the cold December air. She had perspired so much beneath the thick layers of her costume and from the hood over her head that she had become terribly dehydrated. She knew her sister would be dying of thirst as well. She was grateful to hear Corley being lugged out of the van after her, that she was not being driven elsewhere. They would be together at least a little longer, and she would not risk separation by upsetting her captors in any way. She didn't resist when she was grabbed on either side and forced inside…a what? A house? A shed? An apartment? She couldn't tell, but she was out of the van, out of the cold, and her sister was right behind her. Thank God for small blessings.

The door closed and Carrie heard a sizzling sound like something was frying in a skillet and then she got a faint whiff of meat and roasting vegetables. From the sound and smells, Carrie assumed she was in the kitchen. However, they didn't linger, and she was led up a flight of stairs. She stumbled at first because no one instructed her to lift her feet. There was no verbal communication. It was as if these phantom skulls spoke no language humans could hear or understand.

Once she reached the last step, there was a sharp turn before she was taken down what she assumed was a hallway. The shuffling of several pairs of feet nearly drowned out all other sound, but as she moved down the hallway, she thought she heard other voices, female voices. Whatever this structure might be, it had at least two floors and there were other people here besides her and Corley. Maybe it was Leandra.

Then she heard the swoosh of an interior door opening and she was whisked inside a room. Carrie put up enough of a resistance to force her captors to stop advancing into the room until she knew her sister was right behind her. When she heard a group entering the room, she began to grunt as loud as possible. It was the only way she knew how to signal Corley. When Carrie heard her sister moan in reply, a deep relief came over her. They were still together, still connected, and with one final shove, she was placed face-first up against a wall. She was held there by two pairs of strong hands. Then she felt a third presence move in close to the side of her head. This presence did not touch her but took a deep breath and exhaled slowly as if to signal to Carrie that she needed to pattern her breathing after this example. And so she did.

After Carrie synchronized her breathing with the presence behind her, and then the presence spoke. "Are you a good girl, little one?"

Carrie held her breath. She didn't know how to answer.

"Your hands can be free and the hood can come off if you are a good girl," said the disembodied voice. The presence spoke in a hushed yet calm, even gentle, tone. "Will you be a good girl?"

She could not speak with the tape over her mouth, nor could she see or be seen with the hood on her head. So Carrie acquiesced with a soft groan.

"A good girl will not scream or shout or put up a fight when I set her free. She will not even speak. So will you still be a good girl?"

Carrie gave another affirmative whimper, and the presence stepped back. A pair of hands pressing her against the wall let go of her right shoulder and with a knife cut off the plastic restraints from her wrists. Her arms dangled loosely at her side. She did not have the strength to raise them. There was a painful tingling as the blood rushed into her wrists and hands.

When the cord around the hood was untied and being lifted off her head Carrie became terrified at what she might see when the blackness gave way to light. The moment the hood was removed she did not immediately open her eyes. She inhaled and could detect the scent of human sweat and stale, exotic cologne. She barely cracked open her eyes. Even though the hood was off, there was very little she could see. The only source of light came from the opposite end of the room from where she stood. All she could perceive were shadowy forms.

"Good girl," the presence said, then took her shoulders and turned her around.

Carrie clamped her eyes shut as she leaned back against the wall. She felt a hand lightly peel away the tape from her mouth until it was completely off. She could now take a deep breath for the first time since being abducted, but she did not open her eyes. She feared she would start weeping if she opened her eyes and saw this sinister being. She did not want to cry or reveal any weakness.

"Drink, little *princesa*," said the presence, and he raised her arm and put a plastic water bottle in her hand. "Drink."

Carrie put the water bottle to her lips and guzzled the tepid liquid. In seconds she had drained the contents, and the presence took the empty bottle from her hand.

"Open your eyes," said the presence.

Carrie obeyed. She was a good girl. But the face she saw did not match the gentle voice of the presence. It was the mask of a grinning skull, the same Day of the Dead mask of those who surrounded her and tossed her into the van. This one was different from the others. This one spoke in a thick Hispanic accent, and she could tell he commanded authority. From her peripheral vision Carrie could see other skulls pressing her sister against the wall like she had been. Had the two of them been carried off to the underworld by these phantoms? Swallowed by a dark sinister reality?

"Looks like you and your sister stepped right out of the Bible," said the presence followed by a malevolent chuckle as he ran his fingers along the folds of her biblical robe.

Carrie said nothing, but she did raise her arm and pointed to the Day of the Dead specters huddled around Corley.

"You want to see your sister, Little One?" he asked. "I too want to see her."

Carrie still could not speak. She could only nod.

"Then let the little one see her sister." The presence motioned for the skulls to set her sister free.

Corley groaned as the phantoms cut the plastic restraints from her wrists and removed the hood from her head. The presence obstructed Carrie's view when he pushed aside the other skulls and stepped between Corley and her. The moment the presence turned Corley around to face him, he erupted with curses. The presence railed against the others in Spanish. In the violence of his anger, he knocked one of the phantoms to the floor. Carrie panicked. Why this response? What had he seen? Was Corley not breathing. Was she dead?

The presence yanked a phone from his back pocket and held it up to Corley's face. His rage had gotten the best of him, and he was not as gentle with her sister in peeling away the tape from her mouth as he had been with her. Once the tape was removed, Corley bawled in pain inhaling harsh quick breaths. The sound of her sister's suffering caused Carrie's knees to buckle. The presence grabbed a clump of Corley's hair and held up her limp head as he took a picture. In the white flash of the phone camera, Carrie was horrified to see Corley's bruised and swollen face. When the presence released her hair, Corley slid down the wall and crumpled to the floor.

The presence swung around and continued his fury, pushing the others out of the way as he stormed toward the door. Carrie did not understand anything he said, but when he opened the door, all the other phantoms scurried out of the room behind him. The last one rolled a bottle of water across the floor in her direction. When the door slammed, the raging trailed off as the presence and his phantoms marched down the hallway.

Carrie didn't move. She listened to be sure they didn't return. When all was quiet except for Corley's raspy breathing, Carrie dropped to the floor and grabbed the bottle of water. She scooted over to Corley and carefully leaned her up against the wall. She broke the seal on the bottle and tenderly placed the mouth of the bottle on Corley's swollen lips. Even in the dim light of the room, it appeared that Corley's head was almost twice its natural size. When Corley tasted the water, she raised her head to drink.

"I can't cry," Carrie whispered to herself as she held the bottle for her sister to take her tiny sips. "I can't cry."

Corley had trouble swallowing the tiny sips of water. The excess dribbled down her chin.

"I can't cry," Carrie repeated. "I can't cry," but the tears rolled down her cheeks.

Chapter Fourteen

Leandra stood alone behind the island in the large kitchen and poured hot water into a mug. A skillet of chicken fajitas warmed on the stovetop. On the countertop was a stack of plates and eating utensils. Food was available for the taking. She should be hungry. She had not eaten since before the last performance of the Christmas pageant, but her stomach had not settled after the intensity of the last hour.

Leandra placed her hand above the skillet. Warm, but not too warm. She reached in and took a juicy chicken strip nestled inside the colorful peppers and onions. She ignored the roasted vegetables, not her thing. She blew her breath on the chicken to cool it before taking her first nibble. From the kitchen Leandra could see the dining room with a table and chairs. Between the kitchen and the dining room was the foyer and stairway leading to the top floors.

She opened a cabinet and took a packet of hot chocolate and marshmallow mix from the box, ripped open the top, and poured the brown powder into the mug. She took a clean spoon from the drawer and stirred the liquid until the contents dissolved. When Leandra brought the mug to her mouth, she could see her face reflected in the brown water by the ceiling lights. Something was missing. She put her hand to her head and remembered the headdress she had on before the abduction. She was still in her Mary costume sans the headdress. Noise on the floor above made her raise her eyes to the ceiling. The movement in the house meant that Tiana must be rousing the girls, and Leandra wanted to get out of her biblical attire before anyone saw her.

Footsteps coming down the steps tightened her stomach. Leandra tossed the half-eaten chicken strip back into the skillet and wiped her fingers on the costume then took quick sips of the hot chocolate to help settle her nerves. When Tiana hit the bottom step and entered the kitchen Leandra moved back and propped her spine against the kitchen counter. She brought the mug to her lips and continued to sip the warm brew. Tiana was carrying a stack of folded clothes like she had just taken them from the dryer. When Tiana glared at the dirty spoon, empty packet of hot chocolate, and some loose grains of cocoa scattered across the island top, Leandra quickly scooped them up and snatched a paper towel from the dispenser to wipe away the cocoa and the few drops of hot chocolate from the spoon.

Once satisfied with Leandra's tidying up, Tiana set the clean clothes on the island.

"I made some chicken fajitas and vegies for the others," Tiana said. "Slap any leftovers in the fridge."

"Will do," Leandra said, trying to act nonchalantly like she had not already snuck a bite.

"They make you wear those towels or whatever when you lived with them?" Tiana asked. "They in some kind of cult or something?"

The hard knocks on mean streets had aged Tiana and no amount of makeup or risqué wardrobe could provide the flattering attention she craved. Leandra knew her looks and body could become downgraded like Tiana if she lived much longer in the life. She hoped this latest task she had performed for Beltran and the gang had proved her worth, and that she and Esteban could settle into some normalcy within the lawless world she inhabited. These last days with the Crane family was a world completely foreign to her. Benevolent parents, enjoyable siblings, a bedroom, new clothes, good food, and a church, of all things. She had never been inside a church before let alone be able to say she had starred in a church pageant. As bizarre as that had been it was much easier than running the gauntlet of the gang. But she had done both, run the gauntlet and played the Virgin Mary, all for the sake of a brighter future for herself.

"Yeah, pretty weird," was all the answer Leandra gave. She did not want to reveal the secret pride she felt at performing in a church play.

"Well, now you're back with us." Tiana laid out three pairs of jeans and a selection of pullover hoodies. "I figured the other two were close to your size, so I pulled something out of the closet for them to wear."

"I want to take it to them." Leandra began separating the jeans and laying a pullover on top of each pair.

"You got to see the bear first," Tiana said. "He's asked for you."

If Leandra had been rattled about seeing Tiana, she was terrified by the prospect of seeing the bear. She had never laid eyes on him, only heard stories about his size and strength, the tattoos and the scarring. Esteban had told her that he had never seen the bear lose his temper or act unreasonable. But he was still the man in charge, the man with real power over the Death Demons. The man who controlled the order of the world she lived in. And he wanted to see her.

"Why does he want to see me?" Leandra asked trying to control her nerves. "What did I do?"

Leandra watched Tiana's face turn into a smirk. Was her fear that obvious? It was as if Tiana enjoyed seeing her flinch.

"Hurry up. Get out of those rags. He's in the office at the top of the stairs. And take him a plate of food." Tiana started around the corner to head back upstairs, then stopped. "Best not to keep him waiting."

She had given Leandra no clue about the bear's current state of mind other than not to keep him waiting. Leandra slipped out of her costume and hustled into the jeans and hoodie. She filled a plate with the chicken fajitas, then tucked the other clothes for the girls under her arm and scrambled up the flight of stairs. If she was going to be punished in any way, perhaps this plate of chicken fajitas would be a peace offering.

She paused to catch her breath when she reached the top of the stairs. While she could hear movement in the bedrooms down the hall, she saw no one else. She took one final deep breath and softly knocked on the office door.

"Enter," came the voice from inside the office, and Leandra turned the doorknob and leaned inside. She saw the bear seated behind a desk talking into his phone. He spoke Spanish which she did not understand, but he waved for her to enter. She quietly closed the door, and when she turned back to him, he cupped his hand over the phone and said to her, *"en un momento"* then went back to his conversation.

He had a commanding voice without sounding overbearing. He displayed no emotion as he conversed with the other party. The wall behind where he sat was a bank of monitors linked to every room in the house including cameras that were mounted on the exterior corners of the house. The bedrooms had little light, but in one she could see several people. She assumed this could be the room where the Death Demons were holding the sisters. She could only imagine how terrified they were.

The office itself was plain without any decorating pretense, just a nice desk and one chair in which he sat. Leandra's attention was drawn to one of the monitors where she saw Tiana enter a room, flip on the lights, and start rousing the girls asleep on their mattresses. It was time to get them ready for the nightshift. The sisters were not in this room. They must be in the other room surrounded by Death Demons.

With no other chair in the room except for the one occupied by the bear, everyone else must stand when present, a show of respect to his authority. Even with the bear sitting down, Leandra could see his bear-like qualities, large head covered in long curly hair, round and weathered face with bold features. Spiderweb tattoos covered his neck disappearing into his shirt collar, a red-winged Death Demon skull on one forearm and a fierce looking bear standing on its hind legs on the other. There was a scar that began right above his left eye and extended down his cheek. She wondered how his eye had survived such an injury. When he finished his phone call and stood, he towered over her. Leandra dropped her eyes and pressed her back against the door.

"You must be Leandra," he said.

She tried to speak but could not make a sound. When she heard him coming around from behind the desk, she wanted to run out the door, but instead dug her feet into the carpet and pressed her back harder into the door. Where would she run to anyway?

"Good, you brought food. I'm starving." He took the plate from Leandra.

To her surprise, the bear held the plate in one hand and extended his other hand to her. Even though her eyes were lowered, she saw his hand come into view. She couldn't believe he was being so polite by extending his hand in greeting. No such treatment from the Death Demons.

He waved his hand indicating for her to take it. She reached out and he clasped his fingers around what must have felt to him like a puny paw. But his grip was gentle and when he released it, patted her arm with his open hand. Leandra could not believe she was receiving such a reception from this fierce looking bear.

When she finally found her voice, she was only able to say, "Good to meet you Mr. … Mr. … ah…" She was stumped. She had never seen him and only knew him by the moniker of "bear."

"Arturo, please. Just call me Arturo. I would like that."

"Mr. Arturo," Leandra said softly, then her eyes bounced nervously around the room in search of a place to land.

Arturo gave a puzzled look at the plate in his hands. "No fork?"

Leandra froze. A possible peace offering had become her own

sacrifice. How could she have forgotten.

"I…I'll…just let me run back downstairs to the kitchen."

"Forget it," he said poking his fingers into the fajitas. "I'm too hungry to wait."

When he scooped up a finger load of fajitas Leandra suddenly remembered that she had tossed her half-eaten chicken strip back into the skillet when Tiana had come into the kitchen. Arturo the bear did not seem to notice or care.

"These outfits you carry, are they for the sisters?" he mumbled.

"Yes, sir." Leandra held up the clothes. "I was taking these to them."

"Good for you," he said. He set the plate on his desk and licked his greasy fingers. "You have done a great service for us. You are a *tesoro*, a real treasure, and I wish to reward you. You shall live with us here and not at the factory. You will be warm and safe and well fed—" But that was as far as Arturo got with his list of rewards before the door burst open and Leandra saw the Death Demons coming into the room. Beltran was the first to enter and the first to rip off his mask. By his red sweaty face, she knew his trigger temper had taken control. The rest of the group entered and lined up against the wall each one removing their mask.

It was not until Esteban took off his mask and moved beside her that she began to relax. There was never a time she could fully relax. The life she lived did not allow it. She always had a simmering anxiety in her gut that kept her on edge. But the one person who could provide a level of calm was Este. Were it not for him, she would be on the streets living the life of a scavenger.

Beltran said nothing. He held up his phone and went down the line forcing each Death Demon to take a hard look at the screen. When Beltran got to his brother, he took a few extra seconds for Esteban to see the image, allowing Leandra to see the screen as well. She gasped when she saw Corley's bruised face, the swollen eye, and puffy lips. In the chaos of the abduction, she was not aware of what had been involved with subduing the sisters and getting them into the other van. All she knew was that Este had come up behind her, whispered, "It is me, *Chica*," and then whisked her into his van.

When Beltran gave his phone to Arturo, Leandra slipped her left hand beneath Esteban's arm. She knew whatever was going to happen now could be hazardous for one or all, and she wanted to hold on to someone who might protect her. She glanced at Arturo who sat down on the edge of his desk staring at the image of Corley on the screen.

"This was not supposed to happen." Beltran began moving down the line of male and female gang members eyeing each one with his signature scowl. "Score the sisters, bring them back, without a hitch. Now we got a hitch."

Instead of paying attention to Beltran, Leandra watched Arturo who paid no attention to Beltran. He was preoccupied with Corley's face, enlarging it on the screen to better examine the damage, studying the horizontal then vertical image. He seemed to be pondering a different scenario, one more fortuitous than the "hitch" Beltran claimed.

"We got damaged produce. So who's responsible?" Beltran demanded. "Own up."

No one spoke. Everyone looked down at the floor. Leandra's blood turned cold when he said her name, and she dug her fingers into Esteban's arm.

"Was she like this before the snatch?" he asked her.

Leandra could not speak. She just shook her head, which satisfied Beltran. Then she looked on with horror as he went around the opposite side of the desk where Arturo sat and grabbed a baseball bat leaning against the wall behind the desk.

"There is going to be pain here." Beltran spun around to face the group. "Somebody's face is going to look like that girl."

Leandra could not believe Arturo was staring off into the distance deep in thought, disinterested in Beltran's interrogation.

When one of the male Demons began to sob, Beltran grabbed him by the throat and raised the bat. The others quickly moved away.

"No, Brother. It was me," Esteban said, and he jerked his arm out of Leandra's grasp as he stepped forward. "I hit the girl."

Beltran slammed the weeping banger against the wall.

Leandra knew this was not true as did everyone involved in the kidnapping. Esteban was nowhere near the sisters. He had jumped from the van, and to make it look authentic, grabbed Leandra, and whispered his identity into her ear as he pulled her back into the van. Neither of them saw who struck Corley. It could have easily been Beltran who had dealt the blow. He seemed to always be in bad humor, and this incident made it worse. Now Leandra suspected Beltran was looking for a scapegoat.

"You think you can just blow by this cause we're blood?" Beltran said moving toward his brother. "I was in charge of this raid, and because of you, we brought home some bad dope." Beltran pointed to his phone still in the hands of Arturo.

"It's on me," Esteban said.

Leandra knew by Este's steel tone that he was preparing for his brother's wrath. His confession had shifted the attention. His voice did not falter. His posture did not recoil.

"You right, it's on you. It's all on you," Beltran said as he raised the bat in the air. But instead of striking Esteban with it, Beltran sucker punched his brother with a left hook across his jaw knocking him back against the wall beside Leandra. The scapegoat was chosen and now the scapegoat had been punished.

She dropped the clothes she was holding and wrapped her arms around Esteban to keep him from falling to the floor. Other than a few deep breaths, he did not groan or cry.

"We might have a different play here." Arturo tapped his finger on the screen. "Could be solid redemption. Let's clear the room."

No one had to be told a second time. The Death Demons

scrambled out the door. Leandra picked up the clothes she had dropped. When Esteban put his arm around her, she immediately knew it was more out of a need for support than affection. Together they moved toward the door.

"Este, not you. Stay," Arturo said rising off the edge of the desk. He turned to smile at him. "I want your input."

Esteban gently nudged Leandra out the door. The second she stepped into the hallway, she turned around and looked at Este. As he closed the door, she could see the muscles on the side of his face where he had taken the blow begin to spasm and a tear trickling down his face.

Chapter Fifteen

Carrie held the bottle to Corley's lips. Her sister had to be thirsty, but she had only been able to swallow half the contents of the bottle. The act of drinking was too painful, so Carrie couldn't force her. She was careful as she wiped away the water from Corley's quivering chin. In the dim light from the opposite side of the room, Carrie began to make out the contours of Corley's mouth. The tape had left her lips raw and puffy. Her chin drooped as if from anesthesia after dental surgery.

Corley raised her hand so she could take a breath. She leaned her head back against the wall. One eye was swollen shut and she kept the other closed.

"Where are we?" she asked, her voice a slurred rasp.

"I don't know," Carrie said. "Don't talk. Just drink."

Carrie held the bottle up to Corley's mouth again, but her sister waved it away.

"Where's Leandra?" Corley asked.

"I don't know. I didn't see her after they surrounded us."

"Demons from hell," Corley groaned.

"Don't talk like that," Carrie said. "You're scaring me."

Corley leaned into Carrie and barely opened her good eye. "Are you hurt?"

"I'm fine," she said. "My wrists are sore and my mouth hurts from the tape."

"My wrists hurt too, but I can't feel my mouth," Corley said, then leaned back against the wall. "And my ear is ringing where one of them hit me."

Carrie's spine tingled the second she picked up a strange

movement in the room. Had the death skulls returned and she hadn't heard them? Her back was to the room, and she didn't want to turn to see who or what might have entered.

"Hey, do you know where we are?" asked a spectral voice behind her.

Carrie didn't look around. She felt Corley put her hand on her leg and squeeze.

"We don't know where we are. Do you?"

Carrie did not trust her hearing. Was this a trick to get them to let down their guard? Some kind of mental torture devised by their captors to add to their suffering?

"They just brought us in tonight," the same ghostlike voice continued. "You weren't with us, so we thought you'd know where we are?"

"We," Carrie thought. There was more than one. The voice was not distressed or threatening, but curious. Had this "we" been captured like she and Corley? Carrie scooted around beside her sister. She took Corley's hand and leaned against the wall.

As her eyes adjusted to the diffused light, multiple shaded forms and objects became slightly clearer. There was no furniture except for three stools in front of what appeared to be a built-in bar. Two lava lamps on the bar provided colorful but weak illumination. There were mattresses on the floor with duffle bags between them. The dim revolving lava light provided no definition, only sketched outlines of five female shadows seated on the mattresses looking in her direction. It was as if they all had gathered for a slumber party and turned down the lights to play a group game.

"So do you know where we are?" asked the phantom closest to her.

How could you not know where you are, Carrie wondered, yet at the same time she understood the question. On one level, Carrie thought she knew where she was, but on another level, she had been blindfolded, restrained, and taken to an unknown place against her will, that could be anywhere. She knew the city in which she had lived all her life, the neighborhood, school, home, and the familiar territories she moved through. Now everything was disordered, turned upside down. It was as if gravity had ceased to exist, and she and Corley had been flung into space, untethered with no lifeline to grasp.

"We're in Richland, Tennessee," Carrie said tentatively. "At least I think so. We rode around for a while before we came here."

"They turn you out here in Richland?" asked another of the shadows.

"Turn us out?" Carrie asked. "What's that?"

"Get you in the game," answered the shadow.

"I…we…don't know what you're talking about," Carrie said.

Carrie's response brought silence in the room. Corley squeezed Carrie's hand, so she leaned closer to her sister. Her sister tried to speak, but her words came out in a wet garble.

"You got a daddy?" the shadow asked.

"Yeah, we have a daddy," Carrie answered. That question she understood and got her to sit up straight. Maybe the shadow knew how to find their daddy.

"So who's your daddy? He do his pimping in Richland?"

"What are you talking about? My dad's a pastor." Carrie's heart went from hopeful to indignant in a split second.

"Yeah, I bet he a pastor." The shadow giggled which elicited snickers from the other shadows. "Does he preach on the track or do he have his own hen-pen stable?"

"Your daddy sure hemmed you up in some weird kind of Bible clothes. Guess that's cause he's a preacher."

This comment increased the laughter among the shadows.

"Stop it. Stop it. What are you saying?" Carrie cried, her heart had taken a tumble, and she was losing control once again. What was so funny? "We have a house. My sister and I live there with our big brother and mother. Our daddy preaches at a church, The Mercy Seat, a real church. Our church was doing a Christmas pageant. We had a show tonight. That's why we're dressed like this.

What are you talking about?"

Carrie bent forward, hands covering her face. She was heaving and gasping, trying to keep from crying but failing. She felt Corley wrap her arms around her.

"These girls must be new to the game," another shadow offered, and this brought an end to the group laughter. There was silence except for Carrie's broken sobs.

The shadow closest to them crawled off her mattress to get a better look. Carrie straightened up and sluffed out of her sister's arms. She had no understanding of what was going on, but she was going to be tough, fight if she had to, defend herself and Corley.

"Your daddy give you that head cut," the shadow asked pointing to Corley's face.

"Head cut?" Carrie asked completely baffled by the question.

"Give your sister that beat down," the shadow answered.

Carrie started to lunge for the shadow, but the hands of her sister gripped her shoulders and pulled her back.

"Our father has never hit us." Corley forced her swollen lips to shape the words properly.

Carrie could tell her sister was in too much pain to continue giving an explanation, so she took over.

"We've been kidnapped." Carrie sat up on her knees. "Along with another girl, and we don't know what happened to her. Have you been kidnapped as well?"

"Kidnapped?" came the surprised reaction from one of the shadows. "What are you talking about? You saying you and your sister were kidnapped."

Carrie was unsure how to respond. Were they not all in this room against their will? Is that how they'd come to be in this place?

"Weren't you kidnapped too?" Carrie asked.

The shadows did not answer. Their silhouette outlines became frozen. Had her question somehow shut down communication with these shaded ghosts?

"We just want to get back to our family," Carrie said. She put her wrist over her mouth to stifle a bubbling cry, but she could not hold it back. She fell forward onto her stomach and sobbed. The room went still except for Carrie's weeping. She felt Corley tugging on her foot, but then she felt a hand on her shoulder, a comforting hand, a hand from the shadow who had crawled off the mattress and approached them.

"You in the circuit now, baby," the shadow spoke with weary kindness.

"Circuit? What circuit are you talking about?" Corley puffed out the words to her question between her mushroomed lips.

"Several of us started in Tucson. We lost a few along the way…cops, trading up with other pimps, one OD'd." The shadow pointed to two shadows sharing a mattress in the far corner. "We took on those two in El Paso. Coyotes tossed them over the border. They only speak Spanish. We all cousins in the pipeline to New York."

Carrie had heard the words but could not comprehend any of them. This story made no sense. She and Corley had fallen into a deep underground cavern where there was little light and no exit, inhabited by strange-talking ghosts. She was sick with confusion and fear, the pit of her stomach in turmoil. Carrie dug her fingernails into the floor just as a woman she did not recognize came through the door and flipped on the overhead light.

"Rodeo time, ladies—high demand with back-to-back buyers," the lady said. "No curb-crawling tonight."

Carrie raised her head to see a strange woman standing just inside the open door. She wiped her blurry eyes and saw that the shadows had become human shapes, young women, black, brown, white, all in her age-range. The one closest to where she lay was black. They all scrambled for their duffle bags and started pulling out street clothes.

"Bathroom is behind the bar." The woman stepped to the bar and set what looked like a bowl of candy on top. Then she started swiping the screen on her phone. "Brush your hair and paint your face. Want you camera-ready. First stop, the factory for a little movie magic. You girls are stars."

"Who is that?" Carrie asked the former shadow.

"She's "the Bottom," pimp's right hand," she mumbled under her breath. "She got us on the dark web, doing all kind of crazy in front of a camera so perverts can watch us." The young girl removed a jean jacket from her duffle bag and used it to block the view of the woman standing at the entrance. "You got to help me," she whispered to Carrie. "I want to square up and get out of the circuit."

"No talking," snapped the woman not looking up from the screen of her phone.

Carrie pushed herself off the floor back onto her knees and watched the two girls who spoke Spanish disappear into the bathroom, while the others started dressing. She looked at the young black girl who kept glancing at the woman in the door. Carrie saw the fear in her eyes as she kept shifting her gaze from the woman and back to her. What had she meant by 'squaring up?' Carrie had sight but no vision, hearing but no understanding. What could she say or do for her? The woman began rapping her knuckles on the door, a signal to pick up the pace, and the young black girl quickly pulled on her pants. Carrie looked back at Corley to see if she might have heard and understood what had been communicated to her, but when she saw Corley's red, distended face, with the bruise circling her right eye, the thought of helping someone else flew out of her mind. She grabbed the half-empty water bottle and scooted beside her sister.

"Don't forget to take your Roxies. Get your move and your groove tonight, ladies," the woman said pointing to the bowl of candy on the counter. Then she held up her phone. "On-line buyers in the double digits. They are paying for you to put on a show."

As the girls hustled out of the room each one stuck a hand into the candy dish. Carrie tried to catch the eye of the young girl who had asked for help, but her heart froze when "the Bottom" was staring straight at her.

"Got other plans for you two. Stay put," the woman said as the last of the girls dashed out the door. Then a hand appeared through the doorframe. The woman picked up the candy dish and placed it into an anonymous hand, then she left the room.

Carrie dropped the water bottle when Leandra stepped into the room. She jumped to her feet and rushed to this friendly face, this light in the darkness, this angel. Carrie threw her arms around Leandra and gave her a desperate embrace.

"Corley look," Carrie said. "Leandra is here." Corley moaned as Carrie ushered her over to her sister. Carrie dropped beside Corley and Leandra knelt in front of them both. She laid the jeans and hoodies on the floor and looked into Corley's disfigured face.

"Someone did a number on you, girl," Leandra said.

"What is going on, Leandra?" Carrie blurted. "Who are these people? What do they want from us? Did they hurt you?"

Leandra raised a finger to silence Carrie. She looked back at the open door to make sure the woman had gone. When all was quiet, she spoke in a low voice.

"Get out of those costumes and put these on," she said pointing to the clothes. "I don't know what's going to happen or when, but you need to be ready to move fast."

"Look at her, Leandra." Carrie pointed to Corley. "She's bad off."

Leandra offered Carrie the candy dish the woman had given her.

"These are for pain," she said. "Give her a couple. I'll try to get you some food."

There was talking coming from down the hall. When someone called Leandra's name, she raised her hand for Carrie not to move.

"I'm in here," she said, dropping a couple of pills into Corley's hand.

"You're needed." It was a masculine voice, not harsh but insistent.

Carrie felt her gut twist into a knot. She was shocked that someone knew Leandra's name. But when Leandra rose to leave, Carrie grabbed her arm.

"Please don't leave us," she begged. "If you know these people, tell them to let us go. What do they want from us? How do you know them?"

"You've got to trust me." Leandra removed Carrie's hands from her arm.

When Leandra flipped off the overhead light and closed the door, the radiance of the lava lamps was overwhelmed by the sudden darkness. Carrie froze in the primeval glow of the lava lamps, a blind child, helpless to aid her sister, helpless to escape, helpless to bear the burden of this cruel predicament.

Chapter Sixteen

When Leandra entered the hallway, Esteban was standing outside the door to Arturo's office motioning to her. He massaged the spot where his brother's left hook had landed. When she approached, she stood on her toes and kissed the injured side of his face. There was little she could do. There was no time to comfort, no time to reckon with the heart's turmoil, barely enough time for the kiss and a tender smile. She offered the bowl of pills, but Este refused.

"We have a plan," Esteban whispered. "The bear wants your thoughts."

Leandra was stunned to learn her opinions were sought by the bear no less.

Esteban turned the doorknob but she held his arm to keep him from opening it. She set the bowl of pills in the hallway beside the door before following him into the office.

Arturo and Beltran stared at the monitors in the kitchen and the foyer downstairs. There was no sound, but Leandra saw more than a dozen girls corralled in the foyer. While Death Demons stood guard, Tiana gave a quick inspection of the girls then snapped an individual photo of each one. The routine was all too familiar. While driving to the factory, Tiana would attach the girl's photo to the profile of her online buyers on her phone and collect the "peepers" money. Low risk. Low overhead. High return. Just one of the many ways Leandra's associates made their money.

On the monitors, Leandra watched this pack of forced laborers file out of the house. On an exterior screen of the driveway were the same two vans used in the kidnapping. Both were plain white and blemished with dents and scratches. Each one had metal ladders or pieces of scaffolding stacked on the roof to give the impression of being service vehicles. Service yes, but not for home improvement.

Death Demons slid back the doors of each van and funneled the girls into the vehicles. There was no chance for an escape. After each van was filled, Tiana turned out the lights and took shotgun in the first van. This was a well-run operation, one Leandra hoped she would always observe from a distance. She relied on Esteban for that. He was her guardian. Without his protection, she would quickly become just another girl in the pipeline.

Once the vans left, Arturo turned from the screens and asked, "House empty?"

"Just us and the sisters down the hall," Esteban confirmed.

"And how are they doing?" Arturo looked to Leandra for an answer.

She hesitated. Leandra had not recovered from the stress caused by the whirlwind of the last few hours, performing in a church pageant, setting up the kidnapping, and now standing in the presence of a chief power broker of a vast criminal enterprise. Leandra was not sure what to say. She felt vulnerable like the captured sisters.

"You have earned your place here," Arturo assured her. "Speak freely."

"They are confused and scared," Leandra said.

"To be expected." Arturo nodded and smiled which gave her an uptick in self-confidence.

"They don't know what happened or why it happened. They have no idea where they are or who brought them here."

"Good. Good," Arturo said. "Do you think they still trust you?"

"The younger sister suspects something isn't right but can't put it together. The older sister is in too much pain to know what's going on."

"Yes, she was spoiled for our original purpose." Arturo

looked at Esteban with a flash of anger in his voice, Leandra's first tipoff that the bear could show his claws. "But there is a new possibility. What do you think of the Crane family?"

This question Leandra did not expect. What was her opinion of the people who had taken in a stranger, especially under such threatening circumstances? In a staged drama, she had been dropped off in front of the church and for several days had played the victim in the Crane household. The acting required for such deception was more challenging than that of her role in the church pageant. In fact, playing the role of the Virgin Mary helped her play a more convincing role as a victim of human trafficking.

Leandra hadn't been told the purpose behind the kidnapping. She had simply been given this peculiar opportunity as her last assignment before becoming a full-fledged member of the Death Demons. Normally, a final stage initiation for membership would have been a smash and grab or carjacking or some drug related crime. But this was a bigger task, and the local leadership had decided that there was no one else among the ranks of this gang to do this job. She had been chosen. She had done her part well, it had been accomplished, and she could allow herself to believe Arturo's words that she had earned her place at the table and her right to express an opinion on collective decisions. It was a sign of belonging, and she belonged.

Now she was asked to evaluate the people who had fallen under the spell of her performance and whose only desire had been to show her love. Up until then only Este had ever shown her any form of love. That love she understood. She and Este lived in the same world, with the same view of the world at large. The Cranes were part of a different world, a world she had never known.

If Leandra were honest, she would tell Arturo how good she had been treated by the Cranes. That her welcome into the family had been something she had never experienced, had no frame of reference. Leandra had been confused by the open-arms acceptance of the Cranes. The sisters' present situation was cruel by contrast.

"They're a good family and good to me," she said. By committing the crime, she had proven herself to the powers that be, but she would speak truth about the family.

When Arturo dropped his head and sighed, Leandra feared her truthful answer had been received with disappointment.

"This is perfect. It is even better than I expected," he said, and Leandra breathed a sigh of relief the bear seemed pleased by her answer.

"If such a good family, then the pain we bring will hurt that much more," he said.

Arturo's amused response baffled Leandra. She glanced at Beltran. He too was smiling, hissing through his teeth, verifying a perverse amusement at the prospects of what Arturo might be plotting. Esteban gave no reaction. His face was swollen and bruised, and he maintained a stoic expression.

"What pain? What are you talking about?" asked Leandra.

"This good family you speak of caused pain and disruption to our cartel partnership and our alliances within the city and the region. People died because of this good family. A local *Madre* mourns the cruel death of her son, a profitable asset, at the hands of the father of this good family. A pastor who murdered Diego Sanchez, someone very close to me. This caused a ripple effect on the police and political leaders and banking system of this city, all brought down by this good family. This cannot be ignored. Our international partners have called for payback. An example must be made. I shall see to it. And you, my sweet *Chiquita*, you have given us the sisters of this good family. The retribution has begun."

Leandra had agreed to play her role in this drama because she believed this would secure her *bona fides* in the gang, and the success of the mission had enhanced her status and elevated her from ordinary rank and file to one among the inner circle. Yet, it began to dawn on her how she had been used, that Arturo had been planning retaliation against the Cranes all this time, and that she was an unwitting accomplice.

"There is a price that must be paid for what they have done. We will contact the parents of the sisters to see how much they value the lives of their daughters," Arturo continued. "What will they pay to see their daughters alive again?"

"Wait, wait," Leandra said. "Are you talking about asking a ransom for the girls?"

She looked at Este, his features remained solemn while Beltran was beaming.

"Not asking…demanding," Arturo answered. "The Crane family shall pay in money and blood. The preacher will understand an eye for an eye. The daughters shall be used to get to the father."

Behind the smiling, scarred face and calm demeaner, the bear had lethal claws and was prepared to strike again and again to cause the greatest harm, all for revenge.

"But they could call the police," Leandra argued. "What would stop them?"

"There were many causalities in the Richland police force by the actions of this good family. The blue line is drawn, and the Cranes are on the wrong side of it."

Leandra knew the two distraught girls down the hall—desperate for answers, desperate to flee, desperate to return to their family—had given her their hearts, and this new result was one she never imagined. She had never thought through any of this, about what dire consequences there might be. She'd played along with the plan to ensnare the girls, beyond that, she'd never considered potential outcomes.

This had become so much more than her final initiation into the world of the Death Demons. Leandra was now a player in the drama of retribution demanded by powers beyond her comprehension. She retreated a few steps until she felt the wall at her back. She had waded into waters that were beginning to rise and she found she didn't know how to swim.

"How did you contact Beltran to set up the meet tonight?" asked Arturo.

The question was a hard slap that brought Leandra back into the present.

"I called him on the phone from the church office." Her confession brought a knot into her stomach.

"Burn your phone, Beltran." Arturo opened a drawer in his desk and pulled out several phones, sealed in the packaging, and scattered them over the desktop.

Esteban yanked his flip phone from his hip pocket and broke it in half.

"Go back to the sisters," Arturo said. "Tell them we wish to return them to their family. We need a number to call to set it up."

Leandra made her way to the door, but Arturo stopped her once she opened it.

"And Leandra, get them something to eat and drink. I'm sure they are hungry and thirsty. Make them calm and comfortable."

Leandra nodded then closed the door behind her. "Make them calm and comfortable," Arturo told her. Food and water, as if that was supposed to make them feel calm and comfortable like she had been made to feel by the Cranes when they took her into their home.

Down the hall the sisters waited. It was her task to get the number of their parents, and once secured, turn it over to those who would wield great power over the future lives of this family. Then once the number was called, a sinister force would be released, one that was sure to bring mayhem and sorrow before it would ever bring calm and comfort. Food and drink was no substitute for the calm and comfort the sisters required. Leandra took a deep breath and started down the hallway. She would do what she had been instructed to do.

Chapter Seventeen

Maxwell had been thrown into a dark pit, one he had dug himself, one pregnant with emptiness, one so deep he felt it impossible to climb out. He was lost, yet still present in the immediate world. He could recognize faces around him and acknowledge when they spoke, but he could not speak. He could not think of any coherent words to offer in response. He could only discern the sound of panic in other voices, the sound of grief in those around him, the sound of his own guttural drone.

In truth, it was his daughters that were truly lost. But how? They had been right there, right in front of him, within arm's reach, within his grasp, and yet his hands and fingers could not gain purchase. He envisioned the girls reaching toward him, but he could not take hold of an arm, a shoulder, anything, and pull them to safety.

Maxwell retraced his steps back to the church, and then took a different way home. He kept calling out the girls' names, expecting them to appear at any second, that they would jump out and surprise him and then laugh themselves silly at how they had pranked their father. But Maxwell knew in his gut this was no prank, no light-hearted game of hide and seek.

He circled around every building in the Gardens between church and home. He looked behind every tree, behind every dumpster, and God-forbid, inside every dumpster. He slid back the metal doors of every dumpster from The Mercy Seat to his home, calling their names, insisting they stop being childish and answer him. Each dumpster was empty except for the contents of trash, and he marveled at how he could be thankful for the feeling of relief just to see the discarded junk and rubbish.

Before Maxwell began retracing his steps, he had instructed Carlo to take the minivan and drive the adjacent blocks, check every eatery, in case their hunger pangs forced a change of minds while on the way home and they took a detour. Kenda would stay at the house waiting for their hopeful appearance. She would not call the police to file a missing person's report, not until he and Carlo returned from their search. She did insist on calling her brother, Pete, and Rosemary. Their presence was required.

When Maxwell closed the metal door to the last dumpster opposite his house he stepped into the street. He sensed that something unusual had happened right where he stood. He had found the head covering worn by Leandra in this spot. Kenda had taken it with her back to the house. In the cold night air he kept repeating, "Where are they Lord? Where are they Lord?" He might be furious with God for putting him through so much to this point. He might be confused and hurt by what he perceived as God piling more agonizing weight upon his already broken soul with the disappearance of his daughters, but he could not help himself. He had to keep calling out to God. He had to keep demanding that God listen, pay attention. *Don't you see what is happening here?* he thought. *Don't you care?* Who else was he to call upon?

"If you don't care about me, at least care about my girls!" he shouted unable to contain the blue-burning agony in his throat. "Where have they gone, Lord? They are lost to me, but are they lost to you, O Lord? Please help. Please help."

He was addressing God, but it did not feel like a prayer, or a plea, or a demand, only a jumble of desperate words spewing from his mouth. For some time, Maxwell had not known how or what to pray. He had lost his way, lost the ability to communicate with God at all, at least not the way he used to. He had long since given up using the prayers of the old religious formula or speak his "incense" words as if to impress God. He might think about God or mumble a cursory blessing at dinner or acknowledge the presence of God when others spoke of it. But whenever he allowed himself to really mediate on God and give his thoughts over to any deep connection with the Almighty, the only word that ever came to his mind was, "Help."

He would address God, but with no expectation of aid or comfort. He had little strength, little hope his life would become whole again and peaceful, and given this moment of crisis, he felt the walls of the deep pit in which he found himself could collapse upon him at any second.

Maxwell looked down around his feet and saw two HarperIman dolls lying on the pavement. He picked them up, holding one in each hand. In the glow of the streetlight, he could see some tearing of the fabric and smudges of dirt. Carrie could patch them up good as new and pass them on as Christmas gifts to some lucky child.

Maxwell was certain this was where something had happened, a forceful struggle. His sixth sense kicked in. Only Carrie would take every opportunity to check each of the dumpsters on their way home from church. Only Carrie would rescue these dolls from being lost. Only Carrie could see the beauty beneath the tears in the fabric and the smudges of dirt. Only Carrie would fight to protect her prize. She would never toss these dolls onto the ground and walk away. She would never relinquish her scavenger find without resistance. These dolls were either taken from her or she had dropped them to protect herself or Corley and Leandra. These girls had confronted danger on this spot and these dolls bore witness.

Maxwell examined each doll. If only they might speak and tell him what they had seen, just a clue or a hint, but their adorable linen faces remained silent. He would have to take the physical evidence of each doll as the only trace offered as to the fate of the girls. Maxwell was sure Carrie was the last person to hold these dolls.

The sound of an oncoming car caused the hair on the back of his neck to stand on end. He did not get out of the street but spun around to face the approaching headlights. When the vehicle came to a stop, Maxwell raised his arm to deflect the light. When the headlights went out, the two front doors opened. Had they been found? Could it be them? A spark struck his heart with a flicker of hope.

Rosemary jumped from the driver's side and Lin from the passenger side.

"Our girls…what's happened to our girls?" Rosmary said with an aching mixture of perplexed concern.

He did not know what Kenda had told Rosemary, but the fact she came straight from church and asked her question meant she knew something was terribly wrong.

Maxwell had to muster the strength to utter what any father would hate to speak concerning his children. "I don't know, Rosemary. I don't know. I don't know where they are or what's happened. Something bad, I fear, and…I wasn't there to protect them. I have lost them."

Maxwell pressed the two dolls to his chest. How could he not know what happened to his daughters? What kind of a father was he to let them be taken from him? How could he be so distracted, not paying proper attention, absorbed in his own world? Hidden in his heart he had to believe and hope that he had not seen the last of his girls.

Rosemary and Lin hastened to the front of the car and embraced Maxwell. He felt the instant strength of two loving human beings begin to flow into his heart. He knew neither would judge him, scold or accuse him. Only love and comfort him.

"My babies will be coming home." Rosemary wrapped her arms around him. "They'll be coming home."

"We'll find them, Mr. Crane," Lin added. "I know we will."

"Let it be so," Maxwell said. He might be losing his faith in God, but he was able to manage a level of hope at their encouragement.

"Kenda called me." Rosemary released him from her firm

embrace. "Said that Leandra and the girls never got home. I left Ezekiel at church, grabbed Lin on the way out the door, and here we are."

"We can't find them," Maxwell said. "I've looked everywhere between our house and the church."

"Where's Carlo?" Lin asked.

"Taken the car to look for them," Maxwell answered. "Did they say anything to you before they left the church?"

"No. I was with Carlo, and we never spoke with them after the show."

"They said they were going straight home." Maxwell's mind was racing, trying to recreate his last conversation with them as they were walking away from the church, into the Gardens, into the darkness.

"Maybe they decided at the last minute to cruise the neighborhood and get Chinese or Mexican or pizza," Lin offered.

A second set of headlights moved down the street toward them. Instead of stopping behind Rosemary's car, the driver pulled around it and stopped beside them. The electric window on the passenger side of the black SUV slid down.

"We need to get off the street," Pete said. "We're drawing too much attention." It never failed. Pete always came when called, always assessed the potential danger of any situation upon his arrival even with only a minimum of facts. The "always ready" Marine was always ready with a plan.

"Where's your minivan?" Pete asked.

Now a third car was approaching. When the highlights went from bright to dim, the left headlight went dark. Maxwell knew from the single beam it was Carlo. The dimming circuit on the low beam had gone out before rehearsals began, and of course, the mundane details of normal Crane life had been put on hold for the sake of the show.

"It's Carlo," Maxwell said breaking away from Rosemary and Lin and moving toward the minivan.

Pete was immediately out of his SUV and moved beside Maxwell as they watched Carlo come to a stop.

"They're not in there, Pete." Maxwell's voice was cracking just like his heart. "He didn't find them. He didn't bring them home. Oh, God."

Pete grabbed Maxwell on one side and Rosemary slipped up behind him on the other. Lin stepped in front of them. All four waited for Carlo to exit the car.

Carlo bounded out of the minivan. "Did they come home?" he shouted. "I couldn't find them. I asked everyone. No one saw them."

Then a voice from the front porch rose, a cry, the wail of a stricken mother.

"Carlo, where are my girls? Did you bring them home?" she yelled.

There was no need to answer. Everyone knew the answer.

Pete went into action. "Get the cars off the street. Carlo, you first in the driveway. Pull around me and back in. Rosemary, you're next. Do the same."

Lin jumped inside the minivan with Carlo, and he and Rosemary began backing into the driveway. Then Pete turned Maxwell toward the front porch.

"Can you walk through the yard to Kenda under your own power?"

Maxwell nodded, and Pete released him. But what power did he have? He didn't have the power to protect his daughters. He didn't have the power to find them. And if they were in danger, would he have the power to rescue them? The little power he did have was just enough for him to move forward, stumbling at first, and then getting his footing. He was trembling from the biting cold. It felt like he had stepped into an icy mountain stream with his naked feet. The current was swift and threatened to topple him.

He dug his feet into the ground and struggled to move forward, inching his way, moving like the nearly dead. He had to get to Kenda. He saw her bound off the porch and rush toward him. She would rescue him. She would be his sure footing. He could not open his arms to receive her as she rushed toward him. He could not let go of the dolls. He had to keep the dolls close to his chest. When she threw her arms around him gripping so fiercely, it forced the breath from his lungs.

"Everyone, in the house." The strong, sure voice of Pete had spoken.

Chapter Eighteen

Maxwell had to trust someone. He had to put his faith in someone who was tangible, flesh and blood he could touch and see. Someone who he could speak to and who would speak back. Someone who would be rational and take control and offer a way forward. That someone was his brother-in-law. So when Pete said the first order of business was to review the steps that had brought them to this point, everyone inside the house was asked to remember the last known sighting of Leandra and the girls. It didn't take long for Maxwell to realize he was the last one to see them. Everyone else had last seen all three of them inside the church building.

"Was there anything unusual about their behavior?" Pete asked.

Everyone shook their heads. The church had been packed. There was too much excitement and joyful hubbub for them to notice any unusual behavior, let alone a lurking threat.

"Did they mention to any of you that they were heading home?" Pete asked.

Maxwell was the only one who had been given that information.

"At any time before or during the show did any of you notice a break in your normal routine or some weird manner or comment from the girls?"

The others looked to each other for clues and hints and explained their preshow preparations and responsibilities, all normal, all routine, except for Maxwell.

"I came in from the parking lot with you, Pete," Maxwell said. He was focused intensely on the memory in his mind, playing out the details at a slow pace to be sure he missed nothing. "Kenda asked me to get the props for the wisemen from the office before I changed into my costume. I came around the stage and approached the office, the door was nearly closed, and the lights were turned off. The door is always open, and the lights are always on except during the show. Before I flipped on the lights, I heard someone talking. When I flipped the switch, it was Leandra talking to someone on the office phone. She was startled when the lights came on."

"Who was she talking to?" Pete asked.

"I don't know. She didn't say and I didn't ask."

"Did you hear anything of her conversation?"

"Whoever she was talking to, it had something to do with her mother."

"Her mother?" Kenda said. This was a surprise for everyone. Neither Maxwell nor anyone else had ever considered such a connection.

"Yeah, whoever Leandra was talking to, she asked them to keep looking for her, and then she hung up."

"Had she ever asked to use the church phone before?" Pete looked at Rosemary then at Maxwell. Rosemary could not remember Leandra asking to use the phone.

"I haven't been in the office much," Maxwell said.

"What about at home? Did she ever use the phone at home?"

"Pete, we don't have a landline."

"Do the girls have phones?" Pete asked. "We can look at their history."

"They have to wait until their senior year to get a phone," Kenda said.

"If they had a cell phone, we could track them," Pete reflected.

Pete's logical line of questioning felt all too familiar to Maxwell. This process was exactly like the police interrogations he had gone through when he was being questioned regarding his involvement in the death of Diego Sanchez. Different circumstances, but the same devastating feeling of helplessness.

"Think now, Maxwell, once Leandra hung up the phone, did she offer any other explanation or give any hints who she might be speaking with?" Pete asked.

"Just that she wanted to find her mother, try to find out if she was even alive, maybe reconnect. I could tell Leandra was nervous, and even though I was suspicious, I didn't want to give her the third degree. I know what that feels like. I've kept my distance since she's been in our home. I didn't want to come off as threatening, so I let it go. Then Carrie came in to get the props and Leandra left."

"Now that I think about it, I could tell something wasn't right in my scene with her tonight," Rosemary said. "Ezekiel could sense it too."

"What do you mean, Rosemary?" Pete asked.

"Every time in our scene, when Mary, or rather Leandra entered, Ezekiel would jump out of my lap and run to her. Tonight he stayed put, never left me. She must have brought her nerves from the church office onto the stage."

"Sis, did you notice any extra nervousness with her performance tonight?"

"No, I was paying more attention to the audience. I didn't see anything."

"Maxwell, you didn't detect anything in your scenes with her?"

Maxwell tried to remember if he saw a nervous Leandra onstage as well as off but couldn't remember. The Mercy Seat was at full capacity, standing room only. There was too much going on to pay close attention to such subtleties of human behavior. His real concern was seeing Jeff Anderson in the audience and wondering what he might be thinking more than worrying about Leandra's undetectable edgy condition. That required the feline acuity of Rosemary's cat. Perhaps Ezekiel had been on to something.

"Did she ever talk about herself much, personal history, anything?" Pete asked.

"We knew she came from a hard life on the streets, but not much more," Kenda said. "The pageant consumed every waking hour. We figured once the show was over it wouldn't be so crazy and we'd focus on getting to know Leandra and finding out how we might help her. But what's this got to do with my girls? We've got to find my girls."

Pete put his arm around Kenda and drew her close. "Stay with me, Sis. There might be a connection. We're going to find them."

"Why did we let them out of our sight?" she sobbed. "Why did you let them out of your sight?"

Maxwell knew this was coming. It was inevitable, this irrational blaming. He was fully blaming himself, so why not his wife.

"This is not helpful, Kenda," Pete said calmly. "No one is to blame now."

Maxwell wanted to comfort his wife, reassure her, but he was no help at present. He had to defer to Pete. He was still wrestling with this sudden and incomprehensible vanishing. That was the only way he could explain it, a vanishing. His girls could not be lost. They were too smart for that, too responsible. They would go home just like they said they were going to do, not take a spur-of-the-moment detour, yet they weren't home where they were supposed to be.

He looked at his wife sobbing inside Pete's arms. He longed to let her know how broken he felt, how helpless and sorry he was for these frightening circumstances, how he would move heaven and earth to find their daughters and bring them back home.

Maxwell watched Carlo take Lin into his arms. They both were crying and trying to comfort each other. He looked at Rosemary. She had folded her hands and placed them under her chin. Her eyes were closed, and her lips were moving swiftly. She was storming heaven, expressing her rapid-fire prayers. Everyone was connected to someone—brother to sister, boyfriend to girlfriend, Rosemary to the Almighty. But all he was connected to was the brutal force of self-reproach. He could not pray. He could not weep.

He could not comfort or be comforted.

Maxwell looked at his hands and only then realized he was clutching the two HarperIman dolls, one in each hand.

"Could we get the phone company to trace the call from the office phone?" Kenda asked. She had recovered enough to think of the question.

"Private citizens can't do it. Only a judge, and a request has to come from law enforcement. They only do that if there is probable cause or some evidence of a crime," Pete offered. "And to be honest, I doubt the number she called is still valid."

"What are you saying, Pete?" Kenda asked, on the verge of breaking down once again. "Are you saying they were…they are…in danger?"

"Yes, I believe they are in danger," Maxwell said as he held up the dolls.

"Why do you say that, brother?" Pete asked.

"When I found these dolls lying in the street, I got this strange feeling," Maxwell said cradling the dolls in his hands. "We found the head covering Leandra wore in the play. Then I found the dolls. I believe Carrie rescued these dolls from the dumpster on their way home. They got as far as the dumpster across the street before they were…" He couldn't finish the sentence. He could not finish the thought—too terrible to imagine, too painful to speak the words to those around him or to himself.

He felt his hip pocket begin to vibrate. It was his phone. He tucked the dolls under his arm and reached into his back pocket and pulled out his phone. "Unknown," it read. No accompanying number to indicate the location of the call. Just "Unknown." Everyone was silent, looking at Maxwell holding his phone for them to see what was written on the screen.

Pete looked at his watch. "Confirm the time on your phone, Maxwell."

"Ten minutes till eleven," Maxwell said.

"Who could be calling us at this hour?" Kenda asked.

It was bewildering. An unknown caller. Maxwell would normally allow these types of calls to go direct to voicemail. This was different. It was nearing eleven p.m. His girls had gone missing. The vibrating phone was insisting he answer, but he did not have the courage. He was too frightened of who it might be.

"Answer the phone," Kenda blurted, and she reached for it, but Pete stopped her hand. "What are you doing?"

"Do you see a number and location on the screen?" Pete asked.

"It could be the girls!" Kenda knocked away Pete's hand and reached for the phone, but the vibrating stopped. She gave her husband and brother a fierce look of anger.

Seconds later the phone vibrated again, and again only the word "Unknown" appeared, no location, no number of the caller. The phone should have identified the caller if it were the police, or a hospital or a local eatery or where they might have gone to grab a bite to eat or even potential spam. The mystery of the unknown caller could only be solved if Maxwell answered his phone.

"Everyone don't make a sound," Pete ordered. "Put it on speaker, then answer."

Maxwell dropped the dolls on the floor and pushed "answer" on his phone.

"Yes?" he said trying to control his emotions.

There was silence on the other end, then a garbled voice spoke, then a muffled sound, and then the line went dead.

Chapter Nineteen

Carrie slipped out of her biblical costume and put on the clothes Leandra had brought for them to wear, then she aided Corley to her feet. Corley groaned as Carrie delicately helped pull the robe over her head, then Corley braced herself against the wall to slip into her jeans and hoodie.

"Why don't you take one of those pills Leandra gave us?" Carrie asked.

"Not going to do that," Corley said as she gingerly put the hoodie over her head.

"But Leandra said it was for the pain. Those other girls took them."

"That has to be for a different kind of pain, Carrie. We don't know what that is."

Carrie began to fold her costume but then stopped. Why was she doing this? Her world had been shattered. The normal routine of caring for the actor's wardrobe had been forcefully interrupted, so what would be the point?

"What should I do with our costumes?" she asked Corley.

"Hand me mine." Corley extended her hand.

Carrie picked up Corley's robe off the floor and handed it to her. She neatly folded her robe and set it on the closest mattress.

"If the girls we met come back, maybe one of them could use it," Corley said.

Carrie followed her sister's example even though she doubted any one of these girls would ever find use for a Bible costume.

"Now help me get to the bathroom," Corley said, and Carrie

took her sister's outstretched hand. "It's hard to see in this light with one eye."

Carrie held onto her sister as they shuffled between the mattresses on the floor and around behind the bar. The lava lamps on top of the bar provided enough colored light for Carrie to guide Corley to the bathroom on the opposite side. The door of the bathroom had been removed, so once they reached the threshold, Carrie rubbed her hand along the side of the wall searching for a light switch. When she found it, she flipped the switch on and off several times, but the light did not come on.

"Can you see well enough to go to the bathroom?" Carrie asked.

The swelling on the side of Corley's face around her eye had not diminished enough to restore her vision.

"Just get me close enough to the toilet seat," Corley said. "I want to go before Leandra comes back with something to eat."

Earlier, Leandra had returned to their room to get a phone number so their parents could be contacted, and Carrie had given her Maxwell's cell phone number. Then she said she was going to get them something to eat.

"It shouldn't be long now," Leandra had told them as she stood at the door.

"Where are we, Leandra?" Carrie asked. She was becoming more suspicious of Leandra by the minute. "Do you know these people?"

"They will call your parents," Leandra said. "We're going to get you home."

"Who is 'they'? How do you know them?" Carrie asked. "What do they want? How could you do this?"

"Just stay put and stay quiet," Leandra said, and then closed the door behind her.

Carrie positioned Corley at the toilet. The bathroom was too small for two people to fit comfortably. There was a sink attached to the wall with a pile of dirty towels and a couple of rolls of toilet paper underneath. She picked up a roll and handed it to Corley, then she moved back and leaned against the threshold to give Corley some room.

"I don't trust her," Carrie said. "I don't trust her at all."

"What else can we do?" Corley asked.

"I don't know."

"If they do call Mom and Dad, they will at least know we're alive."

"Do you hear what you're saying? You act like being alive in this awful place is some kind of good news. We've been kidnapped. Our lives are in danger."

"I don't know if this would be good news or not, Carrie. These girls who were in the room with us…if they've been kidnapped as well, they've got a mom and dad out there somewhere looking for some sliver of good news."

"Don't say that Corley. I don't want to believe we're in the same situation."

"But the same thing could happen to us. These people could do to us what they are doing to them."

"That can't happen," Carrie insisted. "Mom and Dad would not let that happen. God wouldn't let that happen…would He?"

"We're here, aren't we?" Corley said and her voice began to tremble. "We're here and no one stopped it from happening."

Carrie reached out and placed her hand on Corley's shoulder. Pondering the possibilities of why and how…how they came to be embroiled in these circumstances, why had it happened. All the hope Carrie could offer her sister was a firm grasp on her shoulder. She had nothing else to give, nothing else to say. How could she understand what had happened? How could she explain it? The harsh reality was that no one or nothing had kept this from happening. No one protected them against this harm. If that was the case, then would anyone come to their rescue or help them to escape?

"Do your business, Corley." Carrie moved away from the threshold. She spread her arms across the bar and stared at the gooey blobs inside the lava lamps forming their liquid configurations and then break apart like amoebic cells and rise to the apex of the lamp. It was hypnotizing. This must have been what the universe was like before God began to create, when He hovered over the deep, watery darkness focusing His imagination. Was He hovering over them now? Was He focusing His attention on them and contemplating creative ways to get them out of this trouble?

She broke her stare from the lava lamps and took in the room. For the first time she noticed there was one window with a curtain drawn over it. If she could see out the window, she might be able to tell where they were. She slipped around the bar and over to the window. Before she tried to pull back the curtain she stepped toward the door and listened for the sound of anyone coming down the hall to the room. When she didn't hear anything, she went back to the window.

The single curtain was made from heavy material. No light could penetrate from outside and no one on the inside could enjoy a view of the outside world. She couldn't yank back this curtain like she did those in her room when she got up each morning to let in the sunlight. Instead, she took the edge of the curtain in her fingers and carefully pulled it back just enough to peek outside. But there were Venetian blinds behind the curtain covering the window. She had to pull down one of the blades if there was any hope of seeing any landmark that might give her an indication of their location.

When Carrie retracted a single blade, it appeared they were in some kind of neighborhood. There were trees, and in the distance, there was a floodlight on the side of another house nearby. She could see shadows moving through the trees. Her hopes began to rise that maybe this was a rescue team, but they were quickly dashed when a group of deer walked out of the trees. She lifted herself up onto her toes and looked down onto the driveway. It was empty except for the deer who crossed the drive and disappeared.

The vehicles that had brought them to this place were gone. Carrie assumed these vehicles were the ones that had taken the other girls away. Even in the darkness, she could tell that at this height if she and Corley were able to climb out of the window, the chances were great that they would be injured when they dropped to the ground.

"Get away from that window right now."

Carrie spun around and saw Leandra standing in the door holding a tray of food. Before stepping into the room, Leandra looked down the hall, and then stepped inside and kicked the door closed. She moved over to the bar and set down the tray with two bowls of soup, packets of oyster crackers, and two more bottles of water. She pointed to a corner of the room near the door where the wall and ceiling met. Carrie could see the red dot on the camera mounted on the wall. She had not noticed this until now.

"They can see and hear what's going on," Leandra said. "You'd better be careful."

Carrie remained beside the window. She could feel her heart pounding, not out of fear, but out of anger. Carrie remembered how Leandra was behaving back at the church right after the show was over. She didn't want to hang around at church like she had done the previous nights. She was complaining of fatigue, complaining of hunger, complaining about being in a hurry to get back to the house and get out of her costume. While they walked home through the apartment buildings of the Gardens she was complaining about the cold.

Leandra was several steps in front of Carrie and Corley, and she was impatient, wanting them to hurry. When Carrie had stopped to look inside one of the dumpsters, Leandra's frustration boiled over as Carrie excitedly showed off the found treasure of dolls. But then the headlights came on, the Day of the Dead skulls came flying out of the vans, and Carrie and Corley were whisked away.

"What did you do with your costume?" Carrie asked.

Leandra became flustered. "I don't know. I just took it off."

"You betrayed us. You tricked us and set us up to get taken." Carrie began to inch toward Leandra.

"You don't know what you're talking about," Leandra protested.

"We're not stupid. You know these people here. You worked with them to lure us into a trap."

Her anger gave way to tears. Carrie didn't want to cry. She needed to hold onto her anger and not reveal any weakness in front of Leandra. Carrie wanted to show herself strong and not one that would be compliant, not a victim that could easily be manipulated.

"Carrie, can you help me," Corley said, and then the toilet flushed.

Carrie glared at Leandra as she moved past her and around behind the bar to help her sister out of the bathroom. When she brought Corley up to the bar, Leandra slid the tray of soup and crackers toward them.

"Thank you, Leandra," Corley whispered.

Carrie was infuriated. "How can you thank her after what she did to us?"

"Carrie, please…"

"No. No. Look at her face, Leandra?" Carrie pointed to the distorted and blackened side of Corley's face. "This is on you. You are responsible."

"You don't understand." Leandra lowered her eyes, refusing to look at Corley's face.

"What don't I understand?" Carrie retorted.

Leandra was silent. She may be reluctant to give an answer, but Carrie was going to insist. She would force a reply. If she and her sister were thrust into this frightening predicament, then she wanted to understand why.

"What don't I understand, Leandra?"

"I've been lost and invisible in the world since the day I was born," Leandra said still not raising her eyes to look at Carrie. "The choices I made have finally given me some control over my life. I belong now."

"Belong to what? Your choices have put our lives in danger," Carrie said.

"Leandra, I don't know who these people are you think you belong to," Corley spoke out of the side of her mouth. She stretched her arm across the bar and placed her hand over Leandra's. "But from what I've seen, you don't want to belong to them. You are a victim like those other girls."

Leandra jerked her hand away and began to back up toward the door.

"I'm not a victim because I choose not to be one," she retorted. "I belong now, and I earned my place. I've filled up my pain quota. Now it's your turn."

Leandra whirled around and grabbed the handle on the door and jerked it open. Then she looked back.

"You're in it now, so just ride it out." She slammed the door behind her.

Carrie was quiet. She listened as Leandra's clomping footsteps faded away before she spoke. "What does she mean, 'pain quota filled up'?"

"I don't know. She must mean the pain she's had in her life," Corley answered. "More than we could ever know. Maybe that's why the girls take those pills, help with their pain quota."

"Well, she's right about one thing—we're in it now," Carrie said.

"Yes, we are, and I say, 'Father forgive them for they know not what they do.'"

How could her sister say such a prayer, Carrie wondered? Jesus might be able to say those words, even her sister, but she couldn't. She wouldn't. She would not lay down. She felt no mercy toward Leandra or toward the demons that flew out of the belly of the van or whoever it was that made all this happen. She would not forgive. She would fight. To the last deep breath in her body, she would fight.

Chapter Twenty

Maxwell looked at the screen on his phone. Both calls did not record a number nor identity of a location. The unknown had to be using a special phone, not the normal phones sold to the common customer. Perhaps a military phone, or one used by high-tech security agencies—a phone and number that was untraceable. He knew in his gut this was a purposeful attempt to contact him. This was not a prank call, a wrong number dialed, or a telemarketer. The unknown was someone who wanted to talk with him, and it had to do with his daughters. He willed it to ring again and was rewarded with the vibration and appearance of unknown on the screen. This was the third attempt in a short space of time. It was no mistake. He pressed on the "speaker" and looked at the others to be sure they were still and quiet. Then he answered.

"Yes, this is Maxwell Crane." He did not wait for a voice to speak or to listen for background sounds. He did not want to give the caller the idea he was startled by this late call. He wanted this caller to know who he was, that he was alert and ready to speak.

There were some amplified clicks on the other end, then static, and finally silence. But not the silence of a disconnection, just silence with no ambient sounds.

"You are Maxwell Crane?" spoke the disembodied voice of the unknown.

Maxwell knew immediately the caller had equipment to purposefully distort the human voice. With no background noise, the caller could be anywhere. When Pete gave him an affirming nod, his knees began to weaken. His heart pounded at the thought of who this might be and what they might have to tell him. Then he felt Rosemary place her hand on his back as if to prop him up. Her steady hand was the bolster he needed.

"I am Maxwell Crane," he said.

Again silence. Maxwell's firm declaration must have given the caller some pause, but he knew there was more. If this was going to be the menacing call Maxwell anticipated, he did not want to weaken his position this early. He had to stay strong.

"Who is this?"

There was a deep breath taken. A deep breath that was held by the unknown. Maxwell held his own breath and looked around the circle. The others had done the same.

"You have two daughters," said the unknown. "We have them in our possession."

Kenda collapsed and Pete had to go down on one knee to catch her. He took one of her hands and used it to cover her mouth and stifle her sobs.

The unknown said "we" and "our." More than one individual was involved. Even though the voice was distorted, it sounded male with a Hispanic accent. Saying "possession" indicated nefarious intentions.

When Pete hissed Maxwell looked down at him with his arms wrapped around Kenda. He mouthed the words, "proof of life."

"How do I know the two females you have are related to me?" Maxwell asked.

"Your daughters are not at home. They were collected on the street where you live. Right in front of your house," responded the unknown.

The unknown's accusation was a measure of his inadequacy, accusing Maxwell of weakness, of being so careless as to allow his daughters to be taken right from under his nose. He looked down at Pete again and saw him shaking his head as if to say, "Don't take the bait. Don't let the caller get to you. Don't lose focus."

"That still does not prove that I am related to the females you claim to have," Maxwell said. "Do you have any proof of identity?"

There was now the muffled sound on the other end as if the unknown might have covered the mouthpiece of the phone or pressed it against his body. Maxwell listened hard for any audible clues from the background sounds. Then the unknown returned.

"Your daughters were wearing some kind of Bible clothes. Their names are Corley and Carrie."

Maxwell could hear the intensity of Kenda's sobbing at the mention of the names of their girls. He saw that Pete's hand pressed against his sister's hand covering her mouth was not enough to stifle the snowballing distress in her heart. But he could not be influenced by her pain. He could not falter.

"Names and clothing are not enough," Maxwell said. "I need something more specific to prove their identity and possible association to me. And I need proof of life."

Maxwell kept his voice calm, tamping down all emotion. He needed to ignore what was going on around him, Kenda's breakdown, Carlo and Lin's panicked faces, the constant flow of Rosemary's muted prayers. He needed to stay focused on the unknown, listening and responding with caution. If what he believed was happening, then the unknown would become the most important person in his life until he could bring his girls home.

On the floor sprawled around Maxwell's feet lay the two cloth dolls that he had found on the street. He believed Carrie had collected them from the dumpster. This was the connection, a hard fact that could nearly break him if proved to be true.

"What do you want to prove their identity?" asked the unknown.

Maxwell could tell that there was a slight uptick in the unknown's impatience.

"One of these two females had gotten something out of the dumpster before…before…they became lost."

He could not say abducted or kidnapped. He could not say or believe anything so terrible even though every instinct within him told him that this was true. This caller had his daughters, and the situation was going to become worse before…before…what? He could not allow his imagination to go to such dark possibilities.

"What was found in the dumpster?" he asked. "Then I will know."

Carrie nibbled on oyster crackers while she traversed around the mattresses on the floor in the room. She had to pace, to think. She would glance up at the camera but wouldn't look at it for long. She did not want the "watchers" to think she was frightened by their all-seeing red eye. She wanted them to see her moving about the room and not cowering in some corner. She was glad to see Corley spooning her soup into the side of her mouth and mumbling something between each swallow.

"What are you saying?" she asked.

"Reciting a verse from the book of *Isaiah*," Corley said, and she blew her breath over the spoonful of soup before putting it to her tender lips.

"Which one?"

Corley carefully swallowed and then sat up on the stool. She glanced up at the camera, and then looked back at Carrie as if she was not sure she should say it.

"Say it, Corley." Carrie gave a defiant nod to the camera.

Corley took a breath and closed her eyes.

"I have chosen you and not cast you off. Do not fear, for I am with you. Do not be dismayed, for I am your God. I will strengthen you and help you. I will uphold you with my righteous right hand."

When Corley was finished, she dropped her head and let out a sigh.

Carrie looked up at the camera and whispered, "Take that."

When the door swung open it startled them both.

"What did you get out of the dumpster before they picked us up?"

Carrie was not surprised to see Leandra standing inside the doorway. She had expected her to return, but what she had not expected was the question.

"What are you talking about?" Carrie asked.

"Just before they snatched us, you got something out of the dumpster," Leandra was on edge. "It happened so fast; I couldn't see what it was. So tell me, what was it?"

"Why are you asking me that question?"

"Just tell me what it was." Impatience was turning to anger. "We need to know."

"Who needs to know?"

Carrie was in no position to be stubborn, but that was the impulse that moved ahead of common sense and any consent in answering Leandra's question. It gave her time to think, time to realize that only a handful of people in her life would know to ask such a question of her. Two of them were with her in this room, and only one of them was trustworthy. If Leandra needed to know immediately, then those who needed to know had to be in communication with the one who had asked the question. If the one who had asked the initial question that required her to give the answer, then it had to be a member of her family. Who else could it be? Could they be talking with them at this very second?

The headstrong impulse sent a shot of energy through her entire body and she bolted for the door. Leandra had no time to react as Carrie pushed her out of the way knocking her back into the hallway, against the wall, and onto the floor. Carrie was not thinking of escaping. She did not know where she was or if she could even get away from her captors. But she knew she had to do something to connect with the one whose question had sent Leandra to the room for her answer.

"Daddy!" Carrie screamed as she raced down the hall. "Daddy, we're alive."

A head thrust out of an open door at the end of the hall. Carrie raced for the door and crashed into the stunned male who quickly wrapped his arms around her.

Leandra was right at her heels, and once she bolted into the room, she slapped her hand over Carrie's mouth.

A large man behind a desk held a cell phone above his head. Carrie tried to scream, but Leandra's hand pressed down on her mouth. Then Carrie stretched her mouth open and clamped her teeth down upon Leandra's finger which got the desired result.

"Daddy, I came as quick as I could," Carrie yelled. "I got two dolls out of the dumpster. Corley is hurt, but we're alive."

"Carrie! Carrie!" she heard her father shouting through the phone.

The large man brought the phone to his ear. "There is your proof of life." Then the large man ordered the one who held Carrie to take her away.

As quickly as the burst of energy had shot through her body, it was suddenly gone. Carrie went limp. The man holding her dragged her out of the room and she saw Leandra nursing her fingers as she was carried out the door. Contact was made. She heard her father's voice, and he had called her name. He was fighting for her. He was taking action. There was hope.

The man stumbled into the room and slung her onto a mattress, knocking the breath out of her. Before he closed the door, she could see Leandra standing in the hallway outside the room. The moment the door was slammed shut, vulgar, shrill arguing from the hallway erupted.

Carrie felt Corley drop beside her on the mattress and scoop her into her arms. When the breath returned to Carrie's lungs she looked up into her sister's face.

"Daddy knows," she gasped. "He knows."

Yes, there was hope, and it brought both of them to tears.

Chapter Twenty-One

Maxwell disconnected the call and dropped the phone. He did not have control and did not want the unknown to hear his emotional breakdown and take advantage of his desperate condition. The second Maxwell heard his daughter's frantic cries, a great wave crashed upon him that brought him to the floor onto all fours heaving out his rage and torment. His fractured mind was in so many pieces he felt he would never be put back together, never be whole again. He had to find one thing to grasp. Just one thing. He focused on the certainty that he had heard his daughter's voice and that, without a doubt, it was Carrie. He had asked for proof of identity and proof of life, and he got both.

He scooped up the two dolls on the floor in front of him. These were the last things she'd held, and he crushed them against his chest. But there was something more she had given him, truer than true, and that truth could only come from Carrie. She had shouted "I came as quick as I could." No one ever used that line but the two of them, and no one in the world but the two of them knew the answer.

"And not a moment too soon," he whispered as he rocked back and forth on his knees. "And not a moment too soon."

This was Carrie's clear and true message that she was his daughter. The two dolls and their shared wordplay were a double confirmation. That was enough for him to know that it was time for action.

Maxwell wiped his face with the sleeve of his shirt. He did not have to explain his sudden collapse. Everyone had heard Carrie and everyone around him were now on their knees holding one another, weeping, trying to console, storming heaven with sodden appeals in grief and distress. It was a group prayer because everyone had been brought low by a cruel ambush that no one could have anticipated, and they all had one supplication: God, protect the girls and bring them home safe. Even his brother-in-law kept repeating "Amen. Amen" to Rosemary and Kenda's pleas for intervention.

"Dad, what do we need to do?" Carlo asked as he wiped his own tears away.

Maxwell looked at his son holding Lin in his arms. His son had turned his attention from heaven to him. Heaven might receive the petitions, but all action was to be taken here on earth, and Carlo was looking to him for direction.

"Maxwell, your phone," Pete said. He reached for the phone lying face down on the carpet and turned it over.

Maxwell heard the vibrations and flipped it over. "Unknown" was on the screen. The unknown was becoming the known. He wiped his face again with his shirt sleeve. His eyes had to be clear. His internal system had to be clear before he could continue with the unknown. He picked up the phone and stood on his feet, taking several deep breaths. He tossed the two dolls on the sofa behind him, and then cleared his throat and waved for everyone to be quiet before he answered. Then he tapped the screen.

"You have my daughters. I want them back," Maxwell said with a steely voice. He did not wait for the unknown to address him first. He took the initiative.

"Do you know why we have your daughters?" the unknown asked.

"I do not need to know why," Maxwell replied. He was not interested in the "why." He just wanted to know the "how" and "when" he could get them back. "I know that you have them. That is enough."

"But it is not enough, Padre," the unknown said. "You must

know we only took your daughters to hurt you."

He must not get angry and threaten the unknown. To do so would only show the unknown that his torturous words were getting to him. He wouldn't show such weakness.

"If you want to hurt me, why take my daughters? Why not take me?"

"Ah, now the good Padre wants to know why," the unknown said.

Maxwell could hear the smile of satisfaction in the voice of the unknown.

"Padre, you have caused much pain to my associates here in Richland and our partners in other parts of the world," the unknown continued. "So pain must be given in return."

"How have I caused you pain?" Maxwell asked.

"The blood of Diego Sanchez is on your hands. Blood for blood," the unknown began. "From your actions, the structure of our international business has been disrupted. Important members of our local team have been removed. You are to blame, and you must pay. We have been watching and waiting. Like the rattlesnake hiding in the desert, we struck when you weren't looking. When your daughters were almost home, we struck. You weren't there to protect them, Padre. And now they are in our possession."

There was so much Maxwell could say, or insist the unknown explain his twisted reasoning, but that would require congenial conversation. This was not an amiable moment. This was a dark and sinister moment, and it didn't take great deductive powers to realize that when he entered the church office before the show and found Leandra talking on the phone, she was coordinating with the kidnappers the time and place for the abduction. Leandra must be the liaison for this criminal gang. Had she been dropped off in front of The Mercy Seat for the sole purpose of playing her part in carrying out this elaborate scheme? If so, she was a better actress than he imagined. He had been deceived. The whole family had been deceived and now found themselves inside this bleak pit.

"What must I do for you to return my daughters safely?" Maxwell asked.

"There is a penalty to pay for all the economic disruption and death you have caused, Padre. A ransom must be paid, and it will be painful, but not as painful as what will happen to your daughters if we are not properly compensated for our losses."

"And what if I don't pay?" Maxwell asked knowing that he would pay anything, yet insisting on knowing how far the unknown was willing to go.

"You are testing me, Padre, but I will answer you. I am not interested in a life-for-a-life. Since your actions caused my associates economic loss, if you don't pay the ransom, your daughters will be exploited for commercial purposes. They will be transported far from their home. You will not know where they are. You will never see them again. You will have your whole life to suffer."

Everyone around Maxwell gasped at this threat. It was not simple intimidation. They had succeeded in capturing the girls, so it was conceivable that the harm the unknown intended could become an evil reality. Maxwell fought against despair.

"So I ask you, Padre. Do you wish such a terrible fate for your daughters?"

The pressure inside Maxwell's chest began to escalate. If he allowed it, the pressure would cause his heart to explode. If he allowed it, the mounting rage could cause him to say something that would further jeopardize his girls.

"How much are your daughters worth? I will let you decide, Padre."

Maxwell remained silent. Whatever the price agreed upon would be impossible for him. This was a game being played and to be drawn in was foolish, yet the lives of his daughters were at stake.

"Twenty-five thousand apiece, Padre? Is that a price you would pay?"

Maxwell did not speak. He would still be trapped inside this incomprehensible drama regardless of price.

"Fifty thousand apiece."

Maxwell felt a tugging on his pants leg and looked down to see Kenda glaring at him. She had stopped weeping and pushed Pete's hand away from her mouth.

"Seventy-five thousand apiece. You do not answer, Padre. Shall I keep going?"

Kenda raised up her hands as if to ask what are you thinking? Had he lost his mind? What was he thinking? It was unimaginable that the unknown was forcing him to name a price for his girls.

"One hundred thousand dollars, Padre? I can see you place a high value on your daughters, but the higher the ransom, the more you are in my debt. Or should I say, the longer your daughters will be our indentured handmaidens."

This manipulation was becoming intolerable. There was no monetary value that could be placed on his daughters. Any amount of money was absurd to him. He obviously did not have it and had no idea how to get it.

"What if I go to the police instead?" Maxwell said. It was probably not a viable option, but it was enough to pause this absurd and perverse auction of his daughters.

"The police will be of no help to you," the unknown said.

Maxwell could hear the abrupt shift in tone. The unknown went from deviant playful to sinister threatening.

"Going to the police will only bring you grief. You will hit the "blue wall" in spite of the new commissioner. They have not forgotten what you did by taking down their own. They have not forgotten or forgiven. Just as we have not forgotten or forgiven."

Maxwell looked at Pete who was nodding his head in agreement with the reasoning of the unknown. The police in this situation would be a costly detriment.

"One hundred and fifty thousand dollars, Padre. You drive a hard bargain."

The unknown chuckled at his joke. He had returned again to

deviant playfulness, and Maxwell would not continue to indulge the unknown in such wicked amusement.

"Yes, one hundred fifty thousand." Maxwell cut off this malevolent peddling.

"Apiece?" The unknown needed clarification.

"Apiece," Maxwell said.

"We have a deal then, Padre? Three hundred thousand dollars?"

"Give me two hours to secure the money," Maxwell said. He was not sure why he set that strict time limit, but he didn't want the unknown to have all the power over him.

"I doubt your collection plate brings in that amount, Padre. I see your daughters working for us for a long time, and I will tell them it was their papa who set such a high price for their debt repayment."

"Call me back in two hours," Maxwell repeated. "And I have one condition."

The unknown was unable to restrain himself. Maxwell knew his laughter was coming from the person who thought he held all the cards.

"What is your condition, Padre?"

"Tell my daughter who spoke just now, tell her, 'And not a moment too soon.'"

The unknown's laughter quickly subsided. "What do you mean?"

"Just say her daddy says, 'And not a moment too soon.' That's all she needs to know."

Maxwell disconnected the call. Negotiations were done. The clock was ticking, and he had no more time to waste.

Maxwell reached down and lifted Rosemary to her feet and looked her straight in the eye. "You have to pray like you've never prayed before."

"I don't know any other way to pray," she responded. "I just need some water and a corner of the house."

"I don't want to stay here," Kenda said. "They were right in front of our house and they kidnapped our girls. I don't want to be here."

"Go back to church," Pete said helping Kenda to her feet. "We work from there."

"Such evil let loose in the world. Who can stand unless we stand in God's house," Rosemary said. "We need Rendell to help us fight this battle. I'll call him now."

"We all ride in my vehicle to the church," Pete said. "One car gets less attention."

Maxwell looked into Kenda's puffy face and bloodshot eyes. He wanted to embrace her. He wanted her forgiveness. There was no getting through this unless she offered her pardon. His heart bore the immense weight of his own guilt. If Kenda forgave, he could move forward with greater confidence. He did not open his arms to her. He did not wish to coerce her. But when she held out her hand to him, he took it.

"Was it Leandra?" she asked. "Could she have betrayed us?"

"I believe she did," Maxwell said. "I believe she was talking to the kidnappers when I found her alone in the office with the lights out before the show."

"Then we were all deceived," Kenda said. She stepped closer to Maxwell and placed both hands upon his face. "I was wrong to blame you. It is not your fault. We cannot get our girls back unless we are of one mind. I am sorry I accused you."

This was all Maxwell needed to hear. His heart was strengthened. An invisible heaviness had been lifted. He could walk this treacherous path with a surer footing.

Chapter Twenty-Two

How they got to this point was no longer Maxwell's concern. Getting the girls back safe was all that mattered and assembling the right players to help make it happen was vital. A plan had to be made, an impossible, yet possible plan to confront a dark and mighty force that appeared invincible. This would be a joint venture of heaven and earth—visible and invisible worlds were in contention—so heaven and earth must work together. If Maxwell stopped to comprehend all the forces at play around him, he would be crushed by the reality of it all. His mind had to focus on one—convince Rendell Hardy to make a call to Jeff Anderson. He did not have the relationship with Anderson that Rendell had. He could not make that midnight call and ask for help.

Maxwell greeted Rendell as he entered through the back door of the office.

"What in the world is going on, Maxwell?" Rendell stepped inside. "Rosemary said it was an emergency but couldn't give me any details on the phone."

Maxwell scanned the alley and the back end of the church parking lot where Rendell had parked next to Pete's SUV before he closed the door.

"Everyone is in the sanctuary. Pete insists we keep the lights off so we don't draw attention." Maxwell switched on a flashlight so Rendell could follow him through the office and into the sanctuary.

"Why is Pete here?" Rendell asked.

"Expertise in emergency situations." Maxwell walked one step ahead of Rendell. "We're in deep, Reny, so deep we need to marshal heaven and earth to our side."

Maxwell pointed the flashlight into the front area of the sanctuary as they walked out of the office. Pete and Carlo were in the vestibule checking the front doors and looking through the stained-glass windows for any suspicious activity in the church parking lot or on the street in front of The Mercy Seat. Lin and Kenda were sitting together on a front pew holding hands and quietly talking.

When everyone first arrived, they found Ezekiel howling for his mistress. As soon as Maxwell had unlocked the back door of the office, Rosemary had grabbed her furry companion, a bottle of water, and went straight to pacing around the altar railing storming heaven. She had enough facts to get started and knew enough to go on the offensive. Maxwell trusted Rosemary's ability to solicit heaven's attention on what was going down in the physical world. Rendell's entrance did not interrupt her celestial business.

"Reny's here, Pete." Maxwell ushered Rendell into the sanctuary.

Kenda leapt out of the pew the moment she heard Maxwell announce Rendell's arrival. She rushed over to him and fell into his arms.

"Reny, our girls are gone," she cried. "They have kidnapped our girls."

Maxwell turned off the flashlight and laid his hand upon Rendell's back to counter the force of Kenda's sobbing embrace.

"It's true, Reny," Maxwell said. "You'll need to sit down so we might tell you everything. We need to act fast."

Maxwell did not want to interrupt Rosemary's prayer vigil to ask her to join the group. She knew the story. She was there from the beginning, and her role as intercessor was too important to disrupt. Pete and Carlo joined them down front, and Maxwell began the dramatic account of how Leandra appeared on the doorstep of The Mercy Seat.

"You mean the young woman who played Mary in the Christmas pageant?" Rendell asked. "That is hard to believe."

"I know. We thought she'd escaped from human traffickers, and we agreed to take her home until we could figure out what we might do about her future," Maxwell said.

"Reny, we wanted to tell you once the play was over," Kenda said. "We knew we were in over our heads, but the play took over our lives and it has all happened so fast."

"What is this girl's name?" Reny leaned forward on the pew and clasped his hands together.

"Leandra. She never told us her last name," Maxwell said.

"She probably didn't want us to know it," Kenda added.

"Reny, we believe Leandra was involved in a plot to kidnap Corley and Carrie. She might have been forced into it. We don't know. But they were abducted on our street tonight, in front of our house, as the three of them were walking home after the show."

"You must call the police now." Rendell sat straight in the pew. "We have a new commissioner. She should know about this."

"Impossible," Pete said. "I understand, Rendell, but that call would be ill-advised given the circumstances and the players."

Maxwell allowed Pete to explain all the reasons why, at this point, the police should not be brought into this predicament including the fact that a new commissioner didn't guarantee a favorable outcome in this case. Reny was a vital component to this small band, and Maxwell knew his brother-in-law would be persuasive and trusted him to lay out the facts not overwrought with emotion. Maxwell was all too aware of being on the edge. This night was far from over and there were so many moving parts. He knew how quickly things could go wrong and how quickly people could get hurt, how quickly people could die.

This could not happen, not to his daughters. He knew Corley was hurt, but he didn't know the extent of her injury. He assumed Carrie would have given him some indication if it was life-threatening. But this could not be a repeat of Diego Sanchez. He had to hold onto something solid to help him through, and Pete was solid.

"Given what Maxwell did to protect Carlo, and my involvement in bringing down the police commissioner and the death and arrests of the vice squad in the drug ring, we will get no immediate help with the police even with a new commissioner. A "blue wall" is up. For now, we go with the least number of players. We need more facts to create a plan, but you play a vital role in getting the girls back," Pete concluded.

"Is there anyone you trust?" Rendell asked. "Anyone besides those of us here?"

Maxwell did not have an answer. Nor, it seemed, did anyone else. It wasn't until Rosemary broke the silence with an empathic "God. You can trust God," that Maxwell was reminded how this saintly guardian had one ear locked onto heaven's gateways tuned for divine words and the other ear locked onto the world below ready to provide clarity when needed while never breaking her stride as she wore a path around the altar railing.

"Amen," Rendell whispered, and took a deep breath before continuing. "What else do you need to move forward?"

This was the second hardest "ask" Maxwell would make tonight. If Rendell gave an affirmative answer, then the hardest question would soon follow.

"Reny, we need to know if you will contact Jeff Anderson now and ask him if he will meet us here at the church."

"Now?" he blurted. "It's the middle of the night."

Maxwell knew Rendell would be astonished, but he had to press this good man.

"The kidnappers will be calling back in less than two hours. You will have the opportunity to hear for yourself the type of people we're dealing with. If Jeff is here, then he'll better understand our dilemma. You do not need to ask Jeff for the ransom. That is my responsibility. But I need to be able to assure this person that the money has been secured for our daughters' release."

"How much are they demanding?" asked Rendell.

It was Maxwell's turn to take a deep breath. Such a figure was incomprehensible for him, but then, so was the kidnapping of his girls.

"The kidnappers demand three hundred thousand dollars for both girls," Maxwell answered. He did not bother to reveal how that figure had been reached. He was still smarting from the humiliation of how he got played and did not want to make it worse.

"This is outrageous." Rendell jumped out of the pew. "This is so outrageous. Outrageous."

Maxwell was not sure how to understand Rendell's outburst. He sat quietly as Rendell paced in front of him mumbling to himself. He was encouraged to see that his dear friend seemed as shocked by the circumstances as he, as infuriated as he, and possibly as eager to resolve this as he. But he thought it best to allow this well-respected priest and influential citizen of Richland a brief time to process the "outrageous."

"I don't see how I, the church, can get involved," Rendell said, still pacing while talking out loud, trying to articulate what to say. "The church, I mean. This is not church business. This is a matter for the authorities. We can't…this is not church business."

"Rendell, listen to me." Rosemary spoke with a firm but gentle voice as she stepped over to meet Rendell. The streetlights shining through the stained-glass windows cast refracted shadows on their faces. Rosemary let go of Ezekiel and placed both hands on Rendell's shoulders. She had temporarily taken a break from soliciting heaven, her focus no longer split between two realms. Not the holy Trinity, not the angels, not Ezekiel held her attention. It was riveted upon Rendell Hardy.

"Rendell, this is most certainly church business," she began. "We are in the world, but we are not of the world. We have opened our doors and our hearts to all the hurting and broken people of this world, and on occasion, when we get distracted, something ruthless sneaks past the doors. You know the evil of this world wants to destroy the good. God don't stand for that, so we don't stand for that. This is very much church business because if we, the people of God, the church, don't stand against it, who will?"

Rosemary paused to give Rendell a moment to think. But that seemed to be all he was doing, thinking, so Rosemary gave him a little nudge.

"Rendell. Reny. Make the call to Jeff, please."

Rosemary released her hold of Rendell's shoulders. She bent down and scooped up Ezekiel then returned to her spiritual march around the altar railing.

Maxwell rose to his feet and stood next to Rendell. He did not want to leave him standing alone, and he laid an affirming hand upon his friend's arm.

"Lord have mercy." Rendell heaved a weighty sigh.

"Have mercy indeed," whispered Maxwell.

Rendell slipped his hand into the interior pocket of his coat and removed his phone. Before pressing Anderson's number, he looked at Maxwell.

"Thank you, Reny." Maxwell gave him a reassuring nod.

Rendell pressed the number on his speed dial and brought the phone to his ear.

"Jeff, so sorry to wake you, but we have an emergency at The Mercy Seat."

Chapter Twenty-Three

Jeff Anderson was accustomed to receiving emergency phone calls any time night or day from all over the world. Anderson Design had a global footprint and there was always an emergency, but he had never been awakened from a sound sleep for a church emergency. Not just any church, but The Mercy Seat, of which he was the current board chair, and which he and his wife had experienced a delightful evening watching a Christmas play only a few hours ago. "It was urgent," Rendell had said, and requested he return to the church, "in haste." He gave no reason for the "haste," or the cause that was "urgent."

Had it not been Rendell Hardy who had called him, and had he not told Anderson that he was already at The Mercy Seat with the Crane family along with Rosemary—the one detail he did offer—he would have told Reny that whatever was so urgent could wait till morning. Whatever the details were of the "urgent," it could not wait, and as he drove—in "haste," sans chauffeur—through Richland's quiet streets to the church, his mind raced with the probabilities of the urgent.

Rendell greeted him at the back door of the church office. Maxwell stood behind Rendell. Once Anderson was inside, Maxwell asked if he thought he might have been followed. He had to restrain himself from chuckling at so absurd a question, but he could tell neither Rendell nor Maxwell were in a jovial mood. Maxwell scanned the alley and parking lot before closing the back door, then he switched on the flashlight and instructed Anderson to follow.

"Reny, what is going on?" Anderson whispered as they

moved through the office.

"Wait until we get with the others." Reny motioned for Anderson to walk ahead of him into the sanctuary.

Anderson followed the beam from the flashlight. Before Maxwell turned it off, he could see Kenda and the others clumped around the first pew. From the corner of his eye, he caught sight of Rosemary pacing around the altar railing. All familiar people in a familiar place, but what strange circumstances. His eyes needed a second to adjust to the shadowy light coming through the stained-glass windows.

"You might need to sit down, Jeff," Rendell said motioning for him to take a seat.

When he sat on the front pew, the group formed a tight circle around him. The only one not to join was Rosemary. She was intensely preoccupied, talking softly while pacing, and though he did not hear what she was saying, he assumed she was praying.

"Jeff, Maxwell has something very urgent to tell you," Rendell said.

Anderson had imagined multiple scenarios as he drove to the church of what this emergency might be, but he was shocked by the story Maxwell told him. Anderson was by nature, sanguine, and generally calm in his approach to business and creative decisions, as well as life overall. But this hit hard. He felt his body temperature rising as Maxwell laid out the details of what had transpired. *How could one man and his family experience such hardship?*

It was not that long ago he had come to this church with Rendell to learn how his former political, financial, and law enforcement friends had used him for their nefarious objectives. Because of his so-called friends' reprehensible connections with Mexican drug cartels, this good family was victimized in such a cruel way. It was reasonable to believe that the very agencies who could help them recover their girls would refuse out of spite.

It was reasonable to believe that Joe Cassia, the former police commissioner, now awaiting trial for his crimes, still wielded his influence within the Richland police force, and that the "blue wall" Maxwell referenced was a reality. It was reasonable to believe that the recent appointment of a new commissioner who did not yet have full control over all the departments in the force, could offer much help. And it was reasonable to believe that the Cranes had few people they could bring into their confidence, and fewer still who could offer them a way out.

"Reny, have you listened in on any of these calls?" Anderson was not questioning the veracity of Maxwell's story. He just wanted Rendell's take on the type of people who were holding the Crane girls aside from personal vendetta.

"Not yet."

Then he looked at Maxwell. "And you heard your daughter screaming in the background on that last call?"

"I did. Everyone here did, but Reny." Maxwell raised his phone and pointed it to Anderson. "Jeff, in just a few minutes, the contact should be calling again." Maxwell then knelt down and set the phone on the carpet in the center of this tight circle.

"This is the hardest ask I have ever made. I never thought I would be in such a…such circumstances. The kidnappers are demanding three hundred thousand dollars as a ransom for our daughters. I am now asking you for that amount, with no guarantee that you will ever see that money again."

People and organizations from all over the world had come to Anderson asking for money. His forebearers had established the Anderson Foundation for all philanthropic contributions, and he had never made a decision to refuse or grant a request without consulting Lindy, his wife. This appeal was not for philanthropy. This plea was for rescue. Now he understood why Rendell used such terms as "haste" and "urgent." And he assumed the speed and urgency of the circumstances would only intensify.

"Does anyone outside of this sanctuary know of your situation?" Anderson asked.

"No one but us and those who took our girls," Maxwell said.

"And God," Rosemary said.

Anderson could not tell if this was part of her prayer or a response to his question. Perhaps both. She did not offer an explanation, and Anderson now understood why she had separated herself from the group and to whom she was speaking so intently. She was engaged with God, and if this were so, perhaps God had brought him into this small circle.

Still, the context was so difficult for him to grasp, for him to believe that he was now in the middle of a life and death situation, that he could not unhear what he had just heard, that he was asked by the father of two kidnapped daughters to participate in a very specific way to help bring them home safely.

"What about any other outside help…besides God?" Anderson asked, and then quickly added, "Not to diminish God's help, but maybe others besides the police."

"What are you thinking, Jeff?" asked Rendell.

"I have a private security team. A few of them came here to secure the church after we watched Pete's video detailing the connections with the city leaders and the cartel. They could be of use in case…well, just in case."

Anderson looked around the group, but no one offered an immediate response. Rosemary was occupied in prayer, fully engaged with heaven, and did not respond. Perhaps no one thought that far in advance, that it was an unspoken hope among them that everything would go smoothly if they got the money demanded by the kidnappers. Exchange the cash for the girls, and everyone would go their separate ways. No one wanted to think of possible dire consequences and so remained silent.

"Mr. Anderson, if I may say something."

"Go ahead, Pete." Anderson nodded. He knew that if anyone could fully appreciate this situation it would be Pete.

"The party on the other end of the call has no respect for human life. We are learning this the hard way. Months ago, when I agreed to work with those who were trying to reduce the flow of drugs into Richland, I never thought it would go this far, or that my family would be embroiled in the conflict. But here we are. I don't want to rule out the offer of your security team, but in my military service I learned that with some missions the fewer the number the better. Not always, but many times. I suggest this might be one of those times, and I don't want to put the lives of your personnel at risk."

"Do you have any sort of plan in mind to reduce risk?" Anderson asked.

"Not until we know more, and once we do, we respond quickly, make plans and adjustments on the fly. Until we get more details, I believe more people involved might slow us down and hinder our success. At present, the opposition has the upper hand."

Anderson was impressed with Pete's appraisal and understanding of the current situation. He appreciated Pete's calm demeaner in spite of his two nieces being in harm's way. Anderson remembered what it took for Pete to shoot the film that took down so many of his former friends, how he had put his life in jeopardy, how it had almost cost him his life. He was sure that Maxwell and Kenda were as appreciative of having Pete on the ground as having Rosemary in the heavens.

The ringing of Maxwell's phone captured everyone's attention. The radiance of the light from the phone lying on the carpet acted like a small florescent fire riveting everyone's attention to its glow. Rosemary did not join but paused in her vigil to listen.

"Right on time. Exactly two hours," Maxwell said, but he did not retrieve his phone. He looked at Kenda who covered her lips with her hands, then he looked at Pete.

"One step at a time, brother," Pete whispered.

Anderson clasped his fingers together as he observed Maxwell's trembling hand reaching for his phone. Anderson saw "Unknown" on the screen. Maxwell bowed his head. Before he answered he said, "God have mercy on our girls. God have mercy on us."

Everyone responded with a quiet "Amen."

Anderson leaned forward on the pew as Maxwell took a deep breath and then swiped the screen on his phone to connect with the unknown and put it on speaker.

"This is Maxwell Crane. Tell me my girls are all right. Tell me you have not harmed them any more than you have already."

Anderson was surprised that Maxwell was so assertive with someone who held his daughters hostage. He thought he might be more submissive and less threatening, but he was even more surprised to learn that one of the Crane girls might have been hurt.

"Your daughters are fine. The one who sustained an injury received treatment."

"What treatment? What is the extent of her injury?" Maxwell demanded.

"Bruising and swelling on one side of her face. She is sore but she will be fine."

Kenda covered her head with her arms trying to control her sobs. Carlo and Lin sat on either side of her, and both wrapped their arms around her, comforting and muffling her weeping. Anderson could not imagine the agony going through her heart.

"I want to speak to them. I want proof they are all right. I want to hear for myself."

"You disappoint me, Padre. You don't trust me?" asked the unknown.

Even though the voice on the other end was mechanically altered, Anderson could hear the teasing quality in the question. The unknown held something of great value to the people who sat with him in the sanctuary, and the unknown took an aberrant pleasure in his power to torture them.

Anderson did not know how Maxwell would respond. He understood Maxwell wanted to find out about his daughters' wellbeing, but it seemed to be a ploy to show some type of bluster to the unknown, and it had backfired.

Pete began waving at Maxwell until he caught his eye, signaling to him that he needed to stop demanding more proof. The girls were alive. That was enough for now. It was time to listen. So Maxwell remained silent. Everyone waited for the unknown to speak, but even he was quiet. He seemed to be anticipating a reply from Maxwell, so Pete whispered for him to answer.

"I trust you," Maxwell said. It was a forced reply.

"That is good. That is good," the unknown responded. "Because now it is time for me to trust you. You asked for two hours. I have given you that time. So now, I ask you. Do you have the money we agreed upon?"

"That was three hundred thousand for both of my daughters, correct?"

"The price has not changed, Padre. Do you have that amount?"

Anderson knew the unknown's question was for him. He had avoided eye contact with Maxwell from the moment he answered the phone. Now Maxwell picked up the phone from off the carpet. In the glow of the screen Anderson saw Kenda's head emerge from the cocoon of her arms and of those who embraced her. He saw Pete come to his feet. He looked at Rendell's earnest face. Then Rosemary appeared out of the shadowy darkness from around the altar railing to stand between Rendell and Pete, her divine watch placed on hold.

Anderson felt the focal point of heaven had been diverted to earth and was concentrated upon him. He looked once more at Rendell who provided him with a somber nod of his head. Then Anderson looked at the phone and raised his eyes to Maxwell giving him a nod of affirmation.

"Yes, we have that amount," Maxwell said.

"I want the money in one-hundred-dollar bills. I want it divided in half. One hundred and fifty thousand placed in two metal suitcases that you will bring with you."

Anderson's eyes locked with Maxwell's, and he gave him a second affirmative nod.

"That can be done," Maxwell answered.

"You see what can happen when we trust each other, Padre?"

the unknown added a snarky chuckle.

Maxwell rose to his feet abruptly, his body stiffening. Anderson took his reaction to mean Maxwell might say something that could be detrimental in this complicated procedure. Anderson rose to his feet. He knew the art of negotiation, and he knew not to go beyond the point of agreement once a deal had been reached. He stretched out his hand and laid it upon Maxwell's shoulder. It had its intended affect.

"Yes, I see what can happen when we trust each other." Maxwell's voice radiated tension. "Now where and when do we meet for the exchange?"

"In one hour I will call with the details." A second later the glow of Maxwell's phone went black.

Chapter Twenty-Four

Leandra watched the monitor in Arturo's office that fed into the sister's room. She listened to the conversations Arturo had with the pastor but kept her attention on the girls. The others in the room were focused on the negotiations between their boss and the father. Aside from their monetary value, the Death Demons cared little about the girls, except for Esteban. At one point, he quietly moved beside Leandra and asked what they were doing. "Eating," she answered. Carrie had finally given in to her hunger and sat next to Corley and began eating her soup and oyster crackers. She was surprised when Corley raised her empty bowl to the camera and mouthed the words, "Thank you." Carrie just glared at the camera and shook her head in disgust before going back to her soup.

The second time Leandra pulled Esteban out of the circle hovering around Arturo and pointed to the monitor.

"What are they doing now?" he asked.

"Praying," she whispered. "The family prays a lot."

Leandra had witnessed many moments of prayer while she was a part of the Crane household. Prayers at every family meal. Prayers about the church. Prayers for the community. Prayers about the play. Prayers for her. Spontaneous prayers about anything and everything. Rosemary always seemed to be praying. She found it annoying when Kenda or Rosemary asked if they could pray for her. She had never prayed, never been in church, never given any consideration to God. Then after a carefully devised plot, she had been dropped on the doorstep of The Mercy Seat, taken in by the Crane family, and entrusted with the role of the Virgin Mary. It was all so very strange.

"I've never seen people praying," Esteban said.

"All of them talk like they know God…you know, in some kind of personal way," Leandra said. "It's too weird."

"And they let you act the mother of Jesus?" His eyes widened in amazement.

"I had to. It was the best way to get them to let me stay. I was afraid they might have turned me in to the police or some shelter if I didn't take part in the play."

They both looked at the monitor, but there wasn't a lot to see. Just two girls down on their knees in front of the bar, an arm over each other's shoulder, eyes closed, heads bowed and lips moving. At least, Corley's lips were moving. Carrie said nothing.

"Yeah, weird," Esteban said, and then slipped back into Arturo's circle.

Leandra had surprised herself with her ability to act. She was acting the minute she busted out of the back of the van in front of the church. She had given a convincing performance, but then she got cast in the role of Mary. What a fluke. She would play a double role—the victim while also the mother of Jesus—a play within a play.

Now she didn't have to act anymore. She could be herself with no constraints. She had always been a survivor. She'd survived parents convicted of criminal neglect, survived countless foster homes, survived the streets. She'd survived every test required by the gang including the gauntlet. The reward for this final test of entrapment and kidnapping was full membership. It would be finalized with the gang's insignia of a human skull sprouting red wings tattooed on her right arm. She had fought hard for a place in this coldhearted world, the only world she knew that provided a sense of belonging.

Yet while watching these sisters on their knees praying, she began to realize that there were other worlds out there besides the only one she had known that were not so harsh, not so heartless.

She had been too absorbed in her dual roles to notice the differences. She had to maintain an emotional distance from the Crane world in order to be convincing. She had succeeded. She had duped the family and brought the sisters into her world. Leandra knew that before the night was out, the sisters would witness much more of her world. How much of that reality they would see and how wild it might be, was not up to her. It would be as drastic a difference for the girls as the Crane world had been for her.

Leandra knew she might offer some hope to the sisters that could make the coming hours more bearable. The pastor had requested Arturo give the girls a message, specifically to Carrie. Arturo had laughed it off, but Leandra knew it could be important, especially if the sole outcome of the night was to get the ransom money and give the girls back to their family.

However, Leandra was not in a compassionate mood. She was angry at Carrie for knocking her on the floor as she rushed past her to let her father know she and her sister were alive and in this present danger. Should she pass on this specific message from her father? Would she show a level of kindness to these sisters that had been shown to her while living with the Cranes? She did not know. She would think about it, and while she thought about it, she would relish the power she felt while pondering her decision.

She only halfway listened to the final conversation between Arturo and the pastor. When she heard Arturo say he would call in an hour with details, she was not sure what he meant, but the cheering from the gang huddled around their leader drew her attention away from the monitor. The girls were in prayer. Her fellow gang members, her true brothers and sisters, were congratulating their leader. She would join them. She would soon bear the red-winged skull on her arm. She would soon be a Death Demon.

Arturo waved for quiet. "One hour. Vacate the house and move to the factory."

Arturo opened a desk drawer and pulled out a fist full of black

Balaclava face masks and tossed the individual packages onto the desk.

"Everyone wears one of these, not those plastic Day of the Dead masks."

As Leandra and the others reached for their masks, she noticed Beltran stiffen his back and fold his arms across his chest.

"I like my D.O.D. mask." Beltran snarled a note of defiance. He tapped the synthetic Day of the Dead mask attached to his belt.

"They worked for the kidnapping. That was the easy part," Arturo said. "We've entered a new phase in the plan, more fluid, more dangerous. Fleece beats hard plastic."

Arturo picked up one of two remaining masks on top of the desk and handed it to Beltran. Beltran cleared his throat and did a little insolent swagger with his shoulders and then took the mask from Arturo.

"Leandra, get the sisters ready. Hood them and slap the restraints on their hands."

"I need a minute," Leandra said.

"We don't have a minute," Arturo said.

"I need to calm them down. Get them ready for this."

Arturo glanced up at the monitor. "They're praying. They look calm to me."

"If we all bust in the room wearing masks they could panic."

Leandra waited as Arturo took a moment to consider her point.

"I have to call Tiana to make adjustments to our operation at the factory." He held up his phone. "That's your minute. When I'm done, have the girls ready. Hoods and restraints are in the storage closet." He pointed to the closet door. "Beltran, make sure the SUVs are stocked and armed. Bring them to the side door. Move."

"I need Este to help me." Leandra grabbed Esteban's arm, preventing him from leaving the room with the others.

Arturo gave Leandra an indifferent wave. He was speed dialing Tiana.

Leandra got two hoods and two pair of plastic restraints from off a shelf in the storage closet while Beltran and the others filed out of the office. Once the crew was down the stairs, Leandra and Esteban proceeded along the hallway toward the room where the sisters waited. Leandra paused at the door for Esteban to put on his mask.

"You're not putting on your mask?" he asked.

"What's the point? They know me." She stuffed her mask in her back pocket. "I don't want to scare them any more than they are."

Leandra helped Esteban adjust his mask like she was putting the finishing touches on a child's wardrobe before sending him out to play. Then she handed him the hoods and restraints. These were not the toys of a child.

"Give me a minute with them." She placed a hand on the knob of the door. "I'll let you know when I'm ready for you."

Leandra pinched the lower portion of Este's mask covering his lips with her fingers. She stood on tiptoes and kissed him. She trusted Este not to purposely terrorize the girls like his older brother, Beltran had done. He was the only one she trusted, period.

After the kiss, Esteban gave a sheepish grin and then looked back down the hall as if he were afraid of being caught.

"We better hurry," he said.

When Leandra stepped into the room, Corley had her back against the bar with Carrie's head resting in her lap. Carrie's face was red and puffy from crying. She wasn't quite as tough as she pretended to be. But in the dim light, this tender frieze of the two sisters comforting each other caused a twinge of pity in Leandra's heart. These girls were in a prison and not because of their crimes. She had played a proactive function in this drama. Were it not for her, the sisters would be at home in their beds asleep.

Before Leandra could speak, Carrie sat up and vigorously wiped the tears from her face and eyes. Both girls looked at Leandra, expectant for the news that they would be returning home soon. At that moment she decided to offer some solace.

"We're moving," she said. "I can't give you facts, but we're going someplace that will get you back with your family. There are a few details to be worked out."

"You spoke with our dad?" Carrie said rising to her feet.

"Not me."

"Then the one in the room? The big guy with the scar on his face holding the phone," Carrie said. "He was talking to my dad."

"He was, and he has worked out with him a plan to get you home," Leandra said.

"Do you hear that, Carrie?" Corley said reaching out her hand to Carrie for help. "Answered prayer, Sis."

Corley groaned in pain as Carrie helped her to her feet.

"So what's the plan?" Carrie asked.

"It starts with the move," Leandra said. "But before we can move, we have to put the hoods and restraints back on."

"No," Carrie said. "You said the big guy worked it out…we're going home."

"Carrie, quiet down." Corley calmly placed her hand on Carrie's shoulder. "If this is what's required to get us home, that's an easy thing to do."

"It's just not fair, and you know it." Carrie glared into Leandra's eyes.

Leandra did not flinch, but she came close to changing her mind by not passing on her father's words, but wisdom prevailed. The words could calm Carrie and reduce the risk of further dissent.

"There was something your father said that was just for you," Leandra said.

"What? What was it?" Carrie asked inching toward Leandra.

"He said to tell you, 'And not a moment too soon.'"

It had the desired effect. Carrie froze in place and then her features softened.

"He's coming for us. You hear that, Corley? Daddy's coming for us."

"Of course he is." Corley placed her arm around Carrie.

"Like I said, 'Answered prayers.'"

"You willing to do this now?" Leandra asked.

Without another word the girls turned their backs to Leandra placing their hands behind them. Leandra stepped toward the open door and waved for Esteban to enter the room. She allowed him to cover the sisters' heads then she turned the girls around and took the restraints from Esteban.

"Put your hands together," she said. "Not behind your back like before."

Leandra had opted for this small gesture of kindness. After securing their hands she motioned for Esteban to stand behind Corley as she stood behind Carrie. She placed one hand on the back of Carrie's neck and gripped her arm with the other hand.

"You ready?" she asked.

When both girls nodded their heads, Leandra and Esteban started for the door.

"You'll be home soon, girls," she whispered as they exited the room.

Chapter Twenty-Five

Only someone like Jeff Anderson could make three-hundred-thousand dollars in specified denomination appear on demand, any time day or night. Maxwell could not comprehend such a feat but simply allowed for it to be a small wonder in the realm of mystery. A couple of people would have to get out of bed to get this done. That amount of cash was not just "walking around" money even for Jeff Anderson.

Maxwell could not imagine how all this had happened, or how rapidly it was unfolding, or why. The deep perplexity of "why" was for another time. He could not comprehend how this small cadre of people nestled inside the sanctuary of The Mercy Seat had been brought together for the sole purpose of rescuing his daughters. Each one played a vital role in this dangerous and unpredictable drama.

When the unknown had disconnected the call, Maxwell wrapped his arms around his chest and began to weep. He could not help himself. The pressure of negotiations, the pressure of hoping that Anderson would cover the cost of the ransom, the pressure of what had been and what was to come for them all in the next few hours, was too much for him to bear. He felt Kenda's arms wrapped around him and Rosemary's strong hands resting upon his quivering shoulders, her prayers whispering into his ears.

"What is happening?" he moaned. "What is happening to us?"

No one offered an answer, and Maxwell did not expect one. He could only offer a groan of agony, a lament, uttered like one of the ancient prophets crying out before the enigmatic nature of the Almighty. All answers to such a question would only be trite and glib. This was the rock bottom of despair which few people could speak to. One had to crawl inside this yawning pit and embrace such pain and bewilderment to understand.

"Brother," Pete whispered. "It's time for action."

These words, kindly spoken by his best friend, got Maxwell's attention. He released himself from the comforting embrace of his wife and wiped his eyes with the sleeve of his shirt.

"What do we do, Pete?" Maxwell asked, his voice unsteady.

"Let's walk Mr. Anderson to his car," Pete said. He picked up the flashlight in the front pew where Maxwell had left it and turned it on. "Follow me."

Isn't that what Jesus had said to his perspective disciples when He called them, Maxwell thought. How ironic. Jesus was calling these men and women into a baffling and potential life-and-death future, not unlike these next few hours. Maxwell needed these good people with him, but he needed God more than ever. He had to rely on heaven and earth. He had to give himself over to the visible and invisible and hope the joint forces of the seen and unseen worlds would get his girls home, safe from further harm.

Maxwell, Rendell, and Anderson followed Pete back through the office and out the rear entrance. Pete turned off the flashlight once everyone was standing outside.

Pete pulled out his cell phone. "Mr. Anderson, may I have your cell number?"

"It's Jeff. Call me, Jeff," Anderson replied, and then gave Pete his number.

"Jeff, when you have the money in hand, text me the word, "good.""

"Will do." Anderson nodded.

"Please divide the sum into the two cases as was requested and in the appropriate denomination. We don't want to give them any cause for complaint."

"Will do," Anderson said again. "What must I do once I've texted you?"

"When we know the location for the exchange, then we'll meet up."

"It may take me more than an hour to have it all ready," Anderson said.

"Not an issue," Pete said. "I expect the location to be inside a thirty-mile radius and remote. It will require drive time to get to it, and we can meet somewhere before we get to the location."

"I would feel more comfortable if Reny was with me," Anderson said looking at Rendell. "Just a precaution, I guess. I'm in unfamiliar territory."

"We all are, sir," Pete replied. "I understand."

"I was thinking the same thing, Jeff," Rendell said. "If I'm not needed here."

Maxwell knew he had to be the one to give permission and it was an easy request to grant. These two men had joined him in this dire hour without hesitation. He would do all he could to allow them the personal freedom to navigate this dark night.

"Yes. You and Reny are together. We all need to be together as much as possible."

"Thank you," Anderson replied, then he took a deep breath and sighed. "This is so unfathomable. It feels like the Boy Scouts going up against El Chapo or something."

"But Pete's a well-prepared Boy Scout," Maxwell said. "I've seen him in action."

"Jeff, maybe it's better to think of it as David versus Goliath," Rendell said.

"Yeah. Yeah, I like that better, Reny," Anderson said, then he looked at Maxwell. "The offer of my security team is real, Pete. They come out of MARSOC."

"Then they are my brothers," Pete said. "Jeff, we have no idea yet what we're up against. How many and how well-armed. If they are cartel, then we must assume they are heavily weaponized and many in number. We'll be making it up as we go along."

"Given the situation, I bet they're game," Anderson said.

"Then tell them to suit up just in case," Pete said. "And thank you."

Anderson put his hand on Maxwell's shoulders. "I…we…don't know how this is all going to go down, but I am with you to the end."

It was *Deja vu*. Earlier this night Anderson had done the same thing in this very spot, laid his hand upon Maxwell's shoulder and said, "Anything you need…anything." And here he was hours later doing exactly what he said, though neither of them could have ever imagined what that 'need' would become and how quickly it would arrive.

"Thank you, Jeff," Maxwell said. "Thank you."

"Jeff, I'm hoping that by the time you text me, we will have a fixed location for the exchange. I'll text you a specific drop-off coordinate for us to pick up the suitcases. You and Reny will not be in close proximity of the final destination."

"I'm on my way," Anderson said, and jogged toward his car with Reny trotting behind him. He pulled out his phone as he opened the driver's door of the Bentley. "And I'll alert my guys." Then he hopped inside with Rendell scrambling in on the other side.

"Keep your headlights off, Jeff," Pete said just before he started the engine.

Maxwell and Pete stood quietly as Anderson backed up and silently drove out of the parking lot. Maxwell was thankful for such a quiet engine.

Pete turned to Maxwell. "Maxwell, when you go back inside, tell Carlo and Lin to come out and I'll take them back to get your van and Rosemary's car and return here. Everyone needs easy access to vehicles."

"Where are you going?" Maxwell asked.

"Home to resupply and call a friend," Pete said.

"A friend?" Maxwell asked.

"He's your friend too. He saved Carlo's life. Now go back

inside and send out the kids. I'll be back before the next call."

"What am I to do while you're gone?"

"The hard part…wait…and pray," Pete answered, and then he handed Maxwell the flashlight and waved his phone in the air. "Let me call our friend."

Maxwell understood Pete saying the hard part was waiting, but it surprised him to hear his brother-in-law encouraging him to pray. He could do prayer.

He dashed back inside the church and hustled Lin and Carlo out the door. He walked with them to Pete's vehicle.

Pete was holding his phone to his ear waiting for his party to answer.

"Uncle Pete will explain what's up on the way back to the house," Maxwell said before giving Carlo a firm hug.

Pete waved for Lin and Carlo to get into the SUV, then he spoke into his phone as he got in on the driver's side.

"Hey brother, sorry to wake you," Pete said. "It's an emergency. We're off the reservation for this one. I need you to help me move a mountain."

Pete could not have said it any better, Maxwell thought as he watched Pete and the kids drive away. If there ever was a mountain to be moved, this was it.

When Maxwell walked back inside the sanctuary, he saw Rosemary and Kenda in a tight grip, swaying as they spoke their weeping prayers. He laid the flashlight on the stage and took out his phone. It was less than an hour now before the next call from the unknown, the call that would give him the details of the meeting. In less than an hour so much had to be done, and then after that hour, so much more had to be done to get his girls back home. How would this all work? How could it? Kenda reached out to him as he approached and enfolded him inside a sacred embrace. The prayers of these women, the strength and comfort of their embrace would make the next hour of waiting bearable.

Chapter Twenty-Six

Carrie was thankful for two blessings—she and Corley were not sprawled on the floor of some grungy van but riding upright in a larger, more comfortable vehicle, and that while her hands were still restrained, they were not tied behind her back. She was able to sit next to her sister and they could hold each other's hands. The vehicle was large enough for Corley and her to be sandwiched between Leandra and her companion. It was a snug fit, but at least she was not rubbing her hooded head against smelly carpet.

She wished she understood Spanish. The one seated in the front passenger side of the vehicle was speaking into a phone. It had to be the big man with the scar on his face doing the talking. Carrie could hear a muted female voice coming through the speaker of the big man's phone, also speaking in Spanish. She had no clue what was being said, but she determined right then that she would take Spanish lessons once she was back home.

She and Corley had to be the subjects of this conversation. Even though Carrie had only gotten a glimpse of the big man before she was forcefully removed from the room, she figured he was the one in charge of the situation, and that he would be in charge to the end, whatever that end would be.

Carrie tried to pay attention to where they were going, but there were so many twists and turns after they left the house that it was impossible for her to get any sense of direction. The last location she was sure of was the street outside her own home where they were captured. Then once their hoods were removed, they were inside an interior room of some house. She had gotten a brief look outside a window in the room, but it was too dark to see any notable landmarks. Now they were moving again to somewhere new.

She could only guess how long it had taken to travel from her street to the house. Thirty minutes? An hour? She was so traumatized by what had happened there was no way she could remember how long it had taken. Now she would be more attentive to the time from the undisclosed house to wherever this new location would be. It wasn't until they were on a straight stretch of highway, she began to think they had left the city limits and headed away from Richland. Given the late hour she didn't hear any traffic around the vehicle. Occasionally, there was the sound of a semi-truck barreling past them, but that gave her no indication of their direction.

She felt Corley's head resting on her shoulder and could sense she was moving her mouth close to Carrie's ear.

"Do you know where we are?" she whispered.

Carrie lowered her head and twisted it toward her sister. "No idea."

When she felt an elbow jab her in the ribs, she sat up straight. This was Leandra's not so subtle hint for the two of them not to speak. Carrie squeezed Corley's hands, hoping that was enough of a signal to indicate that they needed to be quiet.

Carrie hated this feeling of helplessness. Yet it was more than just a feeling—it was a reality. She had allowed herself to be suckered. The whole family had been duped, and now she had completely lost her freedom. And it wasn't just the loss of freedom. It had become a matter of life and death for her and her sister. How had her world been turned upside down so quickly? Had she done something that had allowed this evil to sneak into her little sphere while her attention was diverted? This was too much for her to ponder. She would process this experience with her dad. He would know what this all might mean. He had been through something similar not long ago and he was still struggling with the traumatic aftermath of that terrible time.

Her dad had changed because of what he had gone through. Would she too be forever altered by this experience? She could not allow herself to be distracted. She could not let herself slip away from this present reality. She had to pay attention to everything going on around her. She would log every detail, remember every sight and sound, remember every feeling. And she would not be overcome by fear. She would fight.

After what seemed like forever traveling in one direction, Carrie could tell that they were slowing down until they turned off the road and came to a stop. An electric window hummed as it was lowered. The driver spoke and a voice from outside the vehicle leaned in to speak to the driver. After a brief exchange with both the driver and the big man up front, she heard the hiss and squawk of a communication system. Then the voice outside the vehicle gave an order to someone on the other end of the system.

When the order was acknowledged, the voice outside the vehicle shouted to someone else. This time it was not through technical means but to someone near the vehicle. There followed the sound of something like a metal gate clanking open before the driver raised his window and the sound became muffled.

In a moment their vehicle was moving again, but much slower now. It continued for a minute or two at this slow pace before the vehicle veered from its course, took a hard turn to the left and again came to a stop. That was two left turns and two complete stops. She must remember. How long had they been driving? A half an hour at least or longer. And they had to be off the main highway and inside something big, but what was it? At the first stop she heard a metal gate open to let them in, so maybe it was some kind of factory. She had to remember.

The electric window was lowered once more, and the driver stuck his head out and barked at someone in a hostile tone. Again, Carrie heard what sounded like a large and heavy door rumbling open. What happened next, she didn't expect. The driver gunned the engine and accelerated. The force of going forward at a steep incline pressed her back against the seat. What were they climbing?

They had taken off from a standing start and once they leveled off, the vehicle made a sharp right turn. The tires screeched as it sped along a hard surface, and then screeched again when the vehicle came to an abrupt stop. Through the open window Carrie was surprised to hear the echo of the tires once the vehicle had stopped. They were no longer outside on a normal road or highway but were inside some enclosed space, a very large, enclosed space. But what, a garage, a warehouse, some kind of factory?

The moment all four doors flew open Carrie knew they had arrived at their destination. Could her dad be here waiting for them? He had promised to come as "quick as he could." She knew he would keep that promise, and not a moment too soon.

Carrie felt Leandra grab her arm and began pulling her outside of the vehicle. Corley was taken out the opposite side of the vehicle, and for a moment Carrie panicked and cried out her sister's name. Leandra yanked her arm.

"Be quiet," she said with her voice lowered. "She is right behind us. We're all going to the same place, and you won't be separated."

She had panicked. She must not panic. She must keep her head clear, but in that second of panic she had learned that Corley was behind her, that they were going to the same place, and would not be separated. Good news, indeed. She must remember. Carrie was forced to walk at a brisk pace. When she tried to count the number of steps her legs got tangled up and she kept tripping over her feet.

"You can do this," Leandra said. "Don't make it hard on yourself."

"I can't keep up," Carrie said. "You're going too fast."

Carrie felt Leandra yank her arm ignoring her pleas to slow down. She knew they must be inside some kind of building, but how large? She was being forced to walk at such a rapid step she could imagine the space they were in must be vast in size. Then

Leandra jerked her arm backwards and they came to a sudden stop. The big man called for everyone to stand still.

Carrie could feel other people gathering around her. She hoped that Corley was among them, but she didn't dare say her name. Leandra had said they were together and that they would not be separated, so Corley must be among the group of people she sensed around her.

"Take them to stall number four," the big man barked.

The shift from where they stood was several more steps. They moved as a group. By the sound of shuffling feet, Carrie determined there were several individuals in this contingent. After a brief walk, they came to a stop. *This must be stall number four*. At least four stalls, maybe more, but what could be inside this stall? Why would the big man want them to pause here? What did he want them to see?

"Pull back the tarp," he said.

Carrie heard the crumpling sound of a canvass curtain being pulled to one side followed by the rhythms of sensual music and a velvety female voice singing erotic lyrics. She felt Corley rub her shoulder and knew she stood beside her. She could hear her labored breathing through the hood. Then Carrie felt a third presence move in behind her and maneuver its physical bearing between Corley and her.

"Remove their hoods," said the presence.

Carrie clamped her eyes shut. She did not want the mask to scratch her eyeballs as it was yanked off her head.

"Open your eyes, little chiquitas," said the presence. "See the life ahead for you."

Carrie did not want to do the bidding of the presence, and instead, swung her head to one side. Then she heard Corley gasp and say, "Oh please, Jesus, no." Gradually, she opened her eyes. Stall number four was a small cubicle surrounded by dark-colored plastic tarps draped over large sheets of plywood. Inside was a small sofa and sprawled on the sofa was a young African American girl clothed in a sheer white lingerie.

Carrie instantly thought of the young girl who had spoken to her before all the girls were whisked out of their room earlier that night. Was she the same one? She could be. The light was muted, only a string of small red bulbs hanging above the sofa. A few feet from the sofa a camera was positioned on a tripod. Behind the camera was an indistinguishable specter bent over and looking through the lens. When the music picked up the beat, the specter waved its hand, and the young girl stood on the sofa and began a sensual dance.

"Here it begins," the presence hissed. "A profile is created, and your image goes on the "seller's page." We make you a global star on social media. Then the texts come in requesting you by name. After an easy electric payment, like paying a bill, you become the dream of online peepers from around the world…twenty-four seven, three-sixty-five."

It was as if her eyes caught fire as she descended into a place of unbalancing shadows. Carrie was spellbound by this young girl's fluid movement. She had ridden blindly into this darkness, a night so sinister that all natural light had fled. She struggled for breath. She did not want to breathe. If she did, she feared she would inhale the vapors of this hellish pit. It was her sister's words that triggered her intake of air.

"Jesus, protect us in the shadow, in this valley of death," Corley said.

Carrie did not turn her head toward her sister for the face of the presence was positioned between them. It was his breath she smelled. It was his breath that carried the evil pleasure of this torture. She did not want to breathe in this poison, but she had to remain alive and present in this terrible place, and she could hold her breath no longer.

"You are the devil," Carrie gasped.

"No, no. But he is my friend," he chuckled as he stepped back.

"Don't look, Corley," Carrie said. "Just keep your eyes closed."

Over the music. Over the low pitch of Corley's prayers. Over the sound of her own sobbing breath, Carrie detected a noise, a sound foreign to the world into which she had been submerged. What was it? A whistle? It did not originate from inside stall number four. It was an elongated sound. Was it a musical instrument? No, it was a horn. The sound was a horn and while it remained faint, it continued to reverberate. It was the horn from a train engine. It had to be. They were near some train tracks. They had to be.

"Take them to storage," the presence ordered.

The tarp closed in front of them and Carrie was yanked away. She was now able to look out upon a factory of some kind with mounds of recycled products piled high over the vast floor. What and where was this place? As they were hustled along, they passed booth after booth, each one covered with a heavy tarp just like stall number four. But these were not booths set up for a crafts fair to display the creations of an artisan. Carrie could only imagine that each booth contained the same horror she had just witnessed with a different girl in each one. She had to remember.

When they reached the end of the forced march, they were flung into a large room. Carrie locked her legs trying to resist the inevitable. Corley was thrust into the room and against the back wall. Then Leandra shoved Carrie into the room, but Carrie kept her balance and found strength in her legs. She spun around and charged Leandra.

"You said we were going home!" Carrie screamed as she lunged at Leandra.

But Leandra slammed the door and Carrie crashed into it, recoiling onto the floor. In her rage Carrie scrambled across the floor until she ran out of steam. She lay on the floor panting and weeping, but with her exhaustion came a new resolve rising inside her. She would fight. She would get out. She would escape. She would tell her parents everything. She would give the police the best information possible so they could find these locations and arrest these criminals. It was all about rescue, not just of them, but of all those girls they had met earlier tonight, and the one she had just seen, the one who had whispered her desire to get out of "the life." Before tonight she had never heard of "the life." Now she knew.

She did not comprehend the vile chasm she and her sister had fallen into, but she understood enough. It was terrible. It was shattering. She and her sister had to get out of this nightmare, and when she did, she would remember every detail and do everything she could to stop this evil. She would remember. She must remember.

At last, she ran out of steam and lay panting on the floor. Then in the distance she heard the long sharp whistle once again. She took it as a sign. A sign that they had not been lost or forgotten. A sign of hope outside these wicked walls. A sign of rescue.

Chapter Twenty-Seven

Once Carlo and Lin returned with the cars, Maxwell went to his knees at the altar railing in the front of the sanctuary. He was heeding the advice of his brother-in-law. Pete was right, this was the hard part…waiting, being still, his mind racing but unable to be physically engaged in…in what exactly? The energy spent in just being still, in just praying was a physicality he never considered. He had his phone propped up on the tray attached to the back of the altar railing. He could keep his hands folded, but while one eye was cast toward heaven, his other eye zeroed in on the screen of his phone.

Behind him the trio of Kenda, Rosemary, and Lin paced the center aisle arm-in-arm comforting, supporting one another, and exclaiming to heaven the urgent need for intervention. Carlo hovered nearby. Maxwell was so appreciative his son wanted to be near his side. Every few minutes Maxwell could feel the touch of Carlo's hand upon his shoulders or the back of his head. As he passed Carlo would whisper, "I love you, Dad. I'm here, Dad. I'm right here. We'll get them back."

It nearly broke Maxwell. His son, his only son was helping bear his father's sorrow. This was not a docile moment of casual prayer for any of them. These prayers were visceral, muscular, the fraught appeals used by all those in crisis, prayers of bewilderment and desperation. Within the whole madness of this terrible moment, with all this focus on heaven, Maxwell began to allow himself to believe that a mountain could be moved.

He was so engrossed in prayer he was startled when Pete called his name. Maxwell looked into a beam of light atop Pete's head. A second light floated behind Pete.

"You remember Morgan Jackson." Pete set two equipment bags onto the front edge of the pulpit stage.

"How could I ever forget." Maxwell rose to his feet. "You saved my son from certain death when he was about to be killed by those corrupt vice cops."

"Sorry for this situation." Morgan dropped his Pelican case next to Pete's bags. "We cut off the head of the snake six months ago and two more grew in its place."

"And now the snake has my daughters," Maxwell replied. He picked up his phone from the altar railing and set it on the stage next to Pete's bags.

"Not for much longer, brother." Pete gave Maxwell a reassuring pat.

Maxwell had to remind himself how swiftly someone like Pete and Morgan could move when time was of the essence. These two were trained in speed. Both were former team members of MARSOC. Though Pete was in the peer group ahead of Morgan, he had trained Morgan in country during a couple of tours in Afghanistan after Maxwell had retired from duty as chaplain. Both were dressed in full tactical gear, but neither of them carried weapons. Maxwell appreciated such awareness that they were in a church, even though he could not imagine that weapons would not be used at some point in the coming hours if only for show. *Let it be all for show,* Maxwell thought.

"We have just under fifteen minutes before the next call," Pete said looking at his watch. "Maxwell, I need you to unbutton your shirt down to the middle."

Maxwell knew what was required of him. Pete did not need to explain what he intended to do. The more steps that could be taken before the call the better. But when Maxwell began to unbutton his shirt, his fingers were trembling. He had difficulty easing the button out of its hole.

Kenda slipped in front of him and placed her hands on top of his.

"I can do this. I have to be able to do this," Maxwell said. "If I can't, how can I…manage the hard part."

"Every part is hard," Kenda said moving his hands aside. "This is one of many."

"How many more to go?" Maxwell didn't really expect an answer.

"As many as it takes to get our girls home," Kenda replied and unbuttoned the first two buttons on his shirt.

Pete took a small device from a compartment in Morgan's case and attached it to the middle buttonhole inside Maxwell's shirt.

"Check the signal on the camera," Pete said flipping on the surveillance screen fastened to his protective gear in the middle of his chest.

"We're hot," Morgan replied as he adjusted the screen attached to his gear.

"We'll do the audio when we RVP with Anderson," Pete said.

Kenda stepped aside for Morgan to secure the tiny camera, then she resumed her task and began to button the top two buttons on Maxwell's shirt.

"Morgan, did you bring all this gear?" Maxwell waved at the equipment.

"I come with empty hands," he replied. "The FBI doesn't have a lending library."

"So Pete, all this is yours?"

"Yeah. Consolidated and purposed when we need to be quick and nimble." Pete turned to Carlo. "Carlo, I have a job for you."

"Whoa, whoa. What are you doing, Pete?" Maxwell held up his hands after Kenda had finished buttoning his shirt. "I don't want Carlo anywhere near this."

It was only then that Maxwell noticed Carlo was standing next to his uncle. He had changed clothes before he and Lin returned with the cars. He had on his black jeans, dark hoodie, and hiking boots. Not the high end, tactical wardrobe worn by Pete and Morgan, but light and loose-fitting attire acceptable given the situation.

"It's too risky, Pete," Kenda said. "The girls are already in such danger. The thought of Carlo getting deeper into…" She could not finish the thought.

"I know, Sis." Pete gave a firm but brief clasp of Kenda's hand. "But Carlo is already in deep. We all are. Do you remember what you and Carlo did six months ago? You snuck into my house to get the USB port with the evidence that brought down the bad guys. You didn't think about it. You both rushed toward the fight, not away from it."

"You and your son were very brave, Mrs. Crane," Morgan said.

"But still…my son, Pete," Maxwell fought hard to keep his voice calm.

"I need a third man for this task," Pete said.

This was a task now. Maxwell knew this was no task. Pete had used a different word than was normal in his professional experience. "Operation. Assault. Raid. Mission" even, but never a task. "Task" was an everyday word, a household chore or an errand to be run. There was nothing everyday about this night, nothing normal or routine.

"Dad, I want to do this," Carlo said. "I need to do this."

In the light of the two headlamps Maxwell looked into his son's grave face. This was the exact expression of all the young men he had seen go off on their missions when he served as chaplain–sober and resolute. Once a combat operation had been assigned and all preparations were complete, those who wished would gather with Maxwell for prayer. This feeling was just like those combat missions in Afghanistan. People had been in The Mercy Seat filling the sanctuary with prayer for a different mission. In the next few minutes, events would be set in motion from which there was no going back. If Maxwell allowed his son to go into the breech with him, it meant that not only was he putting his own life in God's hands, but also his son's. It was a terrible burden.

Maxwell drew Carlo to his chest. "Son. My son. I will release you."

"Thanks, Dad," Carlo said softly, and Maxwell felt the potency of his son's clasp. The vigor of his son's embrace notched up his flagging courage.

"You still play video games, Carlo?" Pete asked.

"All the time."

"Good, that's your job tonight. You will fly the surveillance drone."

"He can do that from the back seat of your SUV, right?" Maxwell asked.

"He can do that from anywhere," Pete replied, then looked at Carlo. "The drone is in my car. Morgan can give you a tutorial as we drive to meet Anderson."

"You haven't heard from Jeff, have you?" Kenda asked.

Pete pulled out his phone to check for a text from Anderson. "Nothing yet."

"He'll come through, won't he?" Maxwell regretted the words the second he spoke them. He was casting doubt, not just on Anderson, but on everyone in the sanctuary, on Rendell, on anyone who was aiding Anderson in securing such an exorbitant amount of cash in exact denominations in such a short time. Even casting doubt on God, the very one who he and all the others had been begging for aid and intervention. But doubt was natural when the vice grip was tightening its hold.

The screen on Maxwell's phone lit up and the unknown appeared. Maxwell took his phone, but Pete held up his hand.

"Brother, take a breath. Just one step at a time. Confirm the deal, get the G.P.S. coordinates for the meet. Once we get those, we're moving. You with me?"

Maxwell nodded and looked at Kenda. She folded her hands and tucked them under her chin, and then he swiped his phone to answer the call.

"I'm here."

"Do you have the money?"

Maxwell suddenly froze. He was not expecting the question. He was expecting the unknown to simply give him the location of the rendezvous and a time to arrive. In the previous call, Maxwell had told the unknown he had the money, but he did not have it in hand. He did not yet have the confirmation from Anderson that he was able to deliver on his end. Maxwell felt Kenda's hand on his arm and her touch sparked a response.

"The money is guaranteed," Maxwell said. This was a leap of faith. Even though Jeff Anderson had assured the money, he could not fully believe it until he saw it in the cases. Yet, he knew he had to project confidence to the unknown. "We will have it."

The unknown did not speak, just breathed evenly. It was as if he were weighing the veracity of what Maxwell had told him.

"You said that we needed to trust each other," Maxwell said, unable to bear the silence. "I told you that I had the money and I will. Now where do we meet?"

The unknown began to snicker. "I guess I should trust a man of the cloth."

"Where do we meet?" Maxwell repeated his question refusing to get off the point.

"Expect the G.P.S. coordinates to follow," the unknown said. "And come alone."

Maxwell felt Kenda tighten her grip on his arm. She was vigorously pointing to herself, insisting that she go along.

"My wife will come with me," Maxwell said. He spoke the words but could not believe he was saying them. What was his wife thinking? His whole family would be in danger. All of them could be lost. But once he spoke the words, he would not back down.

Again, the unknown went silent except for his calm breathing.

"She drives and I navigate." He did not believe the unknown would accept the condition. "You'll have the money, but we both want to see our girls…together. We need to be together."

"Two by two," the unknown said. "Something for you to preach about, Padre."

The last subject Maxwell would ever want to preach about would be anything that had to do with this night.

"So do we agree?" Maxwell said. "My wife comes with me?"

"What do you drive?" asked the unknown.

"A minivan. A white minivan."

"Your wife best be driving, or we have a new arrangement," the unknown said. "Use your cell phone only. No other. No tricks. You have one hour."

The light went out on Maxwell's phone and the unknown disappeared. But no one moved. No one spoke. Maxwell held his phone in both hands to keep it from falling onto the floor. Pete and Morgan moved in on either side of him raising their phones level with his and waited. These two were his fellow Marines, and Maxwell would never forget their faithfulness.

"*Semper Fidelis*," Maxwell whispered.

"For all battles," Pete responded.

"Past and present," Morgan said.

The screen lit up on Maxwell's phone casting its ambient glow on their faces. Pete and Morgan quickly keyed the coordinates into their phones.

"Got it?" Pete said.

"Got it," Morgan replied.

There was a collective exhale. The sanctuary was filled with the human breath of a desperate people hopeful this night would end with its desired outcome.

"Good job, brother." Pete gave Maxwell a firm squeeze of his arm before closing his bags. "Now, everyone to the cars."

"Thank you," Kenda whispered as she fell into Maxwell's arms.

"I can't believe this is happening to us, but we're a family," Maxwell said. "We have to see this through together."

"Here are the keys, Mom," Carlo said taking Kenda's hand

and offering the keys.

"Take the key off the ring, Sis," Pete said. "Less is best."

While Kenda worked the car key off the metal loop, Maxwell saw Pete's phone light up as he was lifting his bags off the stage.

"Pete, your phone," Maxwell said.

Pete dropped his bags and yanked his phone from the pocket of his protective vest. He gave his phone a quick glance and held it up for the others to see.

"Thank God," Maxwell sighed. "Thank you, Lord."

The word "good" appeared on Pete's screen. While this single word brought Maxwell great relief it did not turn into any kind of celebration. It was way too early for that. It was one step at a time, but this was a big step.

"Morgan, ping Anderson the coordinates and then find a spot five miles back for our vehicles to park to launch the drone and do final checks," Pete said as he typed "Affirmed" in response to Anderson's text. Followed by "Coordinates to follow." Then he enlarged the image on his phone to look at the location. "I estimate the location to be thirty minutes north of Richland on highway forty-seven."

Morgan sent the coordinates to Anderson's phone and then keyed them into his communication system. The screen lit up with its high-tech grid.

"Looks like a lot of nothing on that stretch of highway. A business here and there, a gas station, maybe, a quick stop market. I can take a closer look as we ride." Morgan tapped his finger on the location indicator.

"You're right, not much out there." Pete looked over Morgan's shoulder at the screen.

"Great. Woods and fields." Maxwell sighed.

"Terrain can be an advantage for both," Pete said. "I don't like what we're dealing with, but we're not calling the shots. Which means we need to be ready for anything. What mini-mart business might be in close proximity that's closed this time of night and there won't be much traffic. At this point, the kidnappers are making all the rules and playing to their strength. We are at their mercy so we must be alert."

"We've been here before, haven't we?" Maxwell said remembering those missions in Afghanistan when he prayed over Pete's team before each mission.

"Too many times, brother," Pete said.

"But not with my kids' lives at stake," Maxwell said.

"That much more incentive." Pete patted Maxwell's arm before turning to Morgan. "Moe, did Anderson get the coordinates?"

"Affirmative," Morgan replied.

"If he brought his security team they will travel in a separate vehicle." Pete said.

"Given our situation, Anderson's team may come in handy." Morgan locked his Pelican case. "He can pass the coordinates on to them."

"Copy that," Pete replied. "We do our final checks when we meet up with Anderson and get the money in the minivan. Carlo, you're with me."

Carlo spun around and pulled Lin close to him. "I'll be back."

"Like last time," Lin said. "Just like last time."

"Yeah, just like last time." Carlo kissed her and then followed Pete and Morgan out of the side door of the sanctuary.

When Kenda got the car key off the ring, she handed Rosemary the remaining keys. "Keep praying."

"Just warming up." Rosemary kissed Kenda on her cheek.

"You are our rock, Rosemary," Maxwell said.

"Listen to me now, both of you." Rosemary stared at first one, then the other. "There are people who love the darkness and people who love the light. Jesus is the light of the world. You take His light with you. It shines in the darkness and the darkness can't comprehend it or put it out. He is behind and before you. He is beside you. Take courage."

Maxwell and Kenda hustled out the side exit. He gave one

last glance inside the sanctuary as the door closed and saw Rosemary wrap Lin into her arms. Leaving The Mercy Seat felt like a momentary separation from heaven. He felt a snap in his heart and then he whispered, "I am here, Father. Consume us in Your light."

Chapter Twenty-Eight

Kenda followed her brother out of the church parking lot in the family minivan. She had insisted she go with her husband to get their daughters. It was an easy and instant decision. She wanted to be by his side. She wanted to be there to embrace their girls. That was all that concerned her, get the girls and bring them home. She tried to imagine how she would find them, to imagine their condition, and understand how their exchange might happen. Would it be a simple transaction, just present the money and get their girls. *May it be so, Lord,* she thought. *May it be that easy.*

Now all she had to do was follow her brother as he led them out of the city limits and onto the highway toward their destination. She needed her husband by her side, and she just needed to breathe. She placed her hand on her breastbone and felt the beating of her heart. Then she put her hand on her side and felt it expand and deflate like an insect. Her heart was beating. The air was flowing in and out of her lungs–signs of life, and yet, none of what was happening felt real. It was like a play she would direct, but without a rehearsal. This was not a play. It was the real thing in real time with real people, not created, made-up characters. Lives hung in the balance, her life and the lives of her entire family.

Kenda noticed as she drove that fewer and fewer businesses were on the highway. It was as if she was leaving behind one world and entering another, one less populated. She could not ever remember being on this stretch of road. In fact, it was difficult for her to remember anything. It was as if everything in her world before this moment was the personal history of another human being. Nothing was real. She had no personal history. Leaving Rosemary and Lin behind at The Mercy Seat was a long ago and near-forgotten memory.

Kenda was so fully in the present nothing in the past had any meaning or hold on her. She thought only of her daughters and their physical and mental well-being. *What was going on in their frightened and fragile hearts*? Once she got them home, she would hold them so tight. She did not care what happened to the criminals. She would just bring her girls home and lock them away forever.

"Keep them alive, dear Lord." she prayed. "Please keep them alive."

Kenda felt Maxwell's hand gently take hold of her arm. She needed this real connection, this bond that kept her heart inside her rib cage and her mind from rattling out of control. She could imagine every consequence that would end in tragedy, but she had to vanquish those images. Those pictures must remain in the realm of make-believe. Those scenarios could never be allowed to happen. With Maxwell beside her she could find a hope that provided strength. She was not alone in this terrible moment. She was certainly dazed. It felt like the strange flicker of a looming illness, like the heat of an oncoming fever that stirred frightening dreams. This could not consume her. She could not allow herself to be taken down by her own fears of what might happen.

"Pete's got his blinker on. I see Anderson up ahead." Maxwell released Kenda's arm. "Right under those trees. Kill the lights and pull behind Pete."

It was easy for Kenda to do as instructed. She did not want to think of details. She just wanted her daughters tucked beneath her arms. That was all she wanted to think about. Her brother had said one step at a time, and so it was. She didn't know how many steps it would take before her girls would be returned to her, but with each step taken it meant one step closer to having them back. Kill the lights, one step closer. Pull off the deserted highway, one step closer. Stop behind Pete's SUV, one step closer.

Before she could put the van in park, Pete and Morgan had

jumped out of Pete's SUV and opened the automatic door on the back of it. Pete approached her as she lowered her window.

"Turn off the engine," Pete said, and Kenda turned off the engine. One step closer.

Morgan was leaning inside the back of Pete's SUV. He got a device from his Pelican case and then he rapped his knuckles on the hood of her minivan.

"Release the hood," he said, and she pulled the lever. One step closer.

Morgan raised the hood of the minivan and flipped on his headlamp before bending over the engine.

When she and Maxwell got out of the car, Anderson walked up carrying one briefcase. Rendell was beside him carrying the second briefcase. She followed Pete to the rear of the minivan and unlatched the back door. Pete instructed that the metal cases be set inside and opened. After Anderson opened both lids, he stepped back.

Kenda marveled at the sight of so much money. She marveled at Jeff Anderson's ability to acquire such a sum on such short notice. But she marveled even more that this billionaire had been willing to jump onto this speeding train and offer his assistance. He had come through. Kenda took this as a good sign. In a night when good signs were hard won, she would gladly take this one. She fought back tears. She fought back a weakness in her legs that would cause her to crumble to the ground. There was no time for that.

Pete removed a stack of bills from the case and set it aside. Then flipped out a knife and cut a tiny slit into a layer of foam. He pulled a small device out of his pocket and flipped a switch. When he had tucked the device into the foam, he stuck the money back inside. After closing the lid of the second case, he looked to the front of the minivan just as Morgan shut the hood. Morgan gave a thumbs up.

"Carlo, both homing devices are set and activated. Are we

good?" Pete asked.

It was then that Kenda realized that Carlo wasn't around. But then she heard his subdued voice coming through Pete's earpiece. She didn't understand what he had said until Pete lowered the back of the minivan.

"Okay, Carlo, get out of the vehicle and let's set up the drone."

Kenda saw her son bound out of her brother's vehicle to help Morgan set up the drone away from the vehicles. When Morgan opened the case, Kenda noticed that Carlo wore a protective vest. She started to walk over to him, but her brother stopped her.

"He is in a zone," Pete whispered. "Don't distract him."

Kenda looked into her brother's face. She had to trust him. He had lived these scenarios. This was not where she was needed and not a detail that concerned her.

"My team is here," Anderson said. "Three of my best."

Kenda and everyone looked around but did not see them. Then Anderson raised his arm and waved his hand in a circle. On the opposite side of the highway a vehicle was parked in the empty lot of a strip mall. There was a quick flash of the headlights.

"What's the name of your team leader?" Pete asked.

"Quentin," Anderson answered. "The team will follow your lead."

"Good to have reliable back up." Pete hustled to the back of his SUV. "I've got some earpieces for them so we can stay connected." Then he leaned around the side of the SUV. "Kenda you and Maxwell come here as well. You both need an earbud."

"What else can we do?" Anderson asked, as he and Rendell joined Pete.

Kenda felt the comfort of Rendell's hand upon her shoulders. He placed his other hand upon her husband's shoulders.

"The Lord bless and keep you," he whispered. "The Lord surround you and the girls with His peace."

"Thank you, Reny," Kenda replied.

"Do either of you have contacts in the Richland police force?"

Pete asked taking a small box from the Pelican case. "Higher-ups, not rank and file. Someone you trust."

"The new police commissioner, Cynthia Peale," Rendell offered. "I haven't met her. She is busy finding her way cleaning up the previous mess, but I think she could be trusted. Have you met her yet, Jeff?"

"Not yet, but I know we can get to her."

"Straight to the top. I like it," Pete said handing Anderson three earpieces. "Give these to Quentin and tell him they're preset to our frequency. I'll patch him into the drone once we get her in the air."

"What might the commissioner do, Pete?" Rendell asked.

"I don't know what we're getting into. I hope this is a clean in and out, but we're dealing with criminals, and anything can happen. I know the commissioner will consider this a vigilante opp. She won't like it, but we can justify the situation. Once everyone is safe, we need to alert the commissioner what has gone down."

"As long as we have a positive outcome," Rendell said.

"That's my intention," Pete replied. "We can't let these guys get away with this. We might not be able to take down a cartel, but at least we can disrupt its system and get some of the low-level bad guys off the street."

"I agree." Anderson nodded to Rendell. "We can make that call."

What does a "positive" outcome look like? Kenda didn't ask her brother to define such a thing. She knew Pete didn't know the answer to such an intangible question.

Pete opened another compartment in the Pelican case and took out a smaller box. He opened the lid and took out two remote earbuds. He gave one to Maxwell and Kenda.

"These are flesh-colored," Pete said. "Both of you have long enough hair to cover your ears, so they'll be hard to spot. You both can always hear me, and Maxwell, your camera mic is two-way.

So you can communicate."

"What about me?" Kenda asked as she inserted her earbud inside her right ear. "Don't I need a camera as well?"

"I don't want you to have one, Sis. In case they decide to do a body search. Maxwell has done all the talking with our main player, he will come face-to-face with him. Just trying to minimize our overall risk."

"But I'm worried about Maxwell. What if they find it on him and—"

"Sis, someone has to do it."

Maxwell took Kenda's hand and brought it to his lips. The gesture was meant to calm her, but it only provided a slight reassurance.

"The drone is ready, Uncle Pete," Carlo said.

Everyone's attention shifted and they gathered around the drone. Morgan had positioned it on top of the case. Her son held the operator controls. Never again would she scold him for spending so much time playing video games. How could she have known?

"You got this, Carlo?" She marveled at his dexterity with the controls as he raised and lowered the drone a few feet off the ground.

"I got this, Mom." He didn't take his eyes off the drone. "We're getting my sisters back."

"Will you be able to see us on there?" she asked pointing to the screen.

"We'll be following your car from above. We call it the "overwatch." Pete tapped the screen attached to the front of his protective vest. "Morgan and I are linked in on our screens and through the camera in Maxwell's buttonhole. I just want you to concentrate on driving. That is your number one job."

Kenda stepped aside for her brother to move next to Carlo.

"You comfortable?" Pete asked Carlo.

"Yes, sir," Carlo responded.

"It's just like when we took those nature pictures for my last client," Pete said.

"Only this time it's not." Carlo looked into his uncle's face.

"Only this time it's not." Pete gave her son a gentle slap on the back of his head. "Take her up."

Kenda was surprised at how quiet the drone hummed as the propellers lifted it into the air. She was more surprised by her son's confidence in operating the flying machine. She needed all the confidence she could get. Should her confidence wane, she would remember her son's and take courage.

Pete raised his watch to the beam of light on his headlamp.

"We have eighteen minutes before you rendezvous. That will give our drone time to hit altitude and home in on your minivan. From our current position you are approximately ten minutes to the location. Sis, you need to drive the speed limit. Time it so that you arrive at the exact time you were instructed. Don't want to get there early. Don't want to give them any reason to be spooked."

"What is the battery life on your drone, Pete?" Maxwell asked.

"Two batteries, roughly an hour each," Pete said. "We can hot swap in mid-flight, so we should be good. Now, it's time to move."

Pete grabbed Kenda's arm and guided her back to the driver's seat.

"You're not going to be following behind us?" Kenda asked.

"We can't be right behind you, but we'll be in overwatch right above you," Pete said as he opened the driver's door. "It's like Goldilocks–not too close, not too far back, but just right. Remember, you have a homing device under the hood and in one of the cases. You each have an earpiece, and Maxwell is rigged with the camera."

"See you on the other side, brother," Maxwell said as he climbed into the passenger seat and closed his door.

"When we get to the other side, tell me that all will be well." Kenda studied her brother's calm expression.

Pete gripped Kenda's shoulders.

"No mother should have to do this, and few mothers could, but you are one of those few who could. You have been chosen."

Kenda slipped into the driver's seat and started the engine. It was time to go. Several steps accomplished. Several more steps before the finish. The intangible finish lay ahead. She did not want to imagine what it might be.

Chapter Twenty-Nine

Every time Kenda passed a speed limit sign her eyes shifted to the needle on the speedometer. Her brother told her to stay with the limit. A mile or two over and she would slow down. It was all she could do not to accelerate and get to the location. Keep the speedometer needle directly on the speed limit. She had one task. Drive with precision. Drive as if it was life or death.

She leaned forward, her chin extended over the steering wheel, and looked into the night sky to see if she could see the drone flying overhead. The "overwatch" Pete had called it, but she could not see any sign of the drone. The overwatch had eyes that could see her, but she was unable to see it. This required faith. A motorized flying object was not something in which she would ever consider placing her faith.

"I don't see it." She strained her eyes to see above the glare of the headlights. At this late hour and traveling on an empty highway, Kenda expected to see the drone hovering above her.

"I believe that's the point." Maxwell kept his eye on his phone and checking his watch. "The G.P.S. says were less than five miles from the location. At this speed we should arrive right on schedule."

Kenda leaned back against the seat. Pete told her that she had been chosen for this moment. No mother would want to be chosen for this. No mother would ask for this kind of punishment. No mother deserved this kind of maltreatment. What was it about her character that qualified her to be hammered like this? She had not invited this evil into her world. She was just a mother who loved her husband and children and was trying her best to be a godly woman caring for her family and serving her community. This was not something that should have happened.

Was she not paying enough attention? Had she been distracted and while her back was turned something sinister had slipped through the door? Why wasn't God around to intervene and protect her family. *Why God? Why. I didn't ask for this. I didn't choose this to happen. Did You?*

It was too much for her to ponder. Maybe when it was over and everyone was safe she could indulge in the cosmic ramifications of this incident. If she kept pondering the mystery of this terrible moment, she knew she could become more confused, which could quickly lead to bitterness and anger. But this was not the time. She just wanted her girls back. She was going to do whatever it took to get them back. And whatever this was, this horrible circumstance she and her family were in, she would take up the issue with God once everyone was back home. *Just get us home, God. Home in one piece.*

Out of nowhere a van raced up beside her. A masked passenger in the front seat signaled for her to pull onto the side of the road. Then the van accelerated and swerved in front of her forcing her to slow down. A second van sped up next to her taking the place of the first van. The side door of that van flew open, and Kenda could see two more masked figures each holding a weapon and forcefully pointing for her to pull off the road.

"Pete, are you seeing this?" Kenda shouted. "Are you seeing this?"

"We can see there are two vehicles, one in front and beside you," Pete responded. "Any markings on the vans? Color, detailing, anything?"

"Off-white, hard to tell. No detailing. Both vans have heavy-duty racks on top, but they aren't carrying anything," Maxwell said.

"Are they saying to follow them?"

"No! They want us to pull over." Kenda eased her foot off the gas.

Just then, one of the masked men raised a shotgun over the roof of her van and fired off a round.

"One of them just shot at us!" Kenda screamed and she felt the right two wheels of the van begin to career off onto the side of the road.

"Did they hit the van?" Pete yelled. "Are you hurt?"

"No, they fired over the van, like a warning shot." Maxwell signaled to the one who fired the shot that they would be pulling over.

"We're not hurt," Kenda said.

"Pete, we have to pull over." Maxwell kept both this hands raised. "We don't have a choice."

"Then do it. Do it. Don't resist. It's not what we expected but do it."

Kenda regained control of her vehicle, and she turned on her blinker and vigorously nodded at the shooter that she understood and would do what they asked.

"Maxwell, we can't see the interior of the vans. Can you tell how many of them are there?"

"Four that we have seen, but there may be more inside the vans."

"Can you identify any of them?"

"They're wearing masks and are armed," Maxwell said.

"Then pull over now."

"But we're not at the location yet," Kenda said. "It's where the girls are supposed to be."

"Change of plans, Sis. My guess is this was their plan all along, which means that anything can happen now. They've got the girls somewhere else and probably going to take you there once they confirm the money. We're watching and are right behind you. Just think of your girls. Do as they say. I believe they will take you to them. Now be smart and pull over. You can do this. You both can do this."

Kenda looked at Maxwell and he motioned to the masked

men in the van beside them that they were pulling over.

This was the next step, but it was not the anticipated step. Kenda had played out the easiest of scenarios in her mind—meet at the location, give the money to the kidnappers, get the girls, and go home. None of this was happening. If Pete was right, none of what she imagined was ever going to happen. It was a new set of circumstances with a new set of rules and a new set of steps to follow, none of which was a guarantee that they would see the girls. All she could do was trust the overwatch—more than that, trust the God of the overwatch.

Kenda slowed the van down to a crawl gradually coming to a stop. A new step taken on a new path. *Please dear God, be our overwatch.*

The two jumped from the side of the van while three more jumped out of the back of the van parked in front of her.

"Hold your hands up, honey," Maxwell said. "Hands up, fingers spread."

Kenda's door flew open and one of the masked dragged her over to the back of the first van. She did not resist or struggle except to do the best she could to maintain her balance. She did not want to fall. Two of the masked men grabbed Maxwell and led him toward her. It appeared they would keep them together. *God, let it be so.*

Through the front windshield Kenda saw one of the masked men open the back of her van and grab the two metal cases. He rushed to the side door of the second van and set them just inside. He opened both cases and snapped a photo of the contents with his phone before closing them both. He pushed a number on his phone and waited. Kenda assumed the photo of the money was being sent to the mastermind of this whole scheme, the unknown who had been dealing with her husband.

"Where are my girls?" Kenda blurted unable to remain silent. "You have the money, now where are my girls?"

From her husband next to her and from her brother inside her ear, she heard them both tell her to keep calm, but she could not remain calm. This was not a part of the plan, and she would not be silent.

A masked one moved between Maxwell and her. Since she could not see any expression on his face, only his fierce and glaring eyes, she assumed he would refuse to answer her question. She didn't anticipate that he would strike her with the butt of his rifle, but he raised it with threatening intent. She turned her head and closed her eyes, but Maxwell's scream kept her from receiving the blow.

Then the masked one reached for Maxwell's shirt. Kenda's heart froze in fear that the masked one suspected her husband was wearing a wire. If that device was discovered, then this terrible situation would only get worse.

Maxwell did not flinch when the masked one yanked her husband's phone out of his shirt pocket. He examined Maxwell's recent history of calls seeing only the calls from the unknown and the G.P.S. coordinates. He shut off the phone, thrust it in Maxwell's face, and cursed him. Then he threw the phone onto the ground and stomped it with the heel of his boot again and again. He bent down and scooped the remains off the road and hurled the broken pieces into the woods. Then he turned and made a motion at Kenda as if he would search her for a phone.

"No cell! No cell," shouted her husband. "Only one. Mine. Only mine."

The masked one did not seem deterred by Maxwell's assertion that he had the only cell phone between them. But just as the masked one reached for Kenda, the one who had sent the photo of the money shouted "Vamonos! Vamonos!" He was waving his phone in the air before he shoved the cases deeper into the van and jumping inside.

Then Kenda and Maxwell were spun around and had their arms forced behind their backs. Kenda could feel her hands being tied with plastic restraints. They were spun around again, and while they were held in place at the point of a gun, the masked one ripped a strip of duct tape off a roll and slapped it on Kenda's mouth. The same was done to her husband. Before everything went black, Kenda looked at Maxwell. He gave her a half smile and a nod before a mask was placed over his head and tied off. Then the back of his head was pushed down, and he was shoved into the rear of the van.

She wanted to scream. She wanted to curse. She wanted to threaten the masked ones with the vengeance of God but then a mask was put over her head and tied off. The last thing she saw was the black image of her abductor in front of the bright beams on the headlights of her minivan. *This must be the same people who abducted her girls,* she thought. *This must be the same way they were treated.*

A hand gripped the back of her head and forced it down. Then someone grabbed her legs and shoved her into the van. She tried to kick her assailant once her legs were free but missed, which only caused laughter in the masked ones.

The rear doors were slammed shut and the van bounced along the side of the road until it smoothed out once it was on the highway. In spite of the rumbling sounds all around her, Kenda heard the calm voice of her brother inside her head.

"Kenda, do not be afraid," Pete said.

It took Kenda a moment to realize her brother was speaking through the ear bud he had given her. The frantic tempest she had just gone through had completely disoriented her. But if she was hearing Pete's voice, then so was Maxwell, and this began to calm her frayed nerves.

"Can you speak, Maxwell?" Pete asked, but Maxwell could only groan.

"Got it," Pete said. "Listen carefully. We have eyes on you and are on the move about a mile behind you. They have taken the minivan, so it is a convoy of three vehicles. Between the drone, the homing devices, and the camera on your shirt, we have multiple ways to track you. We don't know where they're taking you. I assume where they have the girls, so we are sticking close. Give me three short grunts if you understand."

Maxwell gave three short grunts affirming that he understood.

"Good," Pete said. "All right now. Stay alert and pray for the little things."

"Mom. Dad," Carlo interrupted. "I love you. I love you. We have eyes on you. We're coming for you. We won't leave you."

Kenda forced herself up on her elbow and dropped her head upon Maxwell's chest. He gave a slight groan at the suddenness of her presence, but when she gently rubbed her head over his chest, Maxwell relaxed.

Kenda was terrified by what was happening to her heart. It was beginning to crack, and she did not want a complete rupture brought on by fear. She held onto the words of her son, "We have eyes on you, we're coming for you, we will not leave you." Even with the tape covering her mouth she repeated the words as though it were a prayer, a prayer that God would be present no matter how deep her family would descend into this hell.

Chapter Thirty

Carrie felt the comfort of her sister's fingers massaging her face and smoothing back her hair as she rested her head on her lap. Once they had been locked inside this room and she had hurled herself against the door, the fight had gone out of her. She'd laid there on the floor beneath the dim light of a naked bulb suspended from the ceiling and just screamed, a last primal scream against the evil forces that had brought her and her sister to this horrible place. Once her screams dwindled down to whimpers, she heard Corley's crunching footsteps moving about the room. Then she felt the strength of her sister's hands underneath her shoulders lifting her to a sitting position.

"Hold still, now," Corley said. "I don't want to cut you with this glass."

Corley had found a sliver of glass on the floor sharp enough to cut away the plastic restraints on Carrie's wrists. When she was free, Carrie did the same for her sister. There was a grungy mattress in one corner of the room and Corley lifted Carrie to her feet and together they stumbled over to it and collapsed.

"Sing to me," Carrie said. "Anything."

Corley took a deep breath and began to hum until the words came to her.

"'Abide with me, fast fall the even-tide.
The darkness deepens, Lord, with me abide.
When other helpers fail, and comforts flee,
Help of the helpless, O abide with me.'"

"Where did you hear that?" Carrie asked.

"I've heard Mama Rose sing it," Corley said. "She knows all those old hymns."

"You think it's true?" Carrie asked. "That He abides with us…even now, in here?"

"I hope so. It's like we're trapped in the underworld with few ways to escape. There's little we can do but hope."

"I never thought anything like this ever existed." Carrie rose up beside Corley and together they leaned against the wall while remaining on the mattress.

"I heard some girlfriends at school talk about this type of life, but that's all," Corley said. "I never really paid attention, and Mom and Dad never talked about it."

"You have any idea where we are?" Carrie asked.

"Not really but think about it. We have to be somewhere in the Richland area," Corley said. "I've lost all sense of time, but it didn't seem that long of a drive to get to that house where we were. And then it took, what, about thirty minutes to get to whatever this place is?"

"We can't be that far from the city," Carrie said.

"Which means that we can't be that far from home."

"I tried to keep up with where we might be going and how long we were in the car," Carrie said. "When we got here, I thought I heard a train whistle, so we could be close to some tracks. But after what we saw that girl doing in the stall, and the thought of us…being forced…to do…what she was doing...or worse…"

Carrie began to weep, and her sister put her arm around her and drew Carrie to her side. An arm with warm strength. An arm that consoled. Could the words to that hymn be true…even in this bleak place?

"I know." Corley wrapped her other arm around Carrie. "I know."

"Are we lost in here forever?" Carrie struggled to catch her breath. "Are we gonna end up like all those other girls we saw tonight?"

"There must be a way out," Corley said. "For all of us. There has to be."

"If we're lost in the underworld then there is no way of escape." Carrie sobbed, a fresh wave of grief and panic overtaking her.

"I said it's like the underworld," Corley responded.

Carrie dug the heels of her palms into her eyes. She wanted to stop the flow of tears, to stop seeing the lurid images seared into her memory.

"I can't erase what we just saw," she said. "I can never not see this…this terrible thing…this horrible thing that has happened to those girls. This can't happen to us, Corley. God wouldn't let that happen to us, would He?"

"I can't answer for God," Carrie said. "I just pray He is abiding with us now."

When Carrie removed her hands from her face, her eyes had adjusted to the faint light in the room. She crawled off the mattress and got to her feet and began to look around the room. There was a broken window that was boarded up from the outside. The shattered glass on the floor must have come from the window. There was metal shelving and several spray paint cans. She stepped back to get a good look at one wall and was startled to see the images of ancient warriors that looked like they might be from Central America. But the one image that stood out was of a large skull with multicolored wings attached on each side. Between the wings above the skull was written "Death Demon."

"Corley, look at the painting on that wall." Carrie pointed to the skull.

Corley crawled over to the edge of the mattress. Carrie helped her to her feet and led her to the center of the room. They both stared at the mural of the "Death Demon."

"That's what we saw tonight," Carrie said. "That's what those people were wearing when they took us."

This was a room like no other. This was a space like no other.

It felt as though Carrie was inside this solitary confinement adrift in hell, floating free, apart from the world, apart from anything she had ever known, anything that was safe and protective. If the door flew open now, could she and her sister flee, would an escape route be provided, or was this place of eternal doom? Was hope abandoned now that they were inside this tomb? Was this their final resting place?

"Let the one who walks in the dark, who has no light, trust in the name of the Lord and rely on her God," Corley said.

"How can you say something like that?" Carrie blurted. "How can you have any hope when we're locked in a dungeon like this?"

When Corley grabbed Carrie by her shoulders and spun her around, Carrie could fully see the damage done to her sister's face for the first time. She had either been hooded or only had the dusky glow of lava lamps, insufficient to illuminate facial detail. Even now in the low wattage bulb, Carrie could see the swelling around Corley's eye and temple and the outline of discoloration on the side of her face. It seemed like it was forever ago since they were abducted in front of their home.

Her sister had tried to stop the kidnappers from taking Leandra and this distended, purplish face, with the deeper shaded bruise encircling her eye, was the reward for her attempt to save the one who had deceived them. They would not be here in this fearful place with the "Death Demon" staring down at them if Leandra had not betrayed them. If Leandra had not been brought into their home. If Leandra had not been dropped at the steps of The Mercy Seat.

"Carrie, I'm as frightened as you are," Corley said. "I don't know why we're here, and I don't know if we'll get out alive, but I will not give up hope. You and I are here together. We're in this awful place together. That is not a little thing. We are together and we must do everything we can to stay together until we are given a way of escape."

"But you said there was no way to escape," Carrie said.

"I said we only needed one way to escape," Corley replied. "Just one way."

The door burst open, and Carrie jumped behind Corley. Bright lights flooded into the room making the painted images on the walls come to life. In the doorway stood the silhouette of Leandra. She was peering into the room flanked by two masked gunmen. When she stepped to one side Carrie had a limited view of the factory floor. She saw the hubbub of activity, people shouting and rushing about while heavy machinery plowed into large piles of debris. This had to be in preparation of something. Could this mean someone was coming? Could this mean her parents were on the way?

Leandra moved back in front of the threshold of the door restricting Carrie's view into the factory. She expected Leandra to summon them. Carrie put her arms behind her back and Corley followed her example. But Leandra seemed not to notice that they no longer had the restraints latched to their wrists. Either that, or she didn't care.

Instead of motioning them to come forward, Leandra told them to move to the back wall of the room. Corley immediately began to retreat as Leandra instructed, but Carrie remained in place in the center of the room. She was not ready to comply. She had lost her will to fight, but she would not be as submissive as her sister.

"Carrie, come back here with me, please," Corley said.

Still Carrie didn't move. She watched the heavy-duty backhoe loaders filling their large scoops with debris and crisscrossing over the factory floor with recyclable trash and dumping them into huge bins clearing out a large space in the middle of the factory. But for what purpose? This couldn't be normal. All this commotion and activity was in preparation for what was about to happen, and whatever it was, Carrie was convinced it had to do with her and her sister. *Was it their parents? And not a moment too soon.*

"Do as Corley told you." Leandra motioned for Carrie to step back.

"Come on, Carrie. Come back here by me."

Carrie would do it for her sister, not for Leandra.

Once she took her place beside Corley, Leandra motioned for someone outside the door to enter the room. To her surprise, Carrie saw the woman who appeared at the door was the same one who had come into the room back at the house and hustled the girls out of the room. She had been called the "Bottom." Whatever that meant, whatever she was, this "Bottom" began to motion for the girls to file into the shadowy chamber.

There was no chatter, no talking, from the girls. They all filed into the room, silent and obedient, and began to find a spot along the walls. A few of the girls were weeping. One or two squealed in pain when their bare feet stepped onto a splinter of glass from the broken window. All were barely dressed, only wearing slinky lingerie or slips or wrapped in fur-lined blankets. These girls were of varied ethnicities, and none of them could have been much older than Carrie or Corley.

Carrie counted them as they filed through the door, but they kept filing in until the room became crowded, and she lost count. There were certainly more of them than the ones they had met back in their holding room at the house.

These must be the girls from the stalls. But how many stalls are there and how many girls? Where have they all come from?

The last girl to enter stopped in the doorway. Carrie thought she looked familiar. Was she the same young woman Carrie had been forced to watch before being brought to this room? It was difficult to tell until she could get a better look.

"Go on," barked the Bottom. "Get inside."

The girl did not move fast enough and was shoved by the Bottom into the middle of the room. She spun around as if she might bolt for the door, but it was slammed shut and locked before she could make a move. She breathed deeply through her nose and blasted each exhale out her mouth like a bull preparing to charge.

Carrie thought the young girl might scream or rush the door and try to fight her way out. Could she be the one who had whispered that she was desperate to escape? Carrie pushed off from the wall and stepped behind the seething girl. She miscalculated what might happen by tapping her on the shoulder. When the young woman spun around, she raised her arm to strike Carrie.

"Don't hit my sister," Corley shouted pushing herself off the wall and standing in front of Carrie. The girl held her fist in the air.

"You the two come in tonight?" she asked, her arm still poised to strike. "Wearing those Bible clothes… Daddy's a preacher."

"We are," Corley said.

"Did we see you tonight in stall four?" Carrie asked.

"What about it? What are you doing watching me? You ain't allowed," she said. "That's for online peeps only."

"We didn't want to watch you," Corley said. "We were forced to. I'm sorry."

"Rather dance for a peeper than meet a john in some skanky motel," she said. Her sister's apology appeased her temper, and she lowered her arm.

"They took you away from the house and brought you here," Corley said.

"Did you see any landmark between the house and this place?" Carrie asked.

"They make us sit low in a van with no windows," she said. "Besides, we just come in from out of town. I wouldn't know where we are…doubt most of us do."

Once again, Carrie began to count the girls pressed against the walls. They were like strays she had seen at the animal shelter, too frightened to call attention to themselves, in dread of painful retribution. Each face bore a weary expression, detached from any reality that would be safe and normal. She counted eighteen in all, at least she thought so, given that they were all huddled together.

"Would you tell us your name?" Corley asked.

The young woman did not respond but looked nervously around the room.

"Nobody got a name in here except whatever the online peeps want to call us," she answered, her face becoming ridged.

"You must have family somewhere," Corley said. "Don't you want to go back…"

"Nothing to go back to. I got no family, no history. Now step off my cloud," she said and turned back to face the door as if preparing to rush it the moment it opened.

"I thought you said you wanted out of this life," Carrie said.

"I never said that!" She spun back around. "Must be somebody else. I never said that. Shut your mouth."

Carrie was startled. She was almost certain this was the one who had whispered to her that she wanted her help to get out of this living hell. Could this girl's hostile overreaction be an attempt to hide her true intention? Could she be mistaken about this girl's identity? Was it a different girl?

"We're sorry," Corley said. "We didn't mean to intrude."

The bright light from the factory floor flooded into the room again and all the girls looked away or covered their eyes.

"The Crane sisters. Come out," Leandra demanded. "Everybody else, stay put."

Leandra stepped away from the door.

Carrie did not see the two gunman that were flanking Leandra earlier. Her view was now unobstructed. Framed within the open door she could see the factory floor. It was still bustling with activity, masked ones and machines moving about the open space. Just because the door was open and Carrie and her sister were told to exit, this was not a kind bidding. This was not Leandra telling them that they were now free to go home. And Carrie certainly didn't think this was their chance to escape. Too many people to outrun.

Corley took the first step toward the door. Carrie followed

close behind her big sister. She would rely on her sister's faith, her courage. Carrie had nothing else. She pressed herself against Corley's back and they moved forward as one. But Corley stopped beside the girl who had been so defiant with them.

"My name is Corley Crane," she whispered.

Carrie peeped around Corley's shoulder to see if Leandra had noticed their pause for Corley to speak to the girl from stall four.

"I don't want to know your name," she responded, but also kept her voice quiet.

"You need to know my name," Corley said. "Be alert. Whatever might happen in the next little bit, be ready to lead these girls to safety. Corley Crane. Don't forget."

Why did Corley say such a thing, Carrie wondered. What was her sister thinking?

Carrie stayed attached to Corley as they moved to the threshold of the door. The factory was a huge space with equipment and bins and mounds of waste destined to be recycled. This was a facility devoted to turning litter into reusable products. Carrie could not understand why such a good business would be involved in such criminal activity.

"Jasmine," said the girl behind them. "My name is Jasmine."

"This way," Leandra said and pulled them forward. She slammed the door and pointed to a masked one standing in front of another door in the back of the factory. It appeared to be an office with a large window that looked out onto the factory floor. There was no light on inside so Carrie could not see what it might be. It couldn't be any worse than the room they had just left. The masked one standing in front of the office door didn't carry a weapon. That too was a relief.

"Follow me," Leandra said and began moving toward the office. Corley followed obediently with Carrie affixed to her sister's back like a child being carried by its mother. As they approached the office, the masked one opened the door and stepped aside for them to enter, but Corley stopped once again and spoke to Leandra.

"The night you came to us, I was the one who chose you," Corley said. If Carrie was surprised by her sister's words, Leandra looked stunned. "You were dropped at the front steps of The Mercy Seat for a reason. I chose to invite you to our home. That too was for a reason. I don't know the reason, but it was not a random twist of fate, and it was not for this."

Carrie's attention shifted to a great commotion coming from the far end of the building. She could see a large sliding door being pushed to one side and the headlights of a vehicle shining brightly from the outside. Standing at the edge of the opened door, a masked one waved for the vehicle to enter.

"Whatever happens now, Leandra, I want you to know, I forgive you."

Leandra's hardened face began to crumble just before she shoved Carrie and Corley into the office and locked the door.

Chapter Thirty-One

The skill Carlo gained by playing video games was swiftly put to the test, but this was no longer a video game. Carlo could not pretend he was fighting aliens or flying a star ship through outer space or that he was living in another dimension and another time. This was real time, in the here-and-now, with real people, his people. He had gotten comfortable with the remote controls while flying the drone above his parents' minivan as they drove to the rendezvous point designated by the G.P.S. coordinates. But it came close to destroying him when he saw his parents being pulled over and taken hostage by heavily armed people in masks. The pinhole camera on his dad's shirt was useless once he and his mom were tossed into the van. Plus, Dad could not communicate as long as his hands were restrained and his mouth covered with tape.

Carlo screamed for his uncle to speed up and get to them before they were taken away or worse. This was not supposed to happen. The plan was to deliver the money and get back his sisters. But given the circumstances and the type of criminals they were dealing with, why should Carlo expect these villains to adhere to any plan? They were the ones in control. The night had taken a dire turn and it about wrecked him.

"We can't take them, Carlo," Pete said. "I'm sorry, but unless they were about to be fired upon, we need to let this play out."

"They'll probably lead us straight to your sisters," Morgan added.

The logic was difficult for Carlo to accept, rational as it was. His entire immediate family was in the hands of malevolent people intent on doing harm, adding more harm than they had already done.

"This is tough to watch, Uncle Pete."

"I know. It's okay if you need Morgan to take over." Pete accelerated so they wouldn't lose the ones who had abducted his parents. "I can get Quinten to—"

"No. No." Carlo took a deep breath. "I got this, Uncle Pete. I got this."

"I know what you can do, son," Morgan said turning around to look at Carlo in the backseat of Pete's SUV. "I saw how you faced a dangerous situation that night in Pete's basement with a dirty cop wanting me to kill you and my gun at your head."

"But that was you," Carlo said.

"Yeah, but you didn't know who I was or what I was going to do. You stood up in the face of great danger, and I know you can do this now."

Carlo had to wipe the moisture from his eyes. The tears had come when he saw his parents being shoved into the back of a van and he panicked. He couldn't help himself. He needed to be reminded that he had the fortitude to see this through. Carlo could not be objective. That was impossible. But he had to channel his emotions and focus all his energy on the task at hand. One objective, rescue. His parents and sisters were in grave danger, but he was not alone in this. He was part of a team.

"Thanks, Mr. Jackson." Carlo ran his sleeve over his nose and eyes.

"Call me Morgan." He gave Carlo a reassuring pat on his knee. "You're invested—head and heart in the game. That's good."

"One thing to remember, nephew," Pete said. "Action disables anxiety. We're taking action and we're getting our family back."

"Yes, sir." Carlo gave his eyes one final swipe before he zeroed in on the screen. He repositioned the monitor on his knees and propped it up against the backseat. "Are you seeing this, Uncle Pete?"

Pete had a screen embedded into the console of his SUV.

"They're turning back toward Richland," Carlo said adjusting the drone's flight path. "It's a four-lane, highway thirty-one south. Looks like a straight stretch of road."

"Where are you guys taking us?" Pete said tapping his finger on the screen. "We're still out of the city limits, but where are we going?"

"Widen out the view," Morgan said.

"This is a part of Richland I've never seen." Carlo pulled the screen back to take in more of the topography. "You recognize any of this?"

"Industrial sites, big warehouses close to railroad yards. Semi-trucks load up their rigs with cargo and haul it all over this region," Pete said. "Perfect place for criminals to hide in plain sight."

"Yeah, but what are they hiding?" Morgan said.

One industry after another. One giant warehouse after another. Each one covering acres of land, and the three-vehicle caravan Carlo was tracking kept driving toward Richland until they began to reduce their speed.

"They're slowing down," Carlo said. "Looks like they're pulling off the road and might be turning into one of the industries coming up."

"Once they make their move, lock in an address and name of business," Pete said.

"Also, find a different route for Quentin to take so we don't piggyback," Morgan said. "It could be useful for him to come up from the other side."

Carlo did a quick maneuver of the screen and found an alternative road.

"There is a parallel route half a mile west of us," Carlo said. "Highway fifty-seven. Also heads back into Richland."

The caravan began to pull off the highway and gradually came to a stop. Pete took his foot off the accelerator to keep from catching up to them. When they came to a stop Pete pulled off the road and also stopped. Then he checked the rearview mirror.

"I've got Quentin fifty yards back," he said.

"Mom and Dad are five hundred yards up ahead," Carlo said.

The caravan was not moving, but no one was getting out of the vehicles.

"What do you think they're doing, Uncle Pete?"

"Could be checking to see if they were being followed," Pete said.

Up ahead, far in the distance, Carlo saw the high beams of an oncoming vehicle. Could a vehicle in the caravan have made a U-turn crossing the four lanes and was now headed back toward them? Had he missed something on the screen?

"Everybody scoot down in the seat," Morgan said.

Carlo scrunched down in the backseat just as a semi-truck barreled down the highway on the other side of the road. Carlo never took his eyes off the screen, and as soon as the semi flew by the caravan, the lead vehicle began to move forward with the other two vehicles right behind, but they never got back onto the road. They didn't go far before all three vehicles made a quick turn into the gated entrance of a mid-size business tucked in between two massive warehouses and came to a stop.

"I think we've got a location," Pete said. "They must be waiting for the gate to open. Where are we, Carlo?"

Carlo typed in coordinates, and Garita Metal appeared on the screen.

"Looks like a scrap metal business." Carlo widened the view on their screens. "The property has one large factory-looking building. There are some smaller buildings, and a lot of equipment scattered around the property. Also, looks like piles of junked up cars ready for the crusher."

"How far down before Quentin can get a connector street to the other highway?" Morgan asked.

"There is a side street in the next one hundred yards, Nebraska Avenue. Turn left on Nebraska, and that will take him over to Highway fifty-seven in three blocks. Then right on fifty-seven south. It's a couple of miles before he gets to Warfield Drive. Take a right on Warfield and that will hook him back onto thirty-one coming toward us."

"Once he doubles back, he can take up a position on the opposite side of the gates," Pete said.

"I'll shoot Quentin the directions and have him stay in place until we need him." Morgan quickly dialed in the directions and sent them to Quentin.

"Let's hope we don't," Pete said. "But still good to have the back-up."

The caravan waited in front of the entrance to the factory. No one was getting out of the vehicles. Carlo could see three guards inside the gates. One of them began to open the gates while the other two directed the caravan to enter. Carlo wanted desperately to talk to his parents, to encourage them, but he was afraid of what it would do to him. He was just barely holding it together. However, his Uncle Pete could talk to them and let them know their current status and the details of what might be ahead. There was no way his parents could speak to Carlo and assure him that they were all right. They weren't all right. There was nothing all right with any of this.

"Uncle Pete, we haven't heard anything from Mom and Dad since they forced them into the cars. Do you think we need to communicate with them?"

"Yes." Pete pressed a button on the console. He kept his voice low as he spoke into the microphone. "Grunt twice if you can hear me and let me know you and Kenda are still okay?"

When Carlo heard the two low grunts coming from his dad, he allowed himself to breathe a sigh of relief.

"You're doing good, brother," Pete said. "We are about twenty miles north of Richland in the industrial area on Highway fifty-seven. You have just passed through the gates of a scrap metal factory. There were three hostiles standing guard. We're about five hundred yards behind you. From the drone, this looks like a pretty big place with one large building and several smaller ones. Once we know where they will take you, Morgan and I will find a way inside. Carlo is manning the drone and we're watching from above. They will take you from the vehicle, but the homing device in the case is activated and I doubt you will be far from the money or the girls. I will try to stay in your ear for as long as I can. Now grunt three times to affirm you've heard and understand."

The sound of his father's vocal grunts were like mini rumbles of thunder, strong and fierce. His dad was ready to face this. Carlo knew that his mom would also be alert and ready. They were going to get their girls back, and after hearing his dad affirm Uncle Pete's directive, Carlo felt a surge of confidence in his own heart.

Quentin's black SUV rushed up from behind them and raced past. Pete's SUV was jostled from the air turbulence of the speeding vehicle. As soon as it reached Nebraska Avenue it took an abrupt turn and disappeared.

"Quentin will meet us on the other side," Morgan said. "I let him know there were three hostiles at the entrance to Garita Metal."

"Now, Carlo, find us a way to get inside." Pete put his foot on the accelerator and got them back onto the highway.

"This place looks surrounded with chain-link fence crowned with razor wire," Carlo said.

"We need to get as close to the property as we can and be as invisible as possible," Morgan said.

"Two hundred yards ahead, I see a road or alley that cuts off the highway and circles around behind the factory to some loading docks." Carlo looked up from the screen. "It's all fenced in."

"We'll take it." Pete sped up until time to take the right turn off the highway.

The road followed along the fence of Garita Metal property, but it was a shared drive with the industry beside it so there were some streetlights.

"We need to find a blind spot." Morgan leaned forward in his seat.

"Up ahead the road splits off and circles to the back of Garita," Carlo said.

When Pete made the turn toward the loading docks there were no more lights. It was dark except for some flood lights on the back of the main factory building inside the compound. Pete did a U-turn and tucked the vehicle next to the corner of the fence where there was little light.

"Carlo, put the drone in hover mode and toss your controls in the front seat." Pete and Morgan jumped out of the front seat. "Then meet us in the back."

The liftback door of the SUV began to rise as Carlo switched the drone into a hover position so he could get set up in the front of the vehicle. He tossed his screen onto the dashboard and set his controls in the front seat. Then he joined Pete and Morgan.

Pete handed Carlo a pair of heavy-duty bolt cutters. "Cut us an opening."

As Carlo began cutting the links in the fence, Pete opened the side panels in the back end and pulled out two pairs of night vision goggles. He and Morgan attached them to their helmets and fastened the chinstraps, then Pete lifted the floor covering and retrieved two military grade automatic rifles. He and Morgan grabbed extra magazines for their weapons and stuffed them into the pockets of their protective gear.

When Carlo was finished cutting a hole big enough for them to crawl through, he tossed the bolt cutters into the backseat.

"Carlo, make sure the drone has the position of the caravan," Pete said, and he and Morgan flipped up the screens on their chests. "Make sure we all see the same thing."

Carlo rushed to the front and yanked the flight controls off the seat. He released the hover switch and let the drone fly forward into the center of the compound.

"I got them," Carlo said. "They're parked outside the front of the main building. No sign of Mom and Dad. Looks like they are about to drive up a ramp and go inside."

"That means they should all be in one location inside the factory." Pete nodded. "But we need eyes on the inside of that building. Find an opening on the second floor. There should be a door on a fire escape or a fan shaft or a window. If you find a window and it's not broken, then use the drone. It has a five-inch blade with tungsten teeth. Break it."

"Quentin said he's in place, one hundred yards from the entrance." Morgan lifted his head from the screen.

"Good." Pete tightened the glove straps around his wrists. "Once your folks are out of the van link us to his camera."

"Best entry point are the loading docks." Morgan scanned the premises through his scope.

Pete put his hand under Carlo's chin and looked him square in the eyes. "The SUV is headed out, if it gets too hot, get out fast."

"I'm not leaving you and Morgan, Uncle Pete," Carlo insisted.

"You're not leaving us. Just getting into a better position. I doubt we'll exit the same way we entered. And we're not leaving here without the ones we came for."

"Rock and roll, brother." Morgan dropped to his knees and pushed his weapon through the opening in the fence before crawling under it.

When Pete dropped to his knees, it startled Carlo to hear his uncle groan in pain.

"Are you all right, Uncle Pete?"

"Just the leg," Pete said. "Not quite healed."

"You need something for the pain?"

"This is a good pain," Pete replied. "Keeps me sharp. Let's me know I'm alive. See you on the other side, Carlo."

Pete handed Morgan his weapon through the fence and crawled through the opening on his belly. Morgan helped Pete get to his feet before handing him his weapon. Pete turned back to Carlo and gave him a thumbs up.

"Get inside that factory," he whispered before he and Morgan disappeared around a pile of flattened vehicles awaiting the crusher.

Carlo rushed back to the driver's side and jumped into the front seat. He maneuvered the screen on the drone and released the hover mode. He zoomed in above the caravan and watched in horror as all three vehicles raced up the ramp and disappeared into the building. When the last van vanished inside the structure, a large sliding door began to close. He had to get inside. He had to be the eyes of Pete and Morgan. He had to help them find his parents and his sisters. He had to be the overwatch.

Chapter Thirty-Two

Through the glass window of the office Leandra could see the Crane sisters huddled in a corner holding onto one another. She had never been held like that, not in any sisterly way. She knew a lover's embrace. Este had been the only one to treat her with any form of love. But this expression of filial love was foreign to her. Leandra observed the sisters as if studying the unusual behaviors of creatures inside a cage.

Why had one of these creatures said she forgave her? This was a new thing, another unusual behavior. Leandra had never received forgiveness for anything in her life. She had never asked forgiveness from anyone. The idea of forgiveness for the choices she made had never crossed her mind. She'd lived her life in survival mode—be strong, survive, or die. There was no room for forgiveness for such an existence. It was weakness.

The short time she lived in the Crane household had been a flurry and bustle. She didn't know what to expect of the family when she was dropped off in front of the church. The plan was for Arturo to make an example of the Cranes. She must embed herself in the family, get the sisters to where they could be captured, and then make the call. What would happen to the sisters after that was out of her hands. She had used her survival instincts to carry out this bold plan, and she had played her part well, a dual part, in fact, that surprised her by how skillfully she performed the victim and the Virgin Mary. It was flawless, worthy of an award.

In spite of the Cranes' fast-paced life with a Christmas production, this family had welcomed her into their world. More than welcomed. Leandra was not treated as an outsider. She had not been required to adjust her behavior or act a certain way. There was no gauntlet to go through. She was absorbed into the fabric of the family and given responsibility as a full-fledged member. Something she'd never expected.

The world she knew and lived in expected her to do their bidding and perform an act of deceit and betrayal. The world of the Cranes expected nothing, treating her with dignity and kindness, and now mercy. Mercy. For the first time in her life Leandra realized she had received something she had never experienced and knew she was not worthy of. What she had done was something that required people to forgive her. The turmoil in her heart was new. Corley's words of forgiveness brought on a new sensation, a tension in her soul, an awakening of her conscience.

"Can you imagine? You're looking at three hundred thousand dollars."

Leandra was startled out of her thoughts. She had not noticed Beltran standing beside her looking through the window at the sisters.

"Arturo is grateful," he said. "And you must show your gratitude to him."

"Leave her alone, Beltran." Esteban gave his older brother a push. "Arturo got what he wanted from her. He gets no more."

Esteban's bold statement only drew a derisive laugh from his big brother.

"Este, you are so stupid," Beltran said. "Arturo gets whatever he wants."

The vehicles pulling onto the factory floor drew their attention. Leandra recognized the Crane family minivan as it parked in front of the metal crushing bin. The other two vans made U-turns on the cleared factory floor and began backing up toward Arturo who stood behind a table awaiting their arrival.

"Time to collect." Beltran covered his head and face with his mask. "You will join us soon. Expect the unexpected."

Beltran moved briskly toward Arturo, but Esteban stayed with Leandra.

"You don't have to be afraid," Esteban said.

"I live in fear, Este. I don't know what it's like to live without fear," Leandra leaned against the glass window and bent over. She rubbed her hands up and down her legs trying to stop the trembling.

"I will protect you." He adjusted his posture and stiffened his back.

Leandra glanced sideways and gave him a brief smile. Then she straightened up and offered him a quick kiss for his bravery. First forgiveness was given her and now her lover's resolve of protection.

"And I love you for it," she said.

Leandra could see fellow Death Demons, all armed and taking up positions around the factory floor.

"It's like we're preparing for a battle." Esteban took his mask from his pocket and pulled it down over his head.

"Remember what your brother said, 'Expect the unexpected.'" She fiddled with her mask as if indecisive about its purpose. "That could mean anything."

"Aren't you going to put on your mask?" Esteban asked.

"The family knows what I look like," she answered. "What's the point?"

What was the point of her mask? Who was she hiding from? A mask hides guilt and culpability. She was certainly culpable for this crime. If truthful, she would have to admit her guilt. Now that her heart was in conflict with the dual discovery of forgiveness and the need for protection, perhaps she should hide behind a mask, if for no other reason than to hide the feeling of oncoming shame.

"Maybe we get out once this is done." Esteban looked over the factory floor.

Leandra's gaze shot up into Esteban's face. All she could see was his eyes inside the oval slit of his mask. But that was enough. The narrow glare of his focus revealed the determination of his words.

"Can we do that?" she asked. "Can we really escape the gang?"

The wheels on the vans screeched to a stop. Several Death Demons leapt from the vehicles. One carried two metal cases, and he went straight to Arturo and placed the cases on the table and then backed away. Two other Demons opened the doors on the back of the van. Then several converged and reached inside to remove the contents inside the van.

Leandra repositioned herself in front of the large office window and peered through the glass. The sisters were still pressed into the corner of the office away from the window, holding each other, oblivious of the activity on the factory floor. If they knew their parents had arrived, Leandra guessed the girls would not be so still and quiet.

"Somehow. We need to find a way of escape," Esteban said.

He made a move toward his brother, but Leandra grabbed his arm.

"Don't leave me. I need your help with the sisters."

The two passengers were forcefully removed from the back of the van and positioned to face Arturo. Both of them were wobbly on their legs and had to be propped up by a Demon on each side.

"Remove their masks," ordered Arturo.

Every Demon in the factory wore a mask except for Arturo and her. *Why didn't Arturo have on his mask?* He was the mastermind of this event, the regional leader of the cartel. He should want to conceal his identity. He displayed no fear, no guilt or shame, and only then did it dawn on Leandra that perhaps Arturo's intent was to have no witnesses. As the masks on the passengers were removed, Leandra quickly put her mask over her head and rolled the material down around her neck.

Chapter Thirty-Three

Maxwell felt like someone had lit a match to his eyeballs the moment the hood was yanked off his head. After bouncing around in the back of a van and being forced to stand on his shaky legs in this unfamiliar location, the bright lights suspended high above completely disoriented him. Through the burning mist of his eyes Kenda's foggy shape came into focus. He could not wipe the moisture from his eyes, so he kept his head lowered until his feet came into focus. When he raised his head, Kenda's wild eyes were a flagrant burn. Her face was contorted by the tape across her mouth and her cascading disheveled hair. She was trying to speak, but with the tape covering her mouth, he could not understand her. The sounds she made were only muted groans, but he could tell her heart was as unnerved as was his own.

Maxwell jerked away from the hands who gripped him, and he stumbled next to his wife. If he could not speak to her or she to him, he would at least try and touch her somehow to calm her frantic heart. He laid his chin upon her shoulders, and she pressed her body close to him. The tremors of two frightened people rumbled through his body.

They were pulled apart and forced to face a crowd of people lined up behind a table where the two metal cases were set. Everyone was masked and armed except for one man who stood in the center of the crowd. *This must be the unknown.* The one he'd dealt with all night. There was a pronounced scar above his left eye extending down his cheek. A bear rearing on its hind legs was tattooed on one arm and a skull with red wings on the other. These were the inked markings of a fierce internal nature—markings

Maxwell could never forget. Maybe that was the point. He was not meant to forget them because he and his family were not meant to get out of here alive.

The horror in Kenda's eyes as she scanned the crowd of people in front of them gave Maxwell an icy chill speeding along his spine. Their girls were not among them, and he could hear her groaning in agony. He grunted to get her attention. When she finally looked at him, her eyes were so sorrowful it almost destroyed him. How did they end up in the middle of this nightmare and how would they ever awaken from it?

He heard applause coming from the unknown. He was applauding their arrival.

"You come bearing gifts, Padre. I've seen the pictures. Now let's see the real thing." He raised the lids of both cases, one at a time.

Maxwell witnessed an expression of triumph as the unknown removed a few stacks of cash from each case. He prayed the unknown would be so distracted by the amount of bills in each case that he would not discover the homing device hidden in one of them. Maxwell could not remember which case Pete had placed the gadget in, but he hoped his brother-in-law had concealed it well.

While the masked people removed the stacks of money and began to count it, randomly checking some of the bills in each stack to be sure they were not counterfeit, the unknown picked up a small, wrapped set of bills off the top and made his way around the table sauntering toward Maxwell and Kenda.

"You must be in good with the man upstairs, Padre," the unknown said. "But I am curious how this came to you. Did it fall from the sky? Did you dig up buried treasure? Did you steal it from your church? Ah, that must be it. You stole God's money to pay the ransom for your daughters. Gutsy, I like that."

While the unknown was amusing himself with his rhetoric, his was not the only voice Maxwell was hearing.

"Mom and Dad, we're here. Dad, your camera is working.

Uncle Pete and Morgan are coming in from the back dock. I'm looking for a window to get the drone into the factory. We're here. We're here."

What grand words to hear. He looked at Kenda to see if she had heard their son's voice. Her head was lowered, but when she raised it and looked at him with a calmer expression, he knew she too heard Carlo's reassuring words. The overwatch was here.

The unknown stopped in front of Maxwell and waved the stack of bills under his nose and laughed. When Maxwell saw the unknown raise his hand to the side of his face, he knew what was coming next and he curled his lips inside his teeth to protect them. The unknown grabbed the edge of the tape on Maxwell's mouth and yanked it away. He could not help but roar from the pain as he stretched out his mouth and lips. The two masked ones tightened their grip on his arms to keep him from dropping to his knees.

When the unknown made his way over to Kenda, Maxwell warned her of the pain that was coming. She too screamed as the tape was ripped from her mouth, but her recovery was quick, and the ferocity of a lioness sprang forth.

"Where are my girls?" she shouted. "I want my girls."

It was as if everything came to a standstill as Kenda's words echoed through the large space. Even the unknown took a step back startled by Kenda's unexpected wrath. When someone called to the unknown, he quickly turned around. One of the masked ones pointed to the piles of bills on the table.

"All three hundred counted. All clean bills."

When the unknown ordered the masked ones to repack the money back into the cases, Maxwell was relieved the homing device had not been found.

"You have the money. We've met your demand." Maxwell's voice and mouth were now functioning. "Now give us our girls."

"Be careful what you ask for," the unknown said as he turned back around to Maxwell with his sinister expression. He gave a sharp whistle through his teeth and waved his hand in the air. Then he walked back to the table and handed one of the masked ones the bundle of bills he had been carrying.

Maxwell looked around frantically for the girls. He heard their voices before he saw them. The sounds of their cries were coming from a far corner of the factory.

"Kenda, where are they?" Maxwell kept swiveling his head.

"I see them. I see them. Over there." Kenda jumped on the balls of her feet.

When Maxwell saw the girls being escorted by two masked ones around a mound of debris, he lunged in their direction. It was all his captors could do to restrain Maxwell and keep him from dragging them toward his daughters. Kenda was also trying to escape her captors, kicking at the two who struggled to keep her under control and prevent her from rushing to the girls, but when the sound of the gunshot rang out, everything stopped. Maxwell looked anxiously at Kenda to see if she had been hit, but she stood frozen in place, her efforts to escape thwarted, her eyes ablaze with fear.

"You are not to move," the unknown said. He held his nine-millimeter weapon in the air. "Now bring the girls to me."

In spite of a threatening weapon, the moans and the quiet weeping could not be helped. When Carrie and Corley were brought into full view, Maxwell could not keep from weeping. Neither could Kenda. Neither could the girls. They were together. So close, and yet under complete domination by this powerful evil and unable to embrace, let alone escape. Everyone's life was in peril. All Maxwell wanted to do was complete this terrible transaction and bring his family safely home.

"Come here my little *Chiquita's*," the unknown said, and the girls were led around the group of masked ones who remained behind the table and placed beside the unknown.

The firing of the weapon was enough to keep Maxwell quiet. He used the moment of the echoes of a fired round bouncing between the walls and rafters of the factory to begin to count every one of the potential hostiles. At least the ones that he could see. Close to fifteen, maybe more, including the four that restrained Kenda and him. He moved his chest from side to side, slowly so as not to make it obvious, so Carlo and Pete might see the size and layout of the interior space, that is if everything was working.

Then Maxwell allowed himself to really concentrate on his girls sandwiched between two masked ones as they clung to each other. He nearly came undone. Carrie was trying hard not to cry but could not help herself as she desperately hung onto her sister's side, and Corley was doing her best to comfort her while putting on a brave face. It was his daughter's swollen face, bruised and red, that enraged him. It was all he could do to keep from charging like a bull. He had to restrain his fury. He had to keep some level of control, or all could be lost. He allowed the firm grip on his arms by his captors to help him refrain from the impulse to attack.

"Girls, tell me you're all right," Maxwell said gently. He wanted to speak with a firm but steady voice. He did not want to set off the volatile temperament of the unknown with the gun in his hand.

"We're fine, Daddy." Corley's voice still quivered underneath her forced bravery.

"I came as quick as I could." Maxwell looked at Carrie.

He saw Carrie's eyes brighten and she stopped sniffling so she might answer.

"And not a moment too soon," she whimpered.

"Good girls. Good girls," Maxwell said giving his daughters a reassuring smile. "Your mother and I, we've come to take you home." He smiled at Kenda, offering her the same promise.

"Do not be hasty, Padre. We've gathered here like church, and since you like to preach, I thought I would give you a little sermon about the dangers of crossing our cartel. There are consequences, Padre, because debts are always paid, and when our blood is shed, then more blood is a price that must be paid in return."

Maxwell had to remain silent. He would not interrupt this sermon, though its source was diabolic, and its inspiration was hellish. To interrupt a man with a gun in his hand was too great a risk when his wife and daughters were all potential victims of his disconcerting personality.

"You caused great disruption to our business, and we do not like disruption. Six months ago, an important member of our organization was killed. Diego Sanchez was murdered at your hand, and then the dominoes fell, the mayor, police commissioner, several of his officers, our financial partners, all casualties because of you."

Do not defend yourself. Maxwell stood silent, only staring at the unknown. *Do not try to reason with this beast.*

"But to make this sermon a short one, Padre, let me just give you a demonstration of what we intend to do to you, your family, and your little church."

Once again, he whistled two sharp blasts of air through his lips and the iron teeth of a giant crushing machine fired up its engine. Then the driver of a second machine swung its forklift claws over to the Crane minivan and hovered above it, waiting for a signal. When the unknown gave the driver the thumbs up, the giant claws were released and dropped on top of the minivan crunching it into its clasp. The vehicle was lifted off the factory floor and deposited into the giant shredder. Maxwell looked on in horror as the massive shredder devoured the family vehicle. This truly was a sermon illustration that needed no interpretation.

Maxwell looked at his daughters and they both crumpled to their knees. He looked at Kenda whose body had gone limp and was being held up by her captors. His own body was nearly quaking out of control. He had to be held up himself by the masked ones gripping his arms.

He had to look away from his women. He had to look away from the minivan disappearing inside the iron gullet of the enormous shredding machine. He raised his eyes to the ceiling above. Where were Pete and Morgan? Where was the overwatch? Where was God?

Chapter Thirty-Four

The sound of the gunshot brought everything into a heightened reality. Carlo could see the man with the gun pointing into the air from the pinhole camera buttoned on his dad's shirt. Through the camera, Carlo had watched the man approach his dad with a stack of bills and then cringe when the man ripped the tape off his dad's mouth. He could not see his mom. She was out of the camera's range. When the gun was fired, Carlo knew this life and death situation for his family could go horribly wrong at any second.

He did not attempt to talk to his dad after his last contact with him or while the man was speaking to him. His father needed to give his full attention to this man with the gun once his sisters were brought into view. Watching as his dad communicated with his sisters was incomprehensible. Even with his restricted view of the pinhole camera, Carlo could still see a line of masked people and Carrie and Corley, prevented from reuniting with their parents. His father kept still as long as the man with the gun was talking, and Carlo could watch the action. However, his focus was divided. He needed to get the drone into the building if Pete and Morgan were going to have a chance of finding a way to get the family out of there.

When the sound of the machines cranked up, his father was able to turn his body just enough for Carlo to see the iron claws of a forklift drop down on top of the minivan and lift it into the air. Then it disappeared from view. He could only listen to the sounds of giant machines grinding and shredding the family vehicle. He could not get a full view from the pinhole camera. Carlo could only see what was directly in front of this dad, and his body was moving too erratically to get a clear picture. He had to get the drone inside the building, but he could not find a broken window anywhere and he was apprehensive that if he used the blade on the drone to bust through the glass that it would create too much noise and jeopardize any attempt at rescuing his family.

"Carlo. Carlo, what is that loud noise?" Pete said coming through the earbuds.

"I don't know, Uncle Pete. It is some kind of forklift. I just saw it crush our minivan through Dad's camera."

"Was that a gunshot I heard a minute ago?" Pete asked.

"Yes, and they brought out Corley and Carrie. They're on the floor with Mom and Dad and bad guys with weapons positioned all around them. I can't tell where you are."

"We're outside on the loading dock. There are three loading docks for semi's and one ramp leading into the factory. It's got a retractable door over it. We're positioned at another door that leads onto the backside of the factory floor, but we don't know where to go from there," Pete said. "Where's the drone? Is it still outside the building?"

"Yes," Carlo replied. "I was afraid of the noise if I busted through the glass."

"Nobody will hear with all that racket inside the factory," Pete said. "Bust through. We've got to get in there."

Carlo found a panel of windows along the western side of the building. The structure was at least four stories high, but with only a single ground floor. He activated the blade on the drone and began cutting into one of the windows. It took less than a minute for the steel blades to cut through and for the pane to fracture into a spider web of cracks. Carlo retracted the blade and then backed the drone up several feet and flew it directly into the center of the pane, shattering the glass.

"I'm through," Carlo said. "I'm through." But in his excitement the drone began to drop, and he had to do some quick maneuvering to regain control before it crashed.

Once he stabilized the drone, Carlo guided it toward the center of the factory, positioning it between the rafters in the ceiling. Widening the screen on the camera, he could view the factory floor, which had to be several football fields in width and length, and large enough to house the machinery used to recycle waste materials and scrap metal. An erector-set of cranes and shredding machines all connected by long conveyer belts enclosed mounds of recyclable materials covering the floor. In the center of the factory, he could see his parents and sisters separated from each other by a good distance. They were surrounded by masked people all of whom carried weapons. His parents were positioned in front of the two vans that had brought them to the factory location of Garita Metal. The sliding door at the front of the building remained closed with a couple of guards posted in front of it. Carlo conveyed all this information to his uncle.

"How many hostiles?" Pete asked.

"Fifteen or more. Hard to tell," Carlo said. "I could try for a better position."

"Negative," Pete said. "We don't want to attract attention. We need to get onto the floor. Can you see any entry points on the back side of the building? That has to be close to our current position."

Carlo panned the camera toward the rear of the factory floor.

"All I can see are what looks to be some interior offices," Carlo said. "I lose visual beyond that but there could be doors to the loading dock."

"Got to take the chance while the noise covers us. Got to shoot out the hinges on the back door," Pete said. "We're going in. Tell me when you have a visual of us."

Carlo took advantage of the distraction on the factory floor. All eyes were riveted, watching the Crane family minivan being devoured and then spit out onto a conveyer belt in bite-sized pieces that were then transported up a steep incline and dumped into a metal container the size of a railroad car. Carlo zoomed in as close as he could on the interior offices without losing focus. When two black figures with weapons poised entered his frame, Carlo began widening out the camera lens.

"I've got you, Uncle Pete," he said. "Just to your left, there are two large mounds of trash between you and the group in the middle of the factory."

"Carlo, before we take up positions do you see any hostiles that might spot us around the mounds of trash?"

Carlo panned the camera over the factory floor to see if there were any other masked figures besides the ones in the center.

"Two guards at the sliding door at the front entrance, and two operating the forklift and the metal shredder. The rest are in the middle of the factory with the family."

"You've got to be our eyes. We can expedite the hostiles around the family, but you have to tell us if others are coming from our blind spots."

"If I'm going to get a better view, I need to drop the drone," Carlo said.

"Slow and easy, Nephew. We'll get in position behind the trash piles."

A better view of the interior of the factory floor required Carlo to lower the drone, which would make it easier to spot. He had to take the risk, but as he began the descent, the machinery stopped. The minivan had been swallowed up and eliminated. While the sounds of destruction of the minivan reverberated throughout the factory, the man with the gun moved to the sisters. He yanked Corley to her feet and put his gun to her head.

Chapter Thirty-Five

How did it come to this? How far would it go? How could Maxwell stop this madness? This was unimaginable. One daughter crumpled on the floor weeping. The other daughter held at gunpoint. His wife restrained beside him. All of them in one place and yet an invincible barrier of evil kept them apart, an impenetrable presence. Not only that, but this evil threatened to destroy the most important people in his life, demolish them just like the destruction of the family vehicle. Nothing mattered except to save his family. Nothing else had any value, not his possessions, not his church, not even his life. Just his family.

"Please don't do this," Maxwell pleaded.

"We make an example of our enemies, Padre." The unknown pressed the muzzle of his handgun into Corley's temple.

"We've done what you asked of us," Maxwell stated. "You have your money."

"You think this is about the money?" The unknown laughed at the absurd humor in such a statement. "We make that much every minute of the day from all over the world. Your money is no good to me, Padre. Your family's blood is what I want."

Kenda bellowed, sending a jolt through Maxwell's body as if he had gripped the live end of a hot electrical wire. He saw Corley's arms go limp and fall to her side. It was as if all the strength had left her body. He too could feel the strength leaving his body, and he had to fight to keep from completely shutting down. He had to regain some strength to keep from losing all hope. There was no theology for this. Nothing in seminary, in church, in the Marines, nothing in his whole life had prepared him for this moment. What was he to do in this moment when his whole family could be crushed and snuffed out right before his eyes?

"Please. Please. Please," Maxwell begged. "If money means nothing to you. If all you want is blood for blood, then take me. My wife and daughters have done nothing to hurt you. It was me. I am the one responsible for Diego's death. So take me. Take me."

Could it be true? Could Maxwell's words have changed the mind of the unknown? Could he believe what his eyes were seeing? The unknown lowered his weapon and pushed Corley forward. She did not get far before she fell, collapsing on her face, her arms and legs sprawled out like the limbs of a rag doll.

"She is damaged goods anyway. Her face will never be right," the unknown said, but then he bent down and grabbed the hair on top of Carrie's head and pulled her up onto her knees. "But this one, on the other hand will do nicely."

Maxwell tried to lunge forward, but the masked ones held him fast, and he was still bound by the restraints wrapped around his wrists. He wished for the strength of Samson, someone who could snap the plastic binders around his wrists, the strength to vanquish his enemies, no, more than vanquish, to punish his enemies. But the strength Maxwell prayed for did not come into his limbs, but into his daughter's instead. It was a marvel of animation as Corley began to gather her deflated arms and legs under her middle and push herself to her knees.

"Daddy, Mommy, I love you," Corley said, but the endearing words that she had spoken countless times did not sound like his daughter. It was a deep guttural sound, like that of a determined beast. "I love you both so much, but I can't leave without Carrie, and I can't leave without the other girls."

"What other girls?" cried Kenda. "I don't see other girls. Where are they?"

"Here, Mommy. Here with us in this building. They are forced to do terrible things. We cannot leave without them."

Here was the strength Maxwell needed manifested in his

daughter, a vibrancy that was stunning to behold. In the harsh lights beaming down from the ceiling fixtures he could see the injury done to Corley's face. He hadn't wanted to believe what Carrie had shouted at him over the phone that Corley had been injured. He hadn't wanted to believe that anyone could ever hurt his children. The right side of her face looked as if it were broken and caved-in on itself. The inflamed skin and bruised eye on one side of her face and neck and the lovely unblemished other side made her appearance like that of the dual natures residing in one person. His oldest daughter was hurt, and he did nothing to prevent it. His youngest daughter was still in the grip of the unknown and he couldn't rescue her. His wife was beside him but rendered as helpless as he.

"Listen to me, Corley," Maxwell said. "Listen honey, we'll figure this out. Just come over here with us."

"I can't, Daddy." Corley slowly turned and faced the unknown and stood defiantly before him. "You must let us go. You must let my sister go. You must let the other girls go. You must let all of us go."

Where had her courage come from? How had this strength appeared in Corley's soul, the strength to face one so powerful, one who held their lives in the balance tipping the scales in his favor? These were not pleas for mercy. This was no appeal for reason. These were provocative demands given by one so young, so innocent, and now so damaged.

A flash of surprise and fear appeared in the eyes and face of the unknown, causing him to hesitate as if, in that second, his daughter's words had given him pause and indicated that he might be reasoned with, something Maxwell had been unable to do. This girl was so outrageous, making such outrageous demands. Maxwell knew his child. Corley's resistance was not borne out of the inner strength of her own nature. This was beyond natural, beyond the scope of human capability. As quickly as the apprehension and shock materialized in the face of the unknown, it swiftly disappeared.

"Well, this one must not be so damaged after all." The unknown raised his gun and pointed it at Corley.

There was no mistaking the intent. The unknown was finished talking. Maxwell would not misjudge or second guess, and he would not retreat. He too was finished with talking. The situation had been forced, and now the strength of the warrior came upon him like a great wave. The strength of his daughter drenched him head to toe. It was enough to catapult him forward out of the tight grip of the masked ones who held his arms. Despite this swift rush of adrenaline, it was not enough muscle to break his wrists free of the plastic restraints. He might not have his hands, but he did have his body, and he used it to rush toward Corley knocking her to the floor with his shoulder.

Just as he was ready to hurl his body at the unknown, Maxwell saw a masked one dive in front of the unknown and grab his hand with the gun. The round fired from the weapon knocked the masked one to the floor, but the force of the projectile was powerful enough to do the same to Maxwell. He felt as if he had been bashed in the shoulder by a sledgehammer. He saw the blood spring from his shoulder like a geyser, and as he fell flat onto his back, he heard the screams of his wife and daughters.

Chapter Thirty-Six

Corley rolled onto her hands and knees and started scrambling for her father who lay bleeding on the floor. From her peripheral vision the man who had fired the shot began marching toward her, but the masked one who had thwarted his initial attempt to kill her, reached out and grabbed his leg. He fired a second round, and the hand dropped to the floor and the masked one lay still. Then the man with the gun kicked the body out of his way. The bullet that was intended for Corley had been deflected by a masked one who lay motionless near her father.

Just before Corley was about to fling herself onto her father's chest to protect him, a hand grabbed her shoulder and tossed her aside. The man with the gun took a firm stance over her father pointing the muzzle at his head.

"Arturo, wait. Don't shoot," a voice shouted from the group gathered around the table. They were all pointing at something above them. "Up in the ceiling. A drone."

Corley looked up and saw a drone hovering just below the rafters.

"Shoot it down." Arturo pointed his weapon at the drone and fired.

Several in the group began firing their weapons at the drone until it exploded in midair, raining the shattered pieces down onto the floor.

"They came with backup." Arturo spun around to address the group. "Beltran, call the front gate. Tell them to expect company. The rest of you get ready for a fight. Vamonos!"

Everyone around the table began to scatter over the factory

floor, taking up positions behind machinery or the huge piles of rubbish. Arturo grabbed Carrie by the back of the neck and dragged her along as he made his way back to Maxwell. He tossed her beside Corley and then repositioned himself over her father, once again threatening to kill him.

"I love you, Maxwell," screamed her mother as she struggled to free herself. She was still being forcibly held by two masked ones. "I love you."

Her father was struggling for breath, but he managed to get up onto an elbow and look back at Kenda to tell her he loved her. Then he looked at Corley.

"Don't worry, girls," he gasped. "Uncle Pete is coming."

Then Arturo kicked her father in the legs, and he plopped onto his back. "Who is Uncle Pete?" Arturo asked. Corley pulled Carrie close to her, and then her eyes widened when the two masked ones beside her mother let go of her arms and abruptly fell to the ground.

"I am." Pete stepped out from behind a van aiming his weapon at Arturo. He moved toward him in his crouched fighting position.

Corley closed her eyes and covered Carrie's face before Pete fired two rounds. When she opened them, Arturo lay on the floor in a pool of his own blood.

"Girls, quick," Pete shouted. Her uncle was dragging her father by his shirt collar back toward two vans while a second person gave cover fire.

As gunfire rang out in the factory, Corley and Carrie rushed forward on all fours to where Pete had stopped between the two vans. Kenda scooted in beside them.

Pete gave his knife to Corley. "Free your mom and dad."

While Corley cut the restraints off her mother's wrists, Pete pulled out some bandages from a side pocket and dropped them on her father's chest.

"Stuff these in the wound to stop the bleeding, then cut him free."

Once Kenda was free, she ripped open Maxwell's shirt so Corley could stuff the wound in her father's shoulder. It was a clean entry and exit.

"Stay between the vans for cover. Gotta go." Pete stepped over them moving toward Morgan who was engaged in a fire fight with the masked ones.

Once the bandages were in place, Carrie helped pull Maxwell over onto his side so that Corley could cut off the plastic restraints from his wrists.

"You came for us," Carrie was shaking uncontrollably. "You came for us."

When Maxwell's hands were free, he cupped a hand on the faces of his daughters. "And not a minute too soon."

Corley heard someone howling over the constant gunfire, howling as if in deep pain. A masked one was kneeling on the floor and clutching the body of the one who dove in front of Arturo and grabbed his arm just before he fired his weapon. The masked one was crying out the name of the one who had taken the bullet intended for her.

"It's Leandra." Corley handed the knife to her mother. "I've got to go to her."

Corley ignored her parents' alarmed cries as she scrambled out into the open with gun fire all around her. When she crawled past Arturo's body, she saw the two open wounds in his chest and his vacant eyes. She could not imagine what his last thought might have been. Whatever it was, her Uncle Pete's face was emblazoned upon it.

The masked one who held Leandra's body laid her on the floor in front of Corley as she scooted forward. She gently removed Leandra's mask so she might breathe her final labored breaths. Then the masked one leapt to his feet and bolted for cover behind a large metal container.

Leandra was barely able to speak, so Corley leaned her ear close to her lips.

"Save the girls," she gasped. "Save them."

A sound like an explosion rocked the entire factory. A black vehicle crashed through the sliding door of the front entrance and screeched to a stop behind the two vans. The driver's door flew open and out leaped her brother. Carlo was driving Uncle Pete's SUV. A moment later a second vehicle burst through the opening and out jumped three people in full combat gear, weapons drawn and began returning fire as all three of them rushed toward the fight. The cavalry had arrived.

Corley dragged Leandra's lifeless body over to where her family was hunkered down between the two vans. The volley of fire was nearly deafening.

"Carrie, we've got to get Jasmine and the girls out of that room," Corley shouted.

"You two are not going anywhere," Kenda cried.

"Where are they located?" Carlo yelled.

"Locked in a room at the end of that row of cubicles covered in blue tarp." Corley pointed in the general direction.

"How many?" asked Carlo.

"I tried to count them," Carrie said. "But I don't know. Maybe fifteen."

Carlo looked at the vans on either side of them, then he locked eyes with Kenda.

"Mom, we can do this," he said.

"Not on your life," Maxwell said. "We stay put."

"Dad, we got to try and get those girls out of here." Corley stretched her head around the front of the van for a quick look, but the gunfire forced her to retreat.

"Honey, we can do this." Kenda grabbed Maxwell's face in her hands. "We got Carrie and Corley back. We can't leave those girls behind."

"You had to say that." Maxwell shook his head. "You just had to say that."

"But we do this together," Kenda said. "We don't get separated again. Agreed?"

"Agreed," replied Corley and her sister.

"What about Pete and Morgan?" Kenda elevated herself for a quick look.

"Feel sorry for the bad guys." Maxwell pulled his wife back down with his good arm. "If we're gonna do this then let's move."

"Mom, you drive that van," Carlo said. "I'll drive the other one.

"Keep the windows down so we don't get hit with flying glass." Maxwell struggled to get on his knees.

"Carrie, help me with Leandra's body," Corley said. "Put her in Mom's van."

Carrie opened the side door of the van and grabbed Leandra's legs while Corley slipped her hands underneath Leandra's arms. Together they lifted her body and placed her inside the van as tenderly as possible. After she closed the door, she helped her dad buckle into the passenger seat of her mother's van. Then she raced around to the passenger side of Carlo's van and jumped inside.

"Your face is messed up, Sis. Can you see?"

"One eye works."

"That's good enough." Carlo started the engine.

"We got a plan, big brother?" Corley asked.

"Get the girls and drive to the back of the factory. Uncle Pete says there is a ramp beside the loading docks. We find the retractable door and bust through."

"Simple enough." Corley leaned over Carlo and shouted at her mother through the open window. "Mom, follow us to get the girls."

"Mom," Carlo yelled from his van. "We've done this before. We can do it again."

"Go, Carlo. Go." Corley directed her brother around the mounds of trash leading him straight along the side of the factory past all the video cubicles and right up to the large room where the girls had been locked inside.

When Carlo came to a screeching halt, Corley jumped out and opened the side doors of each van. Then she ran to the room that held the girls and tried to open it, but it wouldn't budge. She could hear screaming coming from inside the room.

"It won't open," Corley yelled.

"Try Pete's knife," Kenda held up the knife.

Corley dashed over to where her father was seated, and her mother reached across the front handing it to Corley. She rushed back and began plunging the blade around the doorframe so she could insert the blade and slip the lock. After a few stabs she had just enough space to slip the blade beside the latch and pull it back. She smashed her shoulder against the door the same time she jimmied the lock, and the door flew open.

"Come on, girls," Corley shouted brandishing the knife. "We're out of here."

Corley was shocked to see none of them rush toward her. They were crying but remained huddled together plastered against the wall.

"Come on," Corley shouted. "We need to go now. Jasmine, please."

Jasmine pushed herself off the wall and dashed over to the twin girls that had been in the room with Corley and Carrie and grabbed their arms, pulling them toward the door.

"What about the others?" Corley asked, shocked by the girls' fear and refusal to move. "We've got room. We'll take all of you."

"They won't come," Jasmine said. "Too scared."

The firefight on the factory floor was intensifying and Carlo started blowing the horn on the van.

"Just shut the door behind us." Jasmine led the twins out the door. "Keep them safe as long as possible."

Corley said a quick prayer for the girls as she shut the door behind her. Then she led Jasmine and the twins over to her mother's van. When she opened the sliding door to let them in, she saw Carrie holding Leandra's hand. It nearly brought her to tears, but her tears would have to wait.

Once the girls were in the van with her parents, Corley slammed the door and jumped back into the van with Carlo and buckled her seat belt.

"Look, Carlo, Uncle Pete's coming." Corley pointed to Pete running toward them with two metal cases. He pushed them through Carlo's window.

"Get out of here, through the back dock. There's a ramp on the other side of the metal door." He spun around and headed back into the fight.

Carlo tossed the cases into the back of the van and pushed hard on the gas pedal. When he cut a sharp turn to the right, Corley could see her brother was speeding toward a massive retractable door. Her heart was beating so rapidly it might explode any second.

"You know what you're doing, big brother?" Corley shouted.

"Uncle Pete says it's our way out," he roared. "Taking a leap of faith, Sis."

"But we don't know what's on the other side."

"Freedom, baby. Freedom."

Corley braced her hands on the dashboard and clamped shut one good eye. The jolt of the van crashing into the retractable door sent it flying straight into the air. Crashing through the door did little to slow them down. Once they were down the ramp, Carlo slammed on the brakes. Corley unbuckled her seatbelt and stretched out the window to watch her mother charging down the ramp after them.

"Mom's out," she cried pounding the roof of the van with her fist.

"Get back in your seat, Corley. We're not safe yet," Carlo said. "One more gate to go."

Corley plopped back into her seat as Carlo punched the gas pedal. She braced her hands on the dashboard again, but this time she kept her good eye open as Carlo crashed through the double gate of the backlot. She stretched her head out the window to see her mother flying through the crashed gates and following them down the service road around the factory. She could feel the heavy vibrations rumbling through the van, and when she looked down, she could see a metal object had gotten lodged beneath the van and had punctured a rear tire. So many sparks were flying underneath the vehicle it looked like a Fourth of July fireworks display.

"Carlo, we blew a tire. A piece of metal from the gate is caught underneath the van." Corley pointed out her window to the blown tire.

"We need to get to the highway, then we can hop into Mom's van," Carlo said.

The van was slowing down while weaving from side to side as Carlo forced the vehicle forward until they reached the end of the service road. Carlo brought the van to a stop and slammed the gear into park right where the road intersected with the four-lane highway.

"Grab one of the cases and go." Carlo pointed at a case.

Corley grabbed one case and Carlo the other, then they flew out of the van just as Kenda drove up beside them. They jumped into the back of the van and stashed the cases between the front seats as Kenda pulled onto the highway heading back into Richland.

Corley sat on top of the cases lodged between her parents trying to calm her breath. No one was talking. What was there to say? Her dad was wounded, fading in and out of consciousness. He rolled his head toward her and reached his trembling hand toward her wounded face.

"I'm so sorry…so sorry."

Corley took his hand and squeezed it.

"We made it, Daddy. We made it."

Her mother was driving, wiping the tears from her face and offering breathy thanks to God for getting out of there. Her brother and sister were in the back of the van with four girls, one of whom had given her life to save her.

The sound of firing weapons and vehicles crashing through gates was replaced by the quiet sounds of gentle weeping encased inside the low rumble of the moving vehicle. Corley placed one hand on her mom's arm, another on her dad's. Her dad rolled his head over and gave her a weak smile before closing his tired eyes. The great specter of death had been all around Corley and her family, and now it appeared they had evaded its fearful grip.

As they approached the front entrance of the factory, Corley saw the great arch sign of Garita Metal above the gates at the entrance off the main highway. It remained intact but was knocked off kilter when Carlo crashed through, knocking the gates off their hinges. She looked back at her brother sitting quietly with his arm draped over Carrie's shoulder. He was the great gate crasher. *Where had he learned to drive like that*? What Carlo had done was nothing short of miraculous. What all of them had done to survive this night was miraculous. But had they really escaped? Was there a price to be paid by foiling the plot of the wicked?

"Look." Her mother came to a stop in front of the entrance into the factory. "Uncle Pete and the others."

Corley saw two black SUV's barreling toward them. Uncle Pete pulled up beside them. There was a passenger in the front seat with her uncle. She recognized him as the undercover agent who had saved Carlo from being killed by a corrupt police officer. Pete's SUV had the dents and scars from Carlo driving it into the factory to get to them. Her uncle's vehicle was better suited for such punishment from two gate crashes. The second vehicle pulled behind Pete.

"Safe and sound?" Pete got out of his vehicle and opened the passenger door of the van to look at her father.

Corley answered for her family with a soft "yes" as if she were not sure "safe and sound" was an apt appraisal of the condition of her family or herself. Safe, perhaps, for now, but sound? How might that be possible?

"How we doing?" Uncle Pete pulled back the blood-soaked bandages on her father's wound for a quick inspection, which temporarily brought him back to consciousness.

"We got them back, Pete." Her dad gave a wan smile, and then was gone again.

"Your face?" Pete asked Corley.

"Hurts, but I'll live."

"Good girl. I need those cases."

Corley handed them to her uncle and he tossed them to someone outside her view who must have been standing between the vehicles. Pete closed the door to the van and spoke through the window.

"Go to Veteran's Hospital. He's lost a lot of blood. They'll get you both patched up. We can sort details later."

Her uncle did not wait for an answer but jumped back into his SUV. The undercover agent was no longer in her uncle's vehicle. The second vehicle made a U-turn across the highway and sped off in the opposite direction. The cavalry had completed its mission and disappeared into darkness.

"Follow me, Sis," Pete said before pulling in front and starting down the highway.

Her mother eased onto the highway and began to follow her uncle.

Corley scrunched down between the two front seats. She no longer had the elevated position the metal cases had given her. She looked back into the interior of the van. This had to be one of the vans parked in front of her home, the Death Demons inside lying in wait for her and her sister and the dead young woman now lying on the van floor. One of the same vans used to transport the other innocent girls from city to city enslaving them in this terrible life.

Carlo had taken off his hoodie and lay it over Leandra's shoulders and head. On the opposite side of the van, Jasmine leaned her back against the panel and had her arms over the twin girls holding them close like a portrait of a mother cuddling her children. But this was a terrible pose for a portrait. Jasmine and the twins looked to be barely of legal age, if that.

Corley leaned forward to speak to Jasmine. "Jasmine, why didn't the girls go with us when they had the chance?"

She looked at Corley with weary eyes. "Fear. They ain't running off with strangers. They chose bondage to the devil they know."

"And you, what about you?" Corley asked.

"I'd take death over being a slave. Don't want anybody else to live that way." Jasmine gently kissed the foreheads of the twins burrowed inside her arms.

Corley nestled back into the gap between the two front seats. They were driving away from the harrowing death that had tried to close its hungry jaws around them. This quiet drive away from the mayhem of the last hours had to mean they were all safe at last, that they had escaped the valley of the shadow they had fallen into. This had to mean deliverance.

Please God, let it be so, Corley thought. *Please let it be so.*

Chapter Thirty-Seven

Maxwell gradually opened his eyes to the sound of quiet voices. On the way to the hospital, he'd drifted from rattled slumber to a startled wakefulness, never sure what reality he was in. The last thing he remembered was Carlo pushing a gurney toward the van from the entrance to the V.A. as an E.R. doctor was opening the passenger door. He must have blacked out after that. He looked down at his arms and saw each one was plugged into an I.V., one for blood, the other to restore fluid balance. His chest was patched with a couple of heart tabs to monitor his vitals. The antiseptic smells from his surgery and bandages made him want to gag. Maxwell tried to move his wounded shoulder, but it wasn't ready to cooperate.

Near the door, Doctor Peggy Thomas, the director of the V.A. was going over his charts with the E.R. doctor who had helped him out of the van and onto the gurney. The sunlight came pouring through the half-closed blinds on the window. The day was bright. The light was pure. He was never so glad to be out of the darkness.

Sprawled over the sofa beneath the window were his wife and three children. Scattered on the floor around the sofa was the detritus from vending machines. His family did not move, a posture of people in the tranquility of sleep. He gasped when he saw Corley's discolored face, her eye covered with a patch, which caught the attention of Dr. Thomas. She moved over to the side of his bed, bringing the chart with her as the E.R. doctor slipped out the door. Dr. Thomas pulled some tissues from the box on the bedside table and patted Maxwell's damp eyes.

"They're safe." She nodded toward his sleeping family, then

tossed the tissues into the wastebasket.

"My daughter's face. Will she be all right?"

"We drained off some fluid and gave her something for pain and to help with swelling. There was trauma to her eye, but she needs to see an ophthalmologist. The patch is just a precaution."

"Oh my. Oh my," he moaned.

"I know there's a story behind all this, but for now you need to know that your wound was clean, as clean as a gunshot wound can be. You're patched up, and in a day or two you can leave and go about your normal life."

"There is nothing normal about my life, Doctor," Maxwell whispered.

"Given that the entire Crane household camped out here instead of going home, I can attest to the abnormality of your life."

Maxwell tried to raise himself, but did not have the strength to do little more than turn his head toward his slumbering family. "Why didn't they go home?"

"Your daughters refused," answered the doctor. "The younger one began to cry, so I didn't force it. We had the sofa brought in while you were in surgery."

"They've been through…we've all been…" Maxwell paused, the memory of the unprecedented events of these last hours washed over him.

"No need to explain, Maxwell. While you were in surgery, I told your family that they are safe here. But I need to give you a reality update. There are two police officers stationed outside your room, and the new commissioner is waiting at the nurse's station. She didn't seem ready to pin a medal on your good shoulder."

"A medal is the last thing I want." Maxwell reached for the water on the bedside table but a sharp jab in his side caught his breath and he winced.

"Yeah, you're going to be a little sore for a while," she said.

"Would you hand me that water? I'm parched."

The doctor gave Maxwell a Styrofoam cup full of ice water.

He sipped the refreshing liquid which helped to dispel the grogginess in his head.

"I can stall her, but the commissioner is an inevitable force." The doctor held out her hand to take the cup.

Maxwell handed her the cup and cast his eyes to the ceiling. He could not avoid this meeting. He didn't want to avoid it. He would love to come clean with all the facts and all the emotions of what his family had experienced the last twelve hours, but Maxwell didn't know everything. It would require the people on the sofa to help put all the pieces together, but if he was not ready to do that, he knew his team wouldn't be either. He would provide the commissioner the story without being cagey. There were facts about last night and certain people involved that would not want the spotlight. Not every character should be included in his story. The commissioner knew some facts, or she would not be waiting to come in, nor would the two officers stationed outside his door. This would not be the only interview with the commissioner. This would be the first of many, and he needed to start this one on a good foot.

"Yes, Doctor, send her in," Maxwell said. "And Peggy, thank you for everything."

"Seen this type of GSW before, but not on a pastor." She made her way to the door. Then she paused. "You know, I may come to your church sometime. I've never known a pastor like you. The ones I know don't get shot."

"Yeah, I'll do anything to get people to church." He smiled. "I'll reserve you a seat on the front pew."

"And something else." Dr. Thomas placed her hand on the door handle but didn't open it. "The commissioner arrived at the hospital in an unmarked car and came through the service entrance. She instructed me to deny that you and your family are at the hospital. I don't know what happened last night, but none of us wants an army of reporters camped in the parking lot. So when we discharge you, we may have to spirit you and the family away in an ambulance to get you out of here."

"Let's jump off that bridge when the time comes," Maxwell said.

"I'll send in the commissioner." Dr. Thomas slipped out the door.

Maxwell looked toward his family lying peacefully asleep on the sofa. "Thank you, God. Thank you, God. Thank you. Thank you."

He did not want to wake them. They needed their rest. The coming days would be stressful sorting through all that had happened. Meeting the police commissioner would be a first step. She would see his family, and he would give his assurance they would fully cooperate with her. If there were to be ramifications for the actions taken last night, he would bear responsibility.

Maxwell knew all too well the emotional and psychological burdens that come from severe trauma, and how difficult it would be for all five of them to navigate the path of recovery. He had seen it as a chaplain with his fellow Marines and as a pastor with those he served in the community. He personally knew what mental suffering had done to his own soul. There was a long journey ahead, and it was time for him to stand in the gap for his family, but without the strength of his faith, such a brave bearing would be impossible.

"Pastor Crane, may I come in?"

Maxwell turned his head from his peaceful family and saw the somber face of the police commissioner peeking around the door. He motioned for her to come in, then put his finger to his lips for her to enter quietly.

The commissioner closed the door and tiptoed over to the side of his bed. She was dressed in her uniform with her cap tucked under one arm. Four gold stars lined her shirt collar. There was a gold badge pinned to her jacket above the breast pocket that read "City of Richland" on a banner across the top. In the middle of the badge was an eagle with its talons clasping an olive branch in one and a cluster of arrows in the other. Beneath the eagle's talons was inscribed "Police Commissioner." The tops of two gold ink pens rose out of her suit pocket.

She glanced at the sleeping people on the sofa and then gave Maxwell a look he could not read. She would start to speak and then stop as if she did not know how to begin, so Maxwell held out his good arm. He could only reach so far because of it being attached to the I.V.

"I'm Maxwell Crane." He did not have the strength in his hand for her to grip it, so he offered her a fist in hopes she would bump it.

"Cynthia Peele." She looked warily at Maxwell's offered fist, then she bumped it followed by a wave toward the sofa. "How are we doing?"

Maxwell shrugged his shoulders to indicate his uncertainty of an answer to her question. All were not well. All were in shock. And the presence of the police commissioner was a statement of just how not well it would probably be for some time.

"I started my day earlier than usual, Pastor," she began. "Got a call this morning from a source inviting me to pay a visit to the industrial area of Richland. Specifically, Garita Metal. It looked like the owners of that industry and those who worked there were involved in other activities besides recycling scrap metal."

The commissioner paused for Maxwell to respond, but he only nodded his head.

"Looking at you and seeing the condition of your family, begs the question if what happened last night at Garita Metal is connected to you being here at the hospital with a bullet wound in your shoulder. But you might want counsel first."

"Is that what your source told you or are you just trying to fit some puzzle pieces together?" Maxwell asked.

"From what I saw at Garita Metal, this is a big puzzle, Pastor."

"You trust this source, Commissioner?" Maxwell asked.

"Without question, and I want to make sure you and your

family are safe. You are for the moment." She tilted her head toward the sofa. "We want to keep it that way."

"Yes, we do," Maxwell affirmed her statement.

"But I need your help," continued the commissioner. "Six months ago, the city of Richland appointed me to this job." She tapped her badge with her finger. "His Honor, at the time, should have pinned on this badge, but the job went to the Vice Mayor since the former mayor was sitting in a jail cell. I should thank you for this promotion."

"Mayor Barton found his own way to the jail, along with the others." Maxwell shrugged his shoulders as if he had little to do with the circumstances.

"Yes, how the mighty have fallen," she said. "You also spent time in prison for being in the wrong place at the wrong time regarding the death of Diego Sanchez."

"His death will haunt me for the rest of my life." Maxwell bowed his head. He had everything to do with that circumstance.

"We're still sorting through what brought down that criminal house of cards, but the former mayor and police chief Cassia left behind a real mess and a foul stench," she said. "You played a part in that downfall, but you got out with no stink."

"You're wrong, Commissioner. I smell the stink of my actions all the time."

Maxwell saw Kenda roll up her head onto the back of the sofa. Her eyes widened at the sight of the police commissioner. She was about to adjust the pile of kids off her lap and shoulders, but Maxwell held up his hand for her not to move and mouthed that everything was fine. So, Kenda remained still to let the kids continue to sleep.

"Pastor, I didn't become the first Black Police Commissioner of Richland because I kissed up to those above my rank. I walked from the neighborhood beat into the halls of power earning all these stars you see on my collar and this gold badge. But all this brass can't hide the scars I carry. So I'm going to honor my physical and emotional scars as well as these golden honors pinned on my uniform by cleaning up the mess my predecessor made and rooting out every dust ball of corruption I find swept under the carpet of my house."

"Commissioner, I rejoiced to see your appointment, and I had every intention of seeking an audience with you at the first opportunity," Maxwell said. "I knew you were extremely busy doing exactly what you just said, so I waited. Then this happened."

Maxwell pointed first to his wounded shoulder and then towards the sofa.

"I don't know all the facts behind Garita Metal," she continued. "But my sense tells me that there is a connection to what happened six months ago."

"What are the facts, ma'am?" Maxwell gave her a weak smile.

"A slew of dead gang bangers, some girls and video booths and camera equipment with direct links to the dark web of human trafficking, a half-a-million in cash, stockpiles of military weapons, drugs worth seven-figures in street value, and one dead lieutenant in a world-wide cartel with ties throughout Central America that go all the way to Russia. Those are the facts we've gathered just since my team got to the scene. But one fact I can't explain is how in the world you and your family got mixed up in that."

Maxwell looked back at Kenda who nodded for him to continue and then whispered, "Go on." This was the sign of trust he needed.

"We will not need legal counsel, Commissioner, because we will tell you the truth," Maxwell said. "The truth is all we have, and it is painful."

He turned his head when Kenda gasped and saw her put her hands to her mouth as she began to softly weep. Maxwell hated to see Kenda's reaction. The truth was painful and he and his wife would have to bear it for the rest of their lives. This was an unavoidable reality.

"Pastor, I know the pain the truth can cause. Let me tell you one painful truth that you know all too well," she said. "Being a woman of color and put into a high-powered job means I had to work harder to get here, and I have to work harder to stay here. It starts with cleaning my own house, but then I want also to stop the street gangs from poisoning our kids with drugs and trafficking young girls. And I especially want to go after those cartels who mastermind it all."

"Commissioner Peele, we have seen firsthand what destruction these cartels bring to our city and to my family personally. We will do everything we can to help you."

"Daddy." It was Carrie who was the first of the children to awaken. She jumped off the sofa and rushed over to stand by Maxwell's bed and lay her head on his good shoulder.

"I came as quick as I could." She squeezed his hand.

"And not a minute too soon." Maxwell showered the top of her head with kisses. "Not a minute too soon."

The commissioner placed her police hat back onto her head.

"Get well, Pastor. We'll put a plan together to get you out of here. You may need to spend Christmas in a safe house until the dust has settled."

"Thank you, ma'am," Maxwell said.

The commissioner turned to Kenda and nodded her head then went to the door. Before she opened it, she looked back as everyone was rising from the sofa and making their way over to Maxwell's bedside.

"One more thing, Pastor," she said. "I don't care how many good guys you got on your team, no more cowboy, vigilante stuff. If this is going to work, we work together."

"I couldn't agree more, Commissioner, and I look forward to us getting to know each other better."

Once the commissioner made her exit, Maxwell raised his arm for all three of his children to nestle beneath it while Kenda stood at the foot of the bed and gripped her hands around his legs. He felt a refiner's fire burning in his heart, a surge of healing bellowing through his soul. His family was before him. What he saw he could touch, and what he touched was real flesh and blood, alive, and belonging to him. He wanted to speak, to utter forth the thankfulness he felt, but what burst from his lips was a sob, a moan, an inarticulate howl. It was a holy song with no lyric, for no words could express the bowel-deep love and gratitude he knew at this moment.

Chapter Thirty-Eight

Maxwell pressed his Bible to his chest. He sat on the front pew of The Mercy Seat with his family. Like two pillars of strength, Pete sat on one side of him while Kenda sat on the other. Carlo and Lin and Corley and Carrie filled in the rest of the pew. In the row behind him sat Rendell Hardy with Jeff and Lindy Anderson. On the opposite side of the aisle sat Rosemary with Ezekiel nestled in her lap. It was silent inside the sanctuary except for the clanking of the duct work blowing the warm air through the building. Outside a light wind blew against the stained-glass windows with the hissing sound of falling snow melting on heated panes of glass.

They all sat quietly in their pews for some time. No one had spoken, and Maxwell did not wish to break the silence. For if he spoke, it meant that what they had all gone through the last few days was now final, a conclusion no one foresaw or wanted to believe. Maxwell felt a great relief that he and his family had survived, but it had been at great cost, the cost of another life. Leandra's death was not the ending any of them wanted, but then he never wanted any of these last days to have had a beginning.

Maxwell set his Bible on his lap and thumbed through the pages with his good hand until he landed on the passage that had come to his mind. "I was hungry and you fed me. I was thirsty and you gave me something to drink. I needed clothes and you clothed me. I was a stranger and you took me in. I was sick and in prison and you looked after me. If you did it to the least of these, you did it to me." Leandra was all those things. She suffered from all those depravations. She needed all those kindnesses. Maxwell and his family had done all they could to care for her. If these verses were true, then Jesus had been among them this whole time.

And then the gun was fired and the bullet meant for his daughter, had been taken by Leandra. The lethal round had gone through Leandra and then entered his shoulder. The "least of these" had given her life for Corley and Maxwell. Without Maxwell or anyone realizing it, Leandra had led them into the world of Golgotha, but at the last second, she had substituted her life for theirs. This was a life-long bond he and the whole family would share with Leandra, a bond forged in shed blood.

Rosemary rose from her seat and tucked Ezekiel under her arm then moved to the front. She walked with slow and measured steps as though trudging through deep snow until she stopped beside the simple pinewood box in front of the altar. Rosemary rested her hand upon the coffin. She began to hum, more like gurgling sounds of lament that began to smooth out in the measures of musical notes.

"I can't believe I have to sing this for you now," Rosemary spoke, breathing out the words on moist clouds of sorrow. "You came into our lives a stranger at the door, lost and bewildered. You came from a dark world that had a deep hold of your soul. You never knew comfort or peace. But you came to us, you took your place in our hearts, stepping into the light of Christ for one brief moment. But it was enough. It was enough."

Rosemary set Ezekiel on the floor and turned her back to everyone as she placed both hands on the coffin. Ezekiel sat at Rosemary's feet, obedient and still. She lifted her head and continued her musical expression of grief. Then she lifted her arms as if offering Leandra's soul to the Almighty.

"You asked me to sing this song to you, and I promised I would," she cried. "But now I must sing it over you. I hand these words to the heavenly angels as they usher you into the light."

The lyric to the old hymn filled the sanctuary, a vocal incense of a holy offering.

"What a Friend we have in Jesus,
All our sins and griefs to bear!
What a privilege to carry
Everything to God in prayer!
O what peace we often forfeit,
O what needless pain we bear.
All because we do not carry,
Everything to God in prayer.
Are we weak and heavy laden,
Cumbered with a load of care?
Precious Savior, still our refuge—
Take it to the Lord in prayer;
Do thy friends despise, forsake thee?
Take it to the Lord in prayer;
In His arms He'll take and shield thee;
Thou wilt find a solace there."

Maxwell rose to his feet once Rosemary finished singing. Kenda took his arm and they approached the coffin together. Pete and the children joined them along with Rendell and the Andersons. Everyone placed their hand on the lid of the coffin each one uttering their personal quiet words.

When Maxwell and Kenda were finished, they went and stood behind the altar. Rosemary picked up Ezekiel and joined them as did Pete, Rendell, and the Andersons. Carlo went to the side door and propped it open, then came back to the group. He and Lin took the foot of the coffin and Carrie and Corley took the front. They rolled the stand out the side door where the funeral home attendants helped them roll the coffin into the hearse waiting in the parking lot. Once the hearse drove away, the kids came back inside and fell into the open arms of their friends and family.

"What will happen to all those girls that were rescued?" Rendell closed the side door once the kids were inside.

"Some kind of social services program." Rosemary scratched

the top of Ezekiel's head. "Those who don't have family will end up in foster care, most likely."

"Is there nothing better?" Anderson asked. "Is there nothing in Richland that would be better than a social service agency?"

"Those services can do a fair job with all kinds of needs." Rosemary switched Ezekiel to her other arm. "They have a level of understanding about such things."

"Rosemary, could we learn from their programs and maybe come up with something better?" Anderson put his arm around Lindy. "I mean, take the good things these agencies provide and offer something more specific to the needs of young girls and women caught up in this type of crisis…something more…"

"You mean spiritually and emotionally holistic?" Kenda took Maxwell's Bible and gently pressed herself into his side.

"Yes, Kenda. Meeting more than their physical needs. What would that look like?"

"Rescuing trafficked victims is one thing," Maxwell squeezed Kenda's hand. "They've been traumatized and they're scared. The bonds of the old life are difficult to untangle."

"Rescue is not a one-time event," Rosemary added. "It is a long-term process."

"Whatever the healing progression looks like, it will be messy and complicated." Maxwell raised Kenda's hand to his lips. "I know this too well."

Kenda lay her head on Maxwell's good shoulder and placed her hand upon the back of his neck. Her touch, the tender coil of her fingers, the whispered "I love you" from her lips into his ear, brought a calm to his heart. His wife was a called-up angel, her affection able to erase the dark scribbling on his soul like chalk off the sidewalk.

"You're talking about a real commitment."

"Yes, Jeff," Maxwell responded. "Of time and treasure. A commitment to a population that never sees such kindness and with outcomes that are far from certain."

"If we're taking these girls out of something terrible, then we have to replace it with something good." Rosemary cradled Ezekiel in both arms tenderly rocking from side to side. "A place where they feel they belong."

"We should call it 'Leandra's House,'" Corley said.

Everyone was silent and remained still. It was as if his daughter's words had snapped a photo catching everyone in the frozen action of that moment.

Maxwell was stunned by Corley's suggestion. "You would really do that, after what she did and all that happened?"

"Daddy, I don't know how to describe it any other way but honoring her with forgiveness." Corley dropped her eyes.

For the first time, Maxwell felt the phantoms residing in his soul for so long begin to yield. Like a blind man, the darkness behind his eyes was receding.

Lindy Anderson gave a light tug on her husband's arm and he nodded to her.

"I don't know what you need to do or want to do." Lindy cast her bright smile toward Maxwell and Kenda. "But Jeff and I want to invite you and your family to stay in our guest house for as long as you need."

This was unexpected. Maxwell had just gotten out of the hospital. He and Kenda had not discussed the next step. Planning their immediate future was impossible. They were not ready to return home, but the details of finding a safe house had not been determined.

"We discussed it on the way here," Anderson said. "At least spend the holidays with us while we figure out what the time ahead might look like."

"It's hard to think about that, Jeff, after all we've been through," Maxwell kissed the top of Kenda's head. "We need time."

"What better place to take that time." Kenda lifted her head from his shoulder and graced his cheek with her fingers.

Any hesitation Maxwell felt in accepting Anderson's offer was brushed away by his wife's caress. He looked at his kids and all three were smiling as if the idea of spending the rest of the Christmas holidays in what could only be thought of as an earthly paradise in some far-off land was the best Christmas gift ever. A short-term mission trip into the Anderson world.

"That is very generous of you, Lindy, Jeff." Accepting this offer was humbling for Maxwell, but the reality was that the police had only begun to investigate the criminal network discovered at Garita Metal. His home was not safe. His church was not safe. He didn't even have a car. He and his family were completely dependent on the kindness of others in almost everything. He felt like a beggar, but seeing the brightness in the faces of his family, brought him a sense of hope, even joy. "I…all of us, we accept."

"Wonderful." Lindy reinforced her pleasure with a quiet applause. "This will be wonderful."

"Thank you, Lindy." Kenda reached out her hand. Lindy clasped it like a sister and brought Kenda to her side. "We need to get personal items from our house."

"Of course you do. Jeff and I will drive on ahead and open up the guest house."

"And everyone, we want you for Christmas dinner," Anderson announced before he and Lindy walked out the side door. "Pete, Lin, you and your mom are invited, and Rosemary, bring Ezekiel with you. We'd love to spoil you both."

"You hear that, Ezekiel?" Rosmary spoke into her companion's ear. "We're going to be spoiled this Christmas. Thank you, Lindy and Jeff."

It was settled. Maxwell and his family had received temporary shelter. Rendell would drive the family to their home and then on to the Anderson estate. Maxwell sent Kenda and the kids on without him. He asked Kenda to collect what items he needed. He wanted to get some things from his desk and would get Pete to drive him over later.

The snow was beginning to fall in big flakes blanketing the Gardens and the Hells Canyon community. There was no wind to blow it around, so the snowflakes just floated down out of the clouds. The pure whiteness falling from the sky and covering the landscape brought a quiet calm to the neighborhood and to his soul. Maxwell held out his hand and caught one of the snowflakes. He was startled by the wonder of its crystal patterns before it melted in the palm of his hand. For that fleeting second, he was able to enjoy such simple and stunning beauty.

The crunching noise his feet made in the packed snow as he tramped through the playground and down the alley toward the Gardens was a pleasant sound. It was only a few more days before Christmas Eve and he suddenly remembered that he had not done one minute of shopping for his family or Pete or Rosemary. The fact that he had even thought about it startled him. Could it mean that he was able to imagine the return to normal life? The straightforward act of buying gifts. Was this a return to normalcy? Just contemplating what he might purchase for each person brought a smile to his face.

He had told Rosemary for her and Ezekiel to get on home before the snow got worse. He would lock up the church. He did not really have that much to collect from his desk. The costumes for the play were still piled up, but that could certainly wait. He did have some notes that he had jotted down for a Christmas Eve candlelight service that he wanted to remember. He had written sporadically around the bustle of rehearsals for the play as a random thought popped into his head. It had been so long since he had thought about delivering a sermon, let alone writing one. Another sign of potential normalcy, perhaps.

After he locked the door to the church, he went over to Pete's car. He was sitting in the driver's seat, engine running, heating up the inside. Maxwell motioned for Pete to lower his window.

"Won't be long. Some unfinished business." Maxwell handed Pete his Bible with the notes tucked inside. "And read it while I'm gone. You might learn something."

Pete took Maxwell's Bible and laid it in his lap. His smiling face disappeared as he raised the tinted electric window. If Pete could smile, then so could he. More normalcy.

Once past the playground, Maxwell moved out of the alley and into the apartment complexes in the Gardens. He reached into his coat pocket to warm his hands and felt a pack of cigarettes. He removed them from his pocket, and out of habit, put one into his mouth. They had proved to be a go-to during this time of trouble in his heart and soul as he tried to reconcile all his storm-tossed thoughts and emotions. He stopped in his tracks and stared at the half-empty pack. Cigarettes had always been the best street currency when conversing with the homeless or residents of the neighborhood. He had consistently dipped into his supply for several months. Now maybe it was time for a new currency.

There was a dumpster just ahead with the side door open. He couldn't help but look inside to see what treasures he might be able to tell Carrie about. Something she could look forward to, but it was empty. The trucks must have recently come. He took the cigarette from his mouth and tossed it and the pack into the dumpster.

Once he rounded the corner of the double FF building, he began to slow his pace. He had been marching up to this moment, determined to finish the unfinished business, but now his legs had gotten heavier, the old turmoil in his heart returned, and his will had weakened. It wasn't the snow or the cold that made the trembling start. It was fear and guilt that struck with full-force vengeance as if to say, don't you dare to believe such emotions could be so quickly dispelled. Still he moved forward, more like a child creeping toward a dreaded retribution.

Maxwell moved closer to the concrete pad in front of the apartment door. The memories of that night began swirling around him as if the snow became alive, howling up the shapes and sounds of ghosts. The screams of his children, their terrified faces, the blast of gunfire, the blood, the dying, the howling of a distraught mother as she held the body of her dead son in her arms.

He tried to lift his leg onto the concrete pad, but he could not force either leg to move. He needed to knock on the door, but he could not reach it. He was so close, but he was restrained by fear, guilt, all the horrible memories of that night. He was trembling so he knew he was alive. He had not become frozen in this terrible present moment of immobility. If he could not move forward, neither could he move back. He could not flee. He could go nowhere.

Then he saw her shadowy form and her face staring at him through the glass panes on the door. She looked through one pane and then another as if comparing the clarity of the image of this strange man standing a few feet from her door. The sound of clinking metal from inside the door was the sound of locks being opened, but each rattle and clink of the chains and bolts was like a shot being fired straight into his heart. He could have easily been the one to have died that night. In truth, there had been many days in these last months that he wished he had been the one to have taken the bullet. His life would have been so much easier.

The locks were removed, and the door was forcibly opened. It was an act of strength and will for her to open her door frozen by ice and snow. Maxwell looked in amazement as she placed her hand on the doorframe and took a careful step onto the snow covering the concrete pad. She shuffled forward stopping right in front of him.

Maxwell felt his bones rattling inside his body. He tried to shape his mouth and tongue to speak the words, but each time the words moved into position they would not come forth and his face hardened. He needed to breathe. He needed to inhale, warm the air inside him, before he could utter the words. But each time he opened his mouth and took in the air, it was not words that poured forth but a sobbing grief. His eyes became blurry, and he could feel the streams of tears beginning to freeze as they flowed down his face.

He was able to raise his good arm and wipe his eyes. When he did so she came into focus. Now was the moment. Now he had to speak. Now the words had to flow from his heart and out into the world, and the world before him was a somber face, one that seemed to bear a trace of wonder, ready to connect with him, ready to heal with him.

"Mrs. Sanchez…Louisa…I am so sorry. I am so sorry. I am so sorry."

Sorrow was all he had. Grief was all he had, and it came out in a holy lament.

She raised her hand to his cheek. He could feel Louisa's thumb gently digging into his skin wiping away the streaks of his iced tears.

"Come inside," she said. "Come inside out of the cold."

Author's Note

When I was wrapping up the final edits on *The Mercy Seat*, my wife, Kay and I, had dinner with dear friends Bill and Derri Smith at our favorite restaurant. Derri had recently retired as the director of Ancora, formerly known as End Slavery Tennessee, an organization devoted to rescuing victims of human trafficking. I was sharing with them the story of *The Mercy Seat* and that I was considering a sequel that would have human trafficking as a theme, though at the time, I had no hard and fast plot.

Derri was instantly engaged, and when I suggested she first read *The Mercy Seat* to get an idea of my writing, the flow of the story and a feel for the characters, she asked me to send her a copy as soon as the publisher had a pre-released authorized copy available. Once *The Mercy Seat* e-book arrived, Derri read it and committed to "looking over my shoulder" in the writing of *The Stranger at the Door*. Thus began a beautiful back and forth as Derri weighed in, sprinkling her magic dust on each chapter throughout the course of writing.

As with *The Mercy Seat*, *The Stranger at the Door* was plotless when I sat down to write. Because it is a sequel there was much I needed to address. The story begins six months after the ending of *The Mercy Seat* and opens with Maxwell Crane struggling with the emotional and psychological pain he feels as a result of his impulsive choices to defend his son against a real and present danger.

Once I dealt with these aftereffects of Maxwell's trauma, a stranger arrives at the front door of the church and the Crane family takes her in. That's when things took off. I created a world that was dark and dangerous, but one based in a reality that few of us truly know and none of us want to experience. Thanks to Derri Smith, the created world of *The Stranger at the Door* rings true and the twists and turns of the action and the character choices follow a believable and fascinating logic.

I gave my imagination free rein, and the story soon began to write itself. Some days it was hard to keep up. Characters kept showing up wanting to be a part of the story. I always enjoy the process of writing, but this one had a special pleasure because every character (the old ones and the new) had a real and believable persona and came with specific motivations and desires that allowed them to make believable choices to achieve what they desired. I tried to keep out of their way and let the story unfold as they wished for it to be told. I never knew what my characters might do until they appeared in my imagination. I just kept typing and eventually completed the novel filled with surprises.

The Stranger at the Door takes a hard look at human trafficking that happens in plain sight, yet so often is never seen by the general populace except in an occasional news story. We think it happens in other parts of the world or large metropolitan cities, but too often such crimes are just around the corner, well-concealed in picture postcard neighborhoods.

My desire is that the reader will have a meaningful experience in this journey through unfamiliar territory, and while at times it might make you squirm, that it will also give you understanding and hope for those who cry out for rescue from the dark corners of the world.

If you've enjoyed this story, I'd love it if you'd leave a review at any online bookselling sites that carry my book. That's such a help to authors when readers share. You can find out more about me and my books on my website at:

Website: www.henryoarnold.com

Facebook Pages: www.facebook.com

Henry O. Arnold and Chip Arnold Goodreads: www.goodreads.com

Henry O. Arnold Amazon Author: www.amazon.com

YouTube: Henry O. Arnold: www.youtube.com

Bi-monthly Newsletter – Conversations at the Crossroads accessed through www.henryoarnold.com

Instagram: Henry O. Arnold or henryoarnold

Other Books or Works by Henry O. Arnold

FICTION

Biblical fiction series:

A Voice Within the Flame

Crown of the Warrior King

The Singer of Israel

The Fugitive King

Lion of Judah

Hometown Favorite with Bill Barton

NONFICTION

Kabul24 with Ben Pearson

SCREENPLAYS

The Second Chance

Kabul24 with Ben Pearson

God's Ambassador: The Life of Billy Graham

I Go to the Rock: the Gospel Roots of Whitney Houston

www.ingramcontent.com/pod-product-compliance
Lightning Source LLC
Chambersburg PA
CBHW071220210726
48293CB00002B/516